The Bonded Ember

A forbidden romance. A winter night. A love that reshapes destiny.

Aria Linden

Contents

Part 1

The Night Everything Goes Wrong

Chapter 1

Snow fell in slow, drifting spirals that caught the morning light like scattered shards of glass. Mira Thornvale paused at the edge of the herb garden, her breath warming the scarf wrapped tight around her face. Even in early winter the ground here froze hard enough to kill anything but the toughest plants. She knelt beside a small patch of frostroot, coaxing the stubborn leaves apart with gloved fingers.

The roots had survived another bitter night. They always did, which was more than she could say for the rest of her life.

"Cold morning, Maren," old Brenn called from across the path.

Mira lifted her head. She offered him a polite smile behind the false name she had carried for almost a year. The villagers of Whiteharbor only knew her as Maren. A stranger who had wandered in from the northern woods at the tail end of last winter. Quiet, helpful, harmless. She intended to keep it that way.

"Cold enough to crack a man's bones," she answered.

Brenn laughed, a deep and honest sound that wrapped the frozen air in warmth. The man had a way of finding humor even when storm winds closed in. He carried a bundle of firewood on one shoulder and a dripping net of river fish on the other. He nodded toward the frostroot patch.

"Only you could get those cursed things to grow. Makes me wonder what secret trick you have in those hands."

Mira kept her tone even. "No tricks. Just patience."

She brushed her fingers lightly across the plant and willed her magic to remain dormant. It stirred at her touch, a faint cold shimmer beneath her skin, but she forced it back. Letting frost rise in front of Brenn would be a mistake she could never repair.

He said goodbye and continued down the path toward the smokehouse. Mira pulled her scarf higher until her breath fogged the inside of the wool. She waited until he disappeared behind a row of snow-laden pines, then touched the leaves again. A thin layer of ice, nearly invisible, clung to them. Not enough to expose her. Not yet.

Footsteps crunched behind her. Mira stiffened.

"You are up early again," a soft voice said.

She turned. Rilla, a bright eyed girl barely twelve winters old, stood with a basket of kindling balanced on her hip. Rilla's cheeks were flushed pink from the cold. A stray lock of hair had escaped her hat and stuck to her forehead.

"I have chores," Mira said gently.

"Everyone has chores. You do more than most." Rilla bounced the basket against her hip. "Mama says you help too much. She says you work like someone is watching you."

Mira's pulse quickened. "Your mama says many things."

Rilla giggled. "True."

The girl crouched beside the frostroot and picked at the edge of a leaf. "Do you miss your family, Maren?"

Mira's hands stilled.

"I never hear you talk about them," Rilla added. "Did something happen to them? Or do they live far away?"

Mira forced herself to breathe. Rilla meant nothing by the question. Children asked what others tiptoed around. Still, the words pushed inside her chest with unwelcome pressure.

"They live far away," Mira said.

The lie tasted like iron.

Rilla accepted it with the ease of innocence. She straightened, gave Mira a cheerful wave and then skipped down the path toward the storage huts. Mira stayed still until her heartbeat settled.

Far away. Yes, in a sense. Her parents were not dead, but in the eyes of Veris they might as well be. Exile was a living grave. And she, their daughter, had become the ghost that slipped through winter villages under a name not her own.

A sharp gust of wind swept across the garden and lifted the snow in swirling curtains. Mira stood and brushed her gloves together. Her cabin was close enough that she could have gone inside to warm her hands, but something in the air felt charged. The sky held a strange sheen, a subtle shimmer that had not existed the day before. It prickled along her arms.

She lifted her face toward the pale sun. The light bent oddly. It was almost as if threads of energy rippled across the heavens.

No. Not threads. Signs.

She pressed her lips together. She had hoped the rumors were just rural superstition, but the air confirmed what she had been trying not to acknowledge.

The Winter Rite approached, and something about it felt wrong.

A door slammed nearby. Mira blinked as a traveling merchant strode toward the village square, stamping snow from his boots. His pack bulged with trinkets and foodstuffs. People rushed from their cabins to greet him. A merchant's visit was a rare event this far north.

"Maren," Brenn called again from the crowd. "Come hear the news from the south."

Mira considered retreating to her cabin, but avoiding gatherings often made people talk more than attending them. She slipped off her gloves and tucked them into her belt before walking to the square.

The merchant was already at the center of the attention. He had spread a small blanket on the snow and arranged wares upon it. Silver bangles. Dried herbs. Small vials of infused oil. Mira glanced over them without interest.

"What word from the kingdoms?" Brenn asked.

The merchant wiped his nose with the back of his hand. "Plenty. Roads are thick with soldiers and messengers. The Temple of Glass has summoned half the border settlements. They plan a grander Winter Rite this year."

Mira's breath thinned.

One of the fishermen scoffed. "Every year they claim it is grand. Last time it rained ice shards for a day and we had to fix half the roofs."

"This is different," the merchant insisted. "The Ember beneath the temple is restless. Strange lights over the lake. Frost blooms in summer storage caverns. Priests whisper that the rite will be the strongest in generations."

Mira's hand tightened around her scarf.

Someone else asked, "What does that mean for us?"

The merchant shrugged. "Offerings. Assistance. Ritual attendance. They are gathering gifted folk from the outlying villages. Anyone with a touch of magic might be asked to travel south."

Mira stilled completely. She could feel her magic coiling in protest deep inside her chest.

Brenn chuckled uneasily. "We are a quiet place. They will not come this far."

"They might," the merchant replied. "A messenger was seen riding toward the northern routes. Could be here within days."

Mira stepped backward from the crowd. A strange dizziness washed over her. Her vision shifted and a faint pattern of frost flickered across her fingertips. She curled her hand into a fist.

Brenn noticed her discomfort. "Are you well, Maren?"

"Yes," Mira whispered. "Just cold."

She retreated from the square and hurried toward the treeline. When the last voices vanished behind her, she stopped and braced a hand against a pine trunk. The bark bit into her glove.

A powerful Winter Rite could mean exposure. Veris priests were trained to sense magical resonance. Even hidden, her frost signature might reveal her identity. And if the Thornvale name resurfaced, consequences would follow swiftly.

A raven croaked overhead and shook snow from a branch. Mira looked up. The bird's black wings beat a solemn rhythm against the sky.

She needed distance. She needed a plan.

But for now she needed to breathe.

She closed her eyes. Cold flooded her core. Not the natural winter cold she knew so well, but a cold shaped by magic. It pulsed like a heartbeat beneath her skin, steady and ancient.

"Not now," she murmured.

The magic quieted, but only a little.

She exhaled and pushed away from the tree. The routine of daily tasks waited for her. Simple chores, simple disguises. She walked back toward her small cabin with careful steps.

Whiteharbor's houses loomed ahead, roofs bowed under heavy drifts of snow. Smoke curled from chimneys into the crisp air. Children's laughter echoed near the frozen river where they slid across the ice on makeshift sleds.

The scene should have comforted her. Instead it left her hollow. She had carved out a life here, but it was never meant to last. Exile did not grant roots. It granted hiding places.

Her cabin sat at the edge of the village, half sheltered by the shade of an old spruce. She opened the door and let the warmth inside wash over her. Herbs hung drying near the windows. A kettle hummed on the stove. She removed her scarf and gloves, placed them neatly on a hook and sat on the lone stool.

The air tasted of pine resin and dried mint. Familiar scents. Safe scents. She let her shoulders relax.

A knock came on the door.

Mira straightened at once.

"Come in," she said, steadying her breath.

Rilla peeked inside. "Mama says supper will be ready early. She asked if you wanted to join."

Mira softened. "Tell her thank you. I will be there soon."

Rilla nodded and left, closing the door with a muffled thud.

Mira allowed herself a small smile. She had avoided attachments for months, yet the villagers kept pulling her in gentle ways. It was a kindness she did not deserve.

She rose and moved toward the window. Outside, pale sunlight flickered across the horizon. The distant sky shimmered again with that strange veil of light. Something stirred in her magic, like recognition mixed with dread.

The Winter Rite was coming.

And she would not be able to run from it.

Her fingers tightened on the window frame as the light bent once more. A spiral of frost blossomed across her palm, luminous and delicate, forming a pattern she had not seen since the night her family was exiled.

A sign she had hoped never to see again.

Mira closed her hand around it, but the frost did not fade.

The Rite was calling to her.

And she feared she knew why.

* * *

The frost spiral faded only after Mira willed her breathing to slow. She pressed her palm against her thigh to ground herself. It had been years since her magic reacted with such intensity. Not since the night Veris soldiers marched her family through the gates for the last time. She reminded herself that she was not that frightened girl anymore. She was Maren of Whiteharbor. Quiet. Forgettable. Free in her own way.

Still, the weight of the omen clung to her like ice in her lungs.

She set a hand on the kettle to steady her thoughts, then lifted it from the stove and poured the steaming water into a small wooden cup. Fresh mint filled the air. The scent usually helped calm her, but today it barely took the edge off the unease.

A cluster of voices drifted outside. Children shouted as they returned from the river, their boots thudding over packed snow. A dog barked. Sled runners scraped sharply across the ground. Normal sounds of a quiet winter afternoon. Yet Mira felt as if the world inside her cabin was balancing on something thin and fragile.

She drank the mint water slowly. Warmth spread down her throat, then settled like a protective shield across her chest. She closed her eyes.

She would have to leave after the season. Whether or not the Rite touched Whiteharbor directly. She had lingered too long. Even kindness from people like Brenn and Rilla could not shield her if the wrong person recognized the flicker of Thornvale magic.

A distant knock on another door startled her into movement. She set her empty cup aside, wrapped herself in her cloak and headed outside.

The air stung her cheeks. The sky had deepened into a fragile blue. Villagers were gathering near the communal fire pit as they often did at dusk. Mira joined them reluctantly, hoping to melt into the edges of the group.

Flames crackled in the stone circle. Sparks drifted upward in glittering trails. People sat on logs or leaned against snow drifts. Mira took a place behind a stack of bundled furs.

Brenn noticed her and smiled. "Good. You are here. We were about to speak of something interesting."

Mira kept her voice calm. "The merchant's rumors again?"

"Yes, but also more." Brenn poked the fire with a stick. "Odric went to the high ridge earlier. He said he saw lights over the lake. Strange ones."

Odric, a thick bearded fisherman with a shape like a boulder, nodded. "Not lantern lights. These moved like fireflies, but colder. They drifted in patterns."

Mira's stomach tightened. Frost lights often meant a disturbance in the Ember beneath the temple. She hoped the villagers would not guess that.

"Perhaps it is just the sky acting wild," someone said.

"Perhaps," Odric replied. "But in sixty winters I have not seen frost lights move like that."

The fire popped. Mira stared into the flames, trying to gather her thoughts. She needed to remain invisible. Quiet. Calm. No reaction strong enough to draw suspicion.

Rilla slipped onto the log beside her and nudged Mira's elbow. "Mama says the Rite will be powerful. She says we should stay inside that night."

Mira's throat tightened. "That sounds like good advice."

Rilla leaned closer. "Do you think the priests at the temple can control something like this?"

"I do not know," Mira answered.

It was the truth. The Veris priests were trained to manage the Ember's vast energy, but when the Ember stirred beyond prediction, ancient stories suggested nothing could truly harness it. Mira had learned those stories as a child, long before her family's disgrace. Before her father's strained expression and her mother's frantic whispering on the night the soldiers came.

She pushed that memory aside.

The villagers continued to talk. Some speculated that the rite might bring a season of prosperity. Others feared it might signal a change in the kingdom's fortunes. One spoke of an old tale in which the Ember awakened to punish the wicked. Another insisted it was simply a natural shift in the winter's cycle.

Mira kept her gaze on the fire, allowing the chatter to fade into a low hum. Her magic stirred again beneath her skin. It sensed something she could not yet name. Something closer than she wished.

A gust of cold air swept through the circle. The flames shuddered. Several villagers glanced upward.

"Weather is turning again," Brenn murmured.

Mira followed his gaze. Clouds were gathering faster than normal. Heavy ones, swollen with snow. The wind carried a faint metallic scent that raised the small hairs on her arms.

Rilla shivered. "That smell is strange."

Mira forced her heartbeat to stay steady. "Storm winds bring odd scents sometimes."

But she knew it was not the weather. Her magic recognized the signature. It was the echo of ritual energy rising long before the actual Rite.

Someone nearby caught Mira studying the sky. "What do you think, Maren?" a woman asked. Her tone was casual, but her eyes were observant. "You always seem to sense storms before anyone else."

Mira swallowed. "I only listen to the wind."

The woman chuckled. "Well, keep listening. Maybe you can warn us before the next heavy snowfall."

Mira nodded politely. She kept her hands tucked tightly inside her sleeves. Even the smallest slip of frost would draw questions.

A long silence settled over the circle. The fire burned low. Shadows lengthened along the snow. Eventually the villagers drifted back to their homes in pairs and small groups. Brenn remained behind to bank the fire for the night.

Mira lingered on the edge of the clearing for a moment, waiting for her breath to even out. She felt a subtle vibration in the air, similar to the hum before thunder but colder. It traveled through the ground. A sensation that made her stomach shift.

The Rite was building strength.

She turned toward her cabin.

A thin layer of ice crackled under her boots as if forming seconds before her feet touched the ground. Mira stopped.

The ice vanished when she stepped away. The world returned to its quiet stillness.

She approached her cabin with care. A light dusting of snow covered the steps. She brushed it aside, opened the door and entered the warm room. Shadows flickered across the walls from her small lantern.

She removed her cloak and hung it near the door. Her scarf followed. Her gloves she placed on the table. Once the door was securely shut, she allowed her shoulders to sag.

Silence wrapped the cabin like a soft blanket.

She moved to the small basin beside the window and splashed her face with cool water. It shocked her nerves into clarity.

She needed to calm down. She needed to keep her magic still. As long as she remained unnoticed, she could survive whatever the Rite brought.

She lit a second lantern, placed it on the bedside table and sank onto the narrow bed. The mattress creaked. She curled her fingers into the blanket, grounding herself in the texture.

But the stillness did not last.

A faint humming began to shimmer through the walls. Mira lifted her head. She strained to listen. The sound pulsed so gently that she might have imagined it, but it felt real. Like the distant call of a song she did not want to remember.

She rose from the bed and moved toward the window. Outside, the moon hovered between clouds. Its light stretched across the snow like a silver path. Shadows danced along the tree line where the wind brushed the branches.

Her breath caught. For a brief moment the sky above the Temple of Glass shimmered with the same strange veil she had seen earlier. Threads of light braided together and then parted.

The hum inside the cabin grew faint and then vanished.

Mira stared at the horizon long after the sky returned to normal.

She had hoped the Rite would ignore her, that she could hide as she had always done. But she knew better now.

Something in the Winter Rite was reaching. And it was reaching for her.

She backed away from the window, turned down the lantern by her bed and lay under the blankets. She covered her ears, trying to shut out the lingering hum.

Sleep came slowly, wrapped in tension and cold.

When it finally claimed her, she dreamed of spiraling frost, a lake of glass and a pulse of light beneath the ice that beat in perfect time with her own heart.

* * *

Mira woke just before dawn to the muted glow of snow reflecting through her window. For a moment she did not remember the dream, only the cold that clung to her chest like a forgotten hand. She sat upright. Her breath curled in the air even though the fire in her stove still smoldered. She rubbed her arms and swung her legs over the side of the bed, letting her feet find the rug.

Her head felt heavy. Not from sleep, but from the echo of something that did not belong to ordinary dreams.

Spiraling frost. Light under ice. A pulse of power that matched her heartbeat.

Mira pressed her palms against her eyes. She wanted to dismiss the dream as a trick of her mind. Yet the magic within her stirred in a way that felt unmistakably real.

Outside, the first pale streaks of dawn stretched across the horizon. She dressed slowly, layering wool and leather, trying to anchor herself in the familiar routine. She wrapped her scarf around her neck and slipped her gloves over her hands. Then she took a deep breath and stepped outside.

The village lay quiet under a fresh coat of snow. Smoke rose from a few chimneys, thin and lazy. Frost clung to branches like white lace. Mira walked toward the path that led to the river, the crunch beneath her boots steady and grounding.

This was how she had survived for almost a year. Familiar tasks. Predictable days. No sudden movements. Her cabin, her chores and her silence. They had become her shield.

But the world did not feel predictable this morning.

Far off, a line of clouds rolled low across the horizon with a strange shimmer inside them. Not sunlight. Not dawn. Something else. The same unnatural glow she had seen the previous evening.

She bent to collect a fallen branch, but her hand hesitated mid reach. A faint ring of frost formed around her glove even before she touched the wood. Mira jerked her hand back.

Cold spread up her arm. Not painful, but sharp. Alert. A message without words.

Someone called her name.

"Maren. There you are."

Mira turned. Brenn trudged toward her with a basket of tools in one arm. His beard was crusted with frost. His breath billowed into the air.

"You have a visitor," he said.

Her stomach dropped. "A visitor?"

"No need to panic. It is only Eldin from the northern pass. He came to trade hides. Said he needed to speak with whoever tends the winter gardens."

Relief trickled through her, even if only slightly. Mira nodded. "I will meet him in a moment."

Brenn gave her a curious look. "You seem unsettled."

"I did not sleep well," she replied.

"Storm dreams?" he asked.

Mira almost smiled at the simple northern phrase. "Something like that."

Brenn nodded thoughtfully. "A few of us had restless sleep. Perhaps the sky is stirring old powers. You should come to the square when you are ready. Eldin brought news."

Mira hesitated. "News of what sort?"

Brenn lowered his voice. "He says the Temple of Glass is sending envoys across the northern routes. They are closer than we thought."

Her pulse thudded. Hard. Deep in her ribs.

"That is only rumor," she said, trying to steady herself.

"So far," Brenn agreed. "But Eldin claims he passed a patrol carrying banners from Veris. They were heading toward this region."

Mira looked toward the horizon. The shimmering clouds rolled deeper into the morning sky. She swallowed. "I will join you soon."

Brenn left her with a soft wave. Mira stood still until he disappeared around the bend. Snowflakes drifted lazily in the air, though no clouds hung overhead. It was another sign. Another piece of a puzzle she did not want to assemble.

She turned and made her way back to the cabin. Inside, she removed her gloves and stared at her palms. For a moment they were clear. Then the faintest shimmer of frost spiraled beneath the skin.

She whispered, "Stop."

The frost faded reluctantly, like an animal baring its teeth before it retreats.

A knock sounded at her door before she could gather herself. Mira jumped.

"Come in," she called, steadying her breath.

The door creaked open. Rilla entered with a basket of fresh bread and a grin bright enough to chase shadows.

"Mama sent this," she announced.

"Thank you," Mira said. "Tell her she is too generous."

Rilla set the basket on the table and glanced around the cabin as she often did, curious about everything. Her gaze drifted to the window. Her eyes widened.

"Look at the sky," she whispered.

Mira followed her gaze.

The horizon glowed with a pale ribbon of light, not gold like dawn but silver-blue, thin and trembling. It stretched in a perfect line above the distant frozen lake.

Rilla moved closer to the window. "Is that the first sign of the Rite?"

"I am not sure," Mira lied.

Rilla pressed her hand to the glass. "It is beautiful, but it feels strange. Like it is watching."

Mira stepped behind her and gently pulled her hand away. "You should not stare at it for too long. Go back to your mother. The village will gather soon, and you should stay close to her."

"But everyone is talking about it."

"I know. Still, be careful."

Rilla nodded reluctantly and slipped out of the cabin. The door shut behind her.

Mira stood at the threshold for a long moment. Then she picked up her cloak and stepped outside once more.

Villagers were already emerging from their homes. Some pointed toward the glowing horizon. Others whispered nervously. Snow drifted in thin sheets around them, though the air remained still.

The ribbon of light pulsed faintly. Almost alive.

Mira felt it like a heartbeat under her feet.

She walked to the square where Eldin, a broad shouldered hunter with a face lined by wind and age, spoke with Brenn and several others. When Mira approached, Eldin gave her a respectful nod.

"You are Maren. The one with a healer's hands."

"So I have been told," Mira replied carefully. "Brenn said you brought news."

Eldin scratched his beard. "Not certain if it is news or a warning. On my way from the pass, I saw Veris envoys riding south. Their cloaks were trimmed in ceremonial silver. They carried no weapons at hand, which means they were on temple business."

Mira kept her face calm. "Envoys travel often this time of year."

"Not in numbers like that," Eldin said. "They had a sealed crate marked with the sigil of the highest priest. Something is different this winter."

A hush fell around them.

Mira felt a pressure in the air. Subtle but growing. Like the world holding its breath.

Eldin continued. "The Rite will be stronger than any in my lifetime. The priests prepare for something grand and strange. More villages may be called as witnesses. Gifted folk even more so."

Mira felt herself growing cold beneath her layers.

Brenn folded his arms. "Do you think they will send envoys here?"

Eldin's expression carried no comfort. "I think they already have."

A murmur rippled through the crowd.

Mira's heart kicked against her ribs.

Before anyone could speak again, a sharp whistle cut through the square. Every head turned. A figure on horseback approached from the southern path. The rider wore a heavy cloak and the silver clasp unmistakably shaped like the emblem of Veris.

Every thought in Mira's head scattered.

The envoy halted at the edge of the square and spoke in a strong voice.

"The Temple of Glass seeks the assistance of this settlement. All citizens gifted with even the smallest spark of magic must present themselves before me."

A stunned silence followed.

Mira did not move.

The envoy scanned the crowd with a sharp gaze that carried the weight of authority.

"We will depart for the Rite before nightfall," the envoy called.

Mira felt the frost spiral flicker to life beneath her glove.

There would be no hiding now.

The Rite was calling.

And she would have no choice but to answer.

Chapter 2

The wind howled across the northern ridge, carrying icy needles that stung Kael Ashrow's face as he urged his horse onward. Snow whipped at his cloak, clinging to the dark fabric like ash in reverse. He kept his hood low and his posture hunched, both to shield himself from the cold and to avoid catching the attention of any Veris patrol that might be hidden beyond the next rise.

His forged papers were tucked inside the inner pocket of his coat. He tapped the spot once, checking that they were still there, even though he knew very well they were. He had checked a dozen times since dawn. He did not trust anything forged in a kingdom that would happily see him dead.

The border post loomed ahead, a gray slab of stone beside a narrow path carved between two cliffs. Two guards stood beneath a low arch, shaking the snow from their boots and leaning close to a brazier that spat weak sparks of heat.

Kael slowed his horse and inhaled slowly. He had prepared for this moment all winter. He had memorized the false identity, practiced the accent and rehearsed the calm, neutral expression expected of a man with nothing to hide.

His real name carried danger in every syllable. Ashrow blood was unwelcome. Ashrow magic even more so.

Kael guided his horse to the checkpoint. The guards straightened, their breath forming white clouds.

"Name," one guard demanded.

"Kaelen Marris," he said evenly. He handed over the forged papers.

The guard scanned the parchment, lips moving slightly as he traced the seal. The watchman's expression was unreadable. His fingers lingered on the bottom of the page where the sigil should have been. Kael had worried the lack of a proper raised seal might give him away, but the forger in the outer settlements had done a respectable job with ink and craftsmanship.

"Purpose of travel?" the guard asked.

"Work. I am a metalwright. I was told towns near the Temple of Glass need winter repairs after last season's storms."

The guard grunted. "A lot of storms last year."

Kael kept his expression steady, though his heartbeat thudded hard. "That is what I heard."

The second guard approached, glancing over the horse and the saddlebags. For a moment Kael feared he would ask to inspect them. He had packed supplies and tools, but more importantly, wrapped inside a bundle of cloth, he carried a charm that pulsed faint heat. A remnant from his family's old hearth magic. If the guards sensed it, questioning would follow.

The guard only nodded. "Clear enough. Stay on the western road once you cross. Eastern paths are closed. Too much risk with the Rite approaching."

Kael kept his voice even. "I understand."

The guard handed back the papers. Kael saluted briefly, nudged his horse forward and passed beneath the arch just as a gust of cold wind swept down the path. He did not allow himself to relax until the guards were far behind him and the arch had disappeared around a bend.

Only then did he exhale.

The border of Veris was behind him. He was inside enemy territory now.

Cold crept into his gloves as he tightened his grip on the reins. His fire magic reacted to the temperature, flickering within him like a candle threatened by the wind. A faint warmth pulsed beneath his ribs, then flared sharply.

Kael bit back a curse.

He pressed a hand against the inner pocket of his coat, feeling the shape of a tiny carved stone hidden there. The charm had belonged to his sister, Lira. His real reason for making this journey. He needed answers, not for himself, but for her.

The first signs of the curse had appeared near the end of autumn. A tremor in her hands. A glow beneath her skin when she fell asleep, as if embers danced inside her veins. At first he thought it was a natural result of their family's affinity. But then the glow shifted strangely. It darkened, sometimes dimming to the color of dying coals, then suddenly flashing bright enough to illuminate her room.

Lira had grown weaker each week. The healers had no answers. The elders insisted the curse was old and connected to something buried deep in Ashrow history. Something sealed by an ancient pact they no longer fully remembered. Only the Temple of Glass, seat of the Ember's original binding, might hold the knowledge he needed.

So Kael had left the crumbling halls of Ashrow alone, taking the charm his sister always kept near her pillow, promising he would return with a cure.

He gritted his teeth as another icy gust crawled beneath his coat. His fire magic surged again, this time more sharply. Heat pooled in his palms, begging for release. A faint red glow leaked between his fingers before he closed his fists tight.

"Not now," he muttered.

He could not afford an accidental flare, not while traveling near Veris roads. Even the smallest spark of unrestrained fire could draw suspicion.

He guided his horse through a narrow ravine. Frost glittered on the rock walls. Trees clung to the cliff edges, their branches heavy with ice. The path opened into a stretch of open terrain where the wind swept uninterrupted across frozen plains.

A small settlement appeared in the distance, no more than a cluster of cabins and a watchtower. Smoke curled gently from chimneys. Kael directed his horse toward it, hoping to rest and warm himself before nightfall. He needed to be careful. The people in these border villages were often suspicious of newcomers.

He approached the entrance slowly. A wooden arch marked the entrance with modest carvings of winter animals. A hunter sharpening a blade looked up from a bench as Kael passed. His gaze lingered with a mix of suspicion and simple curiosity.

Kael dismounted near a trough and tied his horse. He reached into his saddlebag for a few coins, enough to pay for food and a place to sleep. Before he could enter the tavern, a sharp pain seared along his arm.

He hissed softly, grabbing his forearm.

His fire magic flared beneath the skin, creating a glowing orange ribbon that pulsed before fading. That flash alone could have exposed him if anyone had been watching closely.

He clenched his jaw. The cold season made it worse. Fire mages tended to struggle in deep winter. The temperature threatened to smother their inner flame, forcing the magic to fight for balance. For most, the reaction was mild. For Kael, whose power had always burned hotter and more unruly than it should, the struggle felt like a constant battle.

Focus. Control. Breathe.

He drew in a slow breath, letting the warmth settle. Gradually, the glow subsided.

He pushed open the tavern door.

Warmth enveloped him at once. Fire cracked in a stone hearth. Lanterns cast golden light across wooden tables. The smell of broth and roasted roots filled the air.

A man behind the counter nodded. "Cold day for travel."

"It is," Kael replied.

"Need a meal? Or a room?"

"A room. And whatever food you have ready."

The man gestured to a table near the hearth. "Sit. I will bring you a bowl."

Kael moved to the table, set down his pack and lowered himself onto the bench with a stiff exhale. The warmth seeped into his muscles. His fire magic steadied, content for the moment.

He scanned the room.

Three merchants occupied a corner table, speaking quietly. A pair of hunters played a quiet game of stones near the wall. An elderly woman dozed beside the fire. No soldiers. That was good. He could rest without fear of someone demanding to see his papers again.

The tavern keeper returned with a bowl of thick stew and a crust of bread. Kael nodded in thanks. As he ate, the chatter from the merchants drifted toward him.

"Temple is preparing something unusual this year."

"I heard the same. Strange lights near the lake. Almost like frostfire."

"Rite will be stronger. They say the Ember is stirring."

Kael's spoon froze midway to his mouth.

He listened more closely.

"Envoys are riding through the northern routes," one merchant said. "Gathering gifted folk. Anyone with a hint of magic is being called in."

Kael leaned back slowly. If the temple was summoning those with magic, he needed to reach them before their forces spread too far. If the Rite grew stronger, the energy surrounding the Ember might reveal truths normally hidden. This might be the only chance he would ever have to understand what was happening to Lira.

But it also meant danger. Strong rites sent unpredictable ripples through magic, and Kael's fire was already unstable.

He finished his meal, left coins on the table and headed toward the stairs. He would rest only briefly. He needed to leave before dawn tomorrow if he wanted to reach the Temple of Glass by the night of the Rite.

As he reached his room, another searing pulse shot through his chest. He grasped the bedpost to steady himself. His fire magic flared violently, so hot it felt as if it tried to burn through him from the inside.

His breath tore from his throat.

Not now. Not here.

He gasped, willing the flame inside him to calm.

A faint glow radiated beneath his coat, illuminating the room in a soft orange flicker. The bedpost beneath his grip grew warm. He forced his breathing into a slow rhythm. Gradually the glow faded.

Kael sagged against the wall.

This was getting worse.

The cold season was tightening its grip, and with it, his control slipped drop by drop.

He looked toward the window where a thin line of distant light shimmered along the horizon above the frozen lands. A light he had never seen before.

The Rite was awakening.

And if he failed to master his fire soon, he would meet the Rite unprepared.

* * *

Sleep came to Kael in fragments.

He lay on the narrow tavern bed, staring at the ceiling while the last of the firelight flickered beneath the door. The room held the sour scent of old smoke and herbs. His body ached from the journey, yet his thoughts refused to settle.

Each time he closed his eyes, he saw Lira's face. Pale, drawn, framed by dark curls that had once bounced with restless energy. He saw the faint glow beneath her skin when the curse flared, like banked coals trying to break through the surface.

He imagined her lying in her small room back in Ashrow, listening to the crackle of a hearth that no longer held enough warmth. Their mother's hands would be calloused from tending to her. Their father's shadow would fill the doorway, shoulders sagging under a weight he never spoke aloud.

Kael turned on his side and pressed his forehead against his arm. The charm in his pocket pulsed faint heat, as if echoing his anxiety.

He remembered the night everything changed.

Veris diplomats had come to Ashrow with promises of peace. They carried soft words and sharp smiles. An agreement had been drafted to share certain rights around the Ember's residual power. Ashrow would pledge support and predictability. Veris would offer legitimacy and resources.

Behind the courteous phrases lay a simple truth. Veris wanted control. Ashrow wanted survival.

Kael had been young but not young enough to be blind. He watched the negotiations from the gallery above the great hall, hidden behind carved stone screens. He remembered his father's voice, steady and measured. He remembered the lead ambassador's reply, smooth as polished ice.

Then, weeks later, the treaty failed.

Veris accused Ashrow of breaking key promises. Ashrow claimed Veris altered the terms after signatures were sealed. Military skirmishes flared along the border. Trade faltered. Lira, who loved stories of distant cities, saw the world shrink to a few safe routes.

Kael's mind caught on one memory in particular. A night lit by torches in the courtyard, Veris messengers spreading word of new sanctions. One of them had turned to Kael and said with a thin smile, "You Ashrow folk burn too bright. The kingdom prefers a calmer flame."

Later, when Lira's curse appeared, some in the clan whispered that it was punishment from the Ember itself. Others believed Veris had tampered with old protections in order to weaken Ashrow blood.

Kael believed none of their interpretations, yet he carried all of their anger.

He woke before dawn, sweat cooling on his skin despite the chill in the room. For a moment he was disoriented, unsure if the faint orange glow on the ceiling was from his magic or the dying fire in the hearth downstairs.

He sat up quickly and checked his hands. They were normal. His breathing evened.

Enough. He had wasted enough time in restless thought.

He dressed, strapped his pack to his shoulders and descended to the common room. The tavern keeper was already awake, stoking the fire.

"Leaving early?" the man asked.

"I prefer quiet roads," Kael said.

The tavern keeper nodded. "Rite fever has people restless. Patrols too. Best to avoid large groups."

Kael accepted a cup of weak tea, drank it quickly, left payment and stepped out into the predawn gloom.

The sky was a dark blue, not yet touched by the sun. The strange ribbon of light that had hovered on the horizon the day before was still present, faint but steady, like a scar across the sky. It cast a faint glow on the snow that did not match the natural light of morning.

His horse snorted and stamped as he untied the reins. The animal's breath steamed in the cold. Kael patted its neck, feeling the familiar rhythm of muscle beneath the fur.

"One step closer," he murmured. "Then another."

He mounted and set off along the western road, as the border guards had instructed. The path wound between low hills, then opened onto wider stretches of flat, snow covered land. Frost coated every stone. Sparse trees rose from the white like dark fingers.

As he rode, the cold pressed deeper into his bones. His fire magic responded with stubborn resistance. It flared in protest, then recoiled, trying to maintain balance.

At first it was manageable. His palms tingled. His chest felt warm. Now and then a faint shiver of heat ran down his spine.

But as the light grew stronger and the day brightened, the wind sharpened. Snow began to fall, thick and heavy.

Kael pulled his cloak tighter, though it did little to shield him. The world narrowed to the horse beneath him, the dull crunch of hooves and the swirling storm.

Visibility dropped. He could barely see beyond a few strides. The road became a suggestion rather than a certainty.

His magic strained.

Heat gathered in his core, the way steam built in a sealed kettle. The more he fought it, the more pressure he felt.

"Not now," he gritted out.

A sudden gust slammed into him, nearly unseating him. The horse stumbled. Kael yanked the reins to steady it.

In that moment his control slipped.

A burst of heat exploded from his chest, racing along his veins. His hands flared bright. Flames licked up his sleeves, eating at the frost that had settled on the fabric.

The horse reared, shrieking.

Kael threw his weight forward, gripping the mane with one hand and clamping the other tightly around his wrist to smother the magic.

The fire guttered, then died back, leaving scorch marks on his gloves and a sharp smell of singed wool in the air.

The horse trembled. Kael whispered calm words, stroking its neck until it settled. His own heart hammered against his ribs.

This was madness. His power normally never erupted so fiercely without conscious intent. The combination of deep winter, the approaching Rite and his own inner turmoil had created a dangerous mix.

He dismounted and walked for a while beside the horse, letting the motion steady him. Snow soaked into his boots. Cold seeped through his trousers. Oddly, the discomfort helped. It tethered him to the present.

He thought of Lira again.

When her curse flared, her eyes had taken on a strange light. Not the usual ember glow of their family, but something thinner. Sharper. Almost like the glow now staining the distant horizon over the Temple of Glass.

What if whatever woke the Ember was also affecting Ashrow bloodlines? What if the Rite, rather than offering answers, deepened the curse?

He shook the thought away. He had no choice. Doing nothing guaranteed Lira's decline. Doing something at least offered a sliver of hope.

Eventually the snow eased. The wind softened to a low moan. Kael remounted and continued his journey.

Near midday, he spotted a group of figures ahead on the road. Their cloaks bore the silver clasp of Veris authority. His pulse quickened. He could not avoid them without leaving the main path and risking unknown terrain, yet passing too close could expose him.

He slowed his horse and measured the distance. Three riders. One wagon. The wagon appeared to carry crates wrapped in tarp.

Envoys.

He considered turning aside, cutting across the open field and circling around them, but the snow was deep enough to make that risky. A stumble or a fall would draw their attention.

Better to pass them with the calm indifference of a man with nothing to hide.

He raised his hood, shadowing his face, and guided his horse to the far side of the road, giving them space.

As he approached, the lead rider lifted a hand in brief greeting. Kael inclined his head.

"Traveling to the temple?" the rider asked.

Kael kept his tone neutral. "To the nearby town. I offer metalwork and repairs."

The rider studied him for a heartbeat that felt too long. "Busy times for such work."

"Storms last year did damage," Kael answered. "People pay to fix broken hinges even when rites call them away."

The rider huffed a faint sound that might have been a laugh. "Fair enough. Safe travels."

"And to you," Kael replied.

He passed them, resisting the urge to look back.

Only when the sound of their wheels and horses faded behind him did he let out a breath.

The brief encounter rattled him more than he liked to admit. He was too close to the heart of Veris. Too close to the temple's sphere of influence. The air itself felt charged, like kindling stacked near a spark.

By late afternoon, the terrain began to change. The hills rose higher, shaped by ancient glaciers. Frost coated the rocks in thick, glittering layers. The sky took on a clear, steely tone.

The ribbon of light on the horizon brightened. Up close, he could see it was not a single band but several, layered faintly one above another. They converged near the direction of the Temple of Glass.

His fire magic responded with a strange, uneasy rhythm. It did not flare in anger this time. Instead it hummed, as if some distant force was calling to it.

He did not like that feeling at all.

Near evening he found a sheltered hollow at the base of a cliff and chose it as his camp. He built a small fire, careful to make it appear ordinary. He used flint and steel instead of magic, though his fire power ached to leap into the dry kindling.

When the flames finally caught, casting a modest circle of light, he sat with his back against the rock and took out Lira's charm.

It was a simple stone, polished smooth by years of handling, with a faint ash colored streak running through its center. He cupped it in both hands.

The stone warmed slightly, responding to his touch.

"Lira," he whispered. "Hold on."

He imagined her in Ashrow, clutching her blanket when fear spiked. She had always been braver than he was, even as a child. She teased him about his temper and laughed when he brooded. Their bond had been the one constant in a life filled with shifting alliances and political storms.

He would not lose her to a curse born of secrets and ancient pacts.

The wind shifted. For a second he thought he heard a distant roar, like a faraway crowd or the rush of water under thick ice.

He looked up. The lights in the sky pulsed once, then again, brighter each time.

The Rite approached fast.

Kael closed his fingers around the charm.

Tomorrow he would draw nearer to the temple. Soon, he would stand in the shadow of the glass lake itself.

Whatever waited there, he would face it.

For Lira's sake.

* * *

Morning came thin and gray, seeping over the ridge like smoke. Kael kicked snow over the last of his fire, stamped his boots until feeling returned to his toes and checked his horse's tack with numb fingers. The animal snorted, impatient with the cold and the lingering scent of ash.

"We move," Kael murmured.

The horse flicked its ears as if in answer.

He rode out of the hollow and followed the road as it climbed toward higher ground. The air grew sharper with each rise. The strange bands of light in the sky glowed steadily now, a constant presence on the horizon. They filled him with the peculiar sensation of being watched by something vast and unseen.

By midday, he reached an outpost larger than the scattered villages he had passed before. Low stone walls ringed a cluster of buildings made of timber and rough cut rock. A tall pole near the gate carried the Veris crest, a stylized flame captured inside a circle of ice.

The sight made his jaw clench.

Years ago, that same crest had flown over the courtyard in Ashrow during one of the rare peace delegations. They brought gifts and offers then, sweetened by honeyed words. The morning after the treaties collapsed, those banners fluttered from the spears of soldiers instead.

Kael slowed his horse as he approached the gate. Two guards stepped forward, spears crossed.

"State your business," one said.

"Seeking lodging and work," Kael replied. "Name is Kaelen Marris. Metalwright."

The other guard eyed him, then glanced toward the sky. "You are cutting it close. With the Rite nearly here, most folk are heading toward the temple, not away from it."

"I heard there would be repairs needed in the towns," Kael said, holding his gaze without challenge. "I thought there might be coin in it."

The guard considered this, then lowered his spear. "You can speak with the quartermaster. He always needs someone who can fix a hinge."

They waved him through the narrow gate.

Inside, the outpost hummed with nervous activity. Pack animals shuffled between storehouses. Children ran beside carts stacked with grain and salted meat. A group of robed acolytes crossed the yard, their heads bowed, lips moving in silent recitation.

Kael dismounted near a hitching post outside an inn and tied his horse. The building's sign creaked in the wind, painted with a crude image of a glassy lake. He pushed open the door.

The common room was crowded, but not rowdy. People spoke in low voices, the way they did in places where small details mattered. A map of the surrounding region covered one wall, dotted with markers showing patrol routes and supply paths.

Kael ordered a bowl of stew and a place at the long table near the hearth. As he ate, he listened.

"Envoys reached the northern fishing villages yesterday," one man was saying. "They are calling anyone with a hint of magic to attend the Rite."

"What if someone refuses?" another asked.

"They call it an honor," the first replied with a shrug. "Who refuses honor when priests are watching?"

A woman near the end of the table spoke quietly. "My cousin's daughter can coax water to move. Only a little. Enough to fill a cup without touching it. The priests marked her years ago. The summons came last week. She leaves tonight."

Murmurs of sympathy and pride mingled.

Kael kept his eyes on his bowl. His magic stirred restlessly, as if the simple mention of the Rite was enough to wake it. Heat prickled along his spine. He pressed his knees together under the table, trying to ground himself.

A group of younger soldiers entered, brushing snow from their shoulders. Their laughter rang too loud in the tense room. One of them slammed a hand on the table beside Kael's bowl, nearly knocking the spoon from his fingers.

"You. Traveler," the soldier said. "You look like you have not taken a side yet. Planning to watch the Rite from a safe distance?"

Kael forced a neutral expression. "I am a metalwright. I take the side that pays me."

That drew a few chuckles from nearby listeners.

The soldier leaned closer. His breath smelled of fermented grain. "You know what the priests say this year? They say the Ember will choose again. Not just bless, but choose. Something large is coming."

Kael met his gaze. "Do they ever say anything else?"

The soldier stared at him for a long moment, then grinned. "You have a point. Enjoy your stew, metalwright." He moved away, dragged by a companion toward the counter.

Kael finished his meal quickly. He needed information, not ale, and he needed to make plans.

He found the quartermaster in a cluttered office behind the inn. Shelves groaned under the weight of ledgers and crates of supplies. The man behind the desk wore a stained vest and had the look of someone who measured his patience the way he measured grain.

"You repair metal?" the quartermaster asked, after Kael introduced himself.

"When paid," Kael answered.

The man snorted. "There are hinges and hooks that need work. A few wagon wheels too. I can pay a fair rate." He looked Kael up and down. "You also look like you can handle a blade if trouble comes."

"I can handle my own," Kael said.

"You might need to. Tempers rise before big rites. People get strange, as if the Ember might judge them for every careless word." The quartermaster pushed a bundle of small tasks across the desk, written in quick, cramped script. "Do these by tomorrow and we talk about more. That is, if you are still here and not carted off to the temple with the rest of the gifted."

Kael stiffened. "I have no magic to interest the priests."

The quartermaster gave him a look that said he did not care either way. "Then you have nothing to worry about."

Kael left with the bundle and spent the afternoon tightening bolts, reforging a broken hook and fixing a warped latch. Ordinary work steadied his hands. The rhythm of hammer and anvil soothed him. He enjoyed the simplicity, even as his mind never strayed far from his purpose.

As the sun dropped toward the mountains, the outpost gathered in the yard. An envoy from the temple had arrived. Her cloak carried the silver trim of high authority. Her dark hair was braided with small crystal beads that caught the fading light.

She raised her hands for silence.

"By decree of the Temple of Glass," she called, "all who possess the gift of magic are summoned to stand as witnesses at the Winter Rite. Your presence will strengthen the bond between the Ember and Veris. It is both duty and honor."

Kael stood near the back, hood up, eyes lowered. His heartrate quickened.

Children clutched their parents' hands. A few adults shifted uncomfortably. Some faces showed pride, others fear. A list was read aloud. Names of those already marked by previous tests. The envoy announced that additional screenings would take place in the morning.

"Do not be afraid," she said. "This is an auspicious year. The Ember has stirred. The priests believe a great alignment approaches."

Kael's magic pulsed sharply at the word alignment. Heat flashed in his chest. He gritted his teeth.

The envoy's gaze swept the crowd. For an instant, he thought her eyes lingered on him. His shoulders tightened. He forced his inner flame to stillness, clamping down on the urge to flare.

A faint whisper ran through his mind, unbidden and unwelcome. Not words, but a sensation. As if something far to the south had turned its attention toward him.

When the gathering ended, people dispersed in small knots of conversation. Some hurried back to their homes. Others lingered, talking in anxious whispers.

Kael returned to the corner of the yard where his horse waited.

"Looks like they are rounding up half the province," a young man beside him said. He was tightening the strap on a pack, his brow furrowed. "My sister can weave tiny light threads through cloth. Priests marked her years ago. She is excited. I am not."

"They promise much," Kael replied. "What do they offer in return?"

The young man hesitated. "Blessing. Protection. Sometimes coin. Mostly the promise that the Ember watches kindly."

Kael bit back a bitter remark. For Ashrow, the Ember's gaze had never felt kind.

He checked his own packs, mostly as an excuse to break off the conversation. His fingers brushed the charm in his pocket. It pulsed in time with his heartbeat, as if agreeing with his thoughts.

That night, he could not bring himself to sleep indoors. The inn's walls felt too close, the air thick with speculation. Instead, he made camp beyond the outer fence, within sight of the watch fires but under the open sky.

Stars pricked through the darkness, faint beside the shimmering bands above the southern horizon. The lights there seemed brighter than the night before. They pulsed with slow, deliberate rhythm.

He sat cross legged beside his small fire, the charm in his hand. Heat radiated from it in a steady, gentle glow. Different from his own power, which surged and retreated like a restless tide.

"Lira," he whispered. "If this is as tangled as the elders think, some part of it began here. At the temple. At the Ember's cradle."

Memories rose, unwelcome. The days after the treaty failed. Veris emissaries standing in Ashrow's hall, not with offers this time, but demands. The accusations of breach. The veiled threats.

He remembered standing beside Lira in the shadows, listening.

"They will use our fire when it suits them," he had muttered then. "Then blame us when the heat burns their fingers."

Lira had elbowed him lightly. "Maybe someday we will set the terms instead."

Her smile had been small but fierce. He had believed it for a moment.

Now he wondered if the curse eating at her had roots in that same struggle. Perhaps Veris had tampered with protections in ways they refused to admit. Perhaps the Ember itself had changed when humans started tugging on its power like children fighting over a toy.

The air around him shifted.

He felt it before he saw it.

Heat rose through his body, sharper than before. Not the gradual build he was used to, but a sudden surge that stole his breath. His fire magic flared, pushing against his skin as if trying to break free.

He sucked in a gasp, clenched his fists and gritted his teeth. The flames held beneath the surface, but barely. A faint glow seeped from his wrists, painting the snow in soft orange.

"Enough," he rasped.

The glow dimmed slowly, reluctantly.

Above, the lights on the southern horizon pulsed in answer.

His magic had never felt connected to the Ember's movements in this way. It was as if a thread now linked his inner fire to something awakening near the temple.

He stared toward that distant glow, the charm warm in his hand.

The Rite was not just an event this year. It was a turning point. For Veris. For Ashrow. For Lira.

Perhaps for him.

He rose and stamped out his campfire, leaving only bare earth and a smear of ash. The night air bit his lungs. His magic still hummed under his skin like a restrained storm.

In the morning he would push closer to the Temple of Glass. He would follow the same roads as the envoys and the summoned gifted. Whatever waited at the heart of the Ember, he would face it directly.

For now, he stood beneath the shimmering sky, surrounded by snow and silence, feeling the distant pull of a power that did not belong to any one kingdom.

The cold pressed in. His fire answered.

And somewhere far ahead, on the edge of a frozen lake of glass, destiny shifted in ways neither he nor Mira Thornvale yet understood.

Chapter 3

Snow drifted over Whiteharbor through the late morning, soft and steady like falling ash. Mira worked in quiet rhythm outside her cabin, chopping thin branches for kindling. Each strike of the hatchet sent small cracks through the frozen wood, the sound sharp in the still air. She focused on the task, letting the repetition drown out her thoughts.

It had been only one night since the envoy arrived and announced the Temple's demand. She hoped, foolishly, that the village council might delay. But dawn had come, and no messenger had appeared at her door to release her from the fear coiled in her chest.

She tried to draw comfort from the ordinary sounds of the morning. Children chased each other through the snow. A dog barked at a raven perched on the roofline. Brenn's laugh carried from the communal barn. Life continued, unaware that hers stood on the edge of collapse.

A sharp horn blast shattered the fragile calm.

Mira's fingers froze on the hatchet handle.

The horn was not one used by Whiteharbor. Its pitch was deeper. Commanding. A sound used only by officials of Veris.

Several villagers rushed from their homes, alarmed. Mira stepped back into the shadow of her cabin, heart pounding. She tried to calm the flicker of magic stirring beneath her skin, but the horn's echo pulsed through her like a signal.

A rider emerged between the pines. Snow sprayed from the horse's hooves as it slowed near the square. Behind the rider came two others, each wearing dark cloaks clasped with the silver crest of Veris.

The emissary dismounted with deliberate grace. She removed her hood and shook snow from her dark hair. Her face was sharp, her eyes focused and measuring.

"People of Whiteharbor," she called, voice clear and cold. "By decree of the Temple of Glass, all citizens bearing magical skill must present themselves."

A ripple of unease moved through the crowd.

Beside Mira's cabin, Rilla clutched her mother's coat sleeve. Brenn stepped forward, bowing stiffly.

"We honor the Temple," Brenn said, wary. "But our village is small. We have no marked gifted among us."

The emissary's gaze swept the people. "Every village claims the same. Magic hides in quiet places. It is the Temple's duty to uncover it."

She lifted a hand. One of her attendants stepped forward with a small crystalline orb held in padded gloves. The orb glowed with faint blue light, swirling like mist trapped in glass.

Mira recognized it at once. A Seeker's sphere. Designed to reveal magical resonance in anyone standing within its range.

Her throat tightened.

The emissary raised her voice again. "You will stand before the sphere. It will detect any deviation of the Ember's pattern. Those with the gift will accompany me at once to the Temple of Glass."

A murmur of protest rose from the villagers. Gifts were prized by the Temple, but they were feared here. People avoided attention, avoided the weight of ceremonial summons and the risk of being drawn into Veris politics.

The emissary's expression never changed. "We begin now."

The villagers stepped forward hesitantly, one by one. The sphere reacted to each with nothing more than a dull flicker. Mira watched from the edge of the square, trying to keep her breathing even. If she slipped away now, they might notice. If she stood among the villagers, the sphere might respond to her magic.

She felt the frost spiral twitch beneath her glove.

Brenn stepped before the sphere. It remained dim. Others followed, older women and young men who worked the river. The sphere stayed quiet.

Mira's turn approached.

She kept her eyes lowered, pulling her scarf up to hide her

face. She whispered silently to herself. Hold still. No emotion. No fear. Let the magic sleep. Let it rest.

"Next," the emissary said.

Mira stepped forward with careful steps.

The sphere glowed faintly. Her pulse jumped.

She tried to suppress the flare, but her fear spiked at the worst moment. A thin ribbon of frost traced across her fingertip beneath her glove. The sphere reacted instantly.

Light burst inside the glass, bright as trapped lightning. Gasps rose from the crowd.

"No," Mira whispered.

The emissary stepped closer. "Name."

"Ma... Maren," Mira said.

The emissary's face remained unreadable. "Your real name."

Mira's heart pounded loud enough to drown out the wind. She said nothing.

The emissary gave a small nod, as if confirming something she had already suspected. "You bear the gift. Perhaps even a strong one. You will join the summoned witnesses."

"I am no one of importance," Mira managed, voice thin. "Surely you have enough others to call."

"The Ember is restless," the emissary replied. "Those touched by magic cannot be spared. The Rite requires every source of resonance."

A cold weight settled in Mira's stomach. This was the moment she had feared for almost a year.

Brenn stepped forward. "Wait. She is quiet. She harms no one. She would bring no value to your Rite."

The emissary held up a hand. "Magic is value."

Mira swallowed, her mouth dry. "Let me gather a few things."

"You may take only what you can carry on foot," the emissary said. "We move now. The temple expects us before nightfall."

Rilla tugged on Mira's sleeve, eyes wide. "Maren, you are not leaving us, are you?"

Mira knelt and placed a trembling hand on the girl's shoulder. "I must go for a little while."

Rilla's lip quivered. "You do not look like you want to."

Mira gave a small, brittle smile. "Some things must be done even when we fear them."

The emissary gestured impatiently.

Mira rose and walked toward her cabin. Snow crunched under her boots in a rhythm that felt strangely final. Inside, she grabbed her cloak, a small pouch of herbs and the warmest gloves she owned. Her hands shook as she tied the cloak around her shoulders.

She paused for a moment and touched the wooden table, the drying herbs, the neat rows of supplies she would likely never see again. She had built a fragile life here. Not perfect. Not home. But safe enough to breathe.

Now that breath was being taken away.

She stepped outside. The villagers gathered around her, quiet and tense. Brenn gave her a look filled with worry.

"Stay careful, Maren," he said softly. "Or whatever your true name is."

She nodded once, unable to speak.

The emissary motioned for the summoned to gather. Three others from the village had shown faint glimmers in the sphere: a young fisherman whose hands sparked when angry, a woman with a slight talent for sensing storms and an elderly man who could warm water by touch. They stood in a small, uncertain cluster.

"Walk," the emissary commanded.

The group began its journey along the snow packed path. The village faded behind them, the sound of muffled voices swallowed by the rising wind.

Mira looked back one last time. Rilla stood near the square, clutching her mother's hand, watching until the white curtain of snowfall hid Mira from sight.

The road to the Temple of Glass stretched ahead, cold and unforgiving. Each step carried her farther from safety and closer to a destiny she had never wanted.

The emissary did not look back. The other villagers walked in tense silence.

Mira pulled her cloak tight and followed, her magic trembling within her like a creature waking too soon.

The Temple of Glass waited for her.

And whatever fate the Rite held would find her there.

Chapter 4

Snow swept across the temple valley in long, whispering sheets as Mira and the forced procession descended from the ridge. The path wound between towering pines glazed with frost, leading into a wide basin carved by ancient glaciers. The Temple of Glass rose at the far end like a shard of frozen sky, its crystalline towers catching pale sunlight and reflecting it across the lake.

Mira had seen sketches of the temple when she was a child, but none of them had prepared her for the real sight. The structure looked alive, as if sculpted by winter itself rather than human hands. The outer walls shimmered in shades of silver and blue. Frost clung to the spires in delicate arcs, making the entire building appear suspended between earth and storm.

The emissary strode at the front of their small group, her cloak snapping behind her. The other summoned villagers trailed close by, clutching their meager belongings with nervous fingers.

A chill slid down Mira's spine that had nothing to do with the cold.

The frozen lake stretched before the temple like a vast mirrored field. Light shimmered beneath its surface. Not sunlight and not reflection. Something deeper. Something breathing.

A faint hum vibrated through the air, rising and falling like a distant pulse.

The emissary halted near the lake's edge and turned. "You will wait here for instruction from the high priests."

Mira and the others nodded. Some stood with rigid backs, trying to hide their fear. Others stared in awe at the glimmering temple towers. Mira kept her gaze low. Eyes watching invited questions. Questions revealed cracks. Cracks revealed danger.

As she stood near the lake, an unexpected wave of heat brushed her senses.

Heat. Not frost. Not Ember cold. Heat.

She frowned and glanced around.

A cluster of figures approached from the western path. Soldiers. Their armored boots crunched over the snow. Behind them walked a young man with dark hair and a storm battered cloak, his posture rigid and alert. His breath steamed sharply in the cold. His hands stayed close to his sides, his fingers flexing as if resisting some inner impulse.

Mira's magic stirred.

A soft pulse of frost rippled beneath her glove. Barely visible, but present.

Her gaze snapped to the young man.

For a heartbeat their eyes met across the snowy clearing.

A jolt shot through her. A ripple of frost and heat collided in her chest. Her magic quivered, stretching toward something it did not recognize.

The young man's expression flickered. Surprise. Confusion. A moment later his right hand glowed faintly through the fabric of his glove. A soft orange shimmer pulsed at the edges of his fingers before he quickly clenched them into a fist.

Heat and ice.

The reaction was unmistakable.

She looked away quickly, pulse pounding.

She had never encountered another gifted so near that their powers reached for each other. It was forbidden for them to bond or resonate in such a way outside of controlled circles. Only certain bloodlines in Veris were allowed to form magical alignments. Anyone else risked accusations of instability and threat.

Yet the moment their gazes touched, her frost magic had responded as if recognizing a call.

She took a step back from the lake, steadying her breath.

She did not know him. She wanted no connection with him. She wanted no connection with anyone here.

But her magic whispered otherwise.

The emissary approached the Ashrow group, her expression tight. She spoke with the guards in clipped, formal tones. The soldiers responded with equally cold politeness, neither side yielding ground. Mira could feel the tension stretching thin, like a brittle sheet of ice about to crack.

"Only authorized envoys may cross the lake," the emissary said sharply.

"Our orders are from Ashrow's council," one soldier replied. "We observe the Rite to ensure our interests are represented."

"Your interests are irrelevant here," the emissary snapped. "The Rite is a Veris ceremony."

The Ashrow soldier bristled. "The Ember's influence does not end at your borders."

A low murmur rippled through the Veris acolytes gathered near the lake. Mira watched them with wary eyes. Political conflict between Veris and Ashrow was common, but seeing it play out at the steps of the temple made her stomach twist.

The young man with the dark hair stood slightly behind the front line of Ashrow observers. His eyes scanned the area methodically. He seemed to measure every path, every guard, every possible threat.

A man used to moving through enemy territory.

When his gaze returned to her for a second time, Mira felt her breath catch.

She turned away again, trying to focus on the lake.

The ice shifted beneath the surface with a low groan. Light rippled across it like a slow wave. The hairs on Mira's neck rose. She had grown up hearing stories of the Ember sealed beneath the glass lake, but she had never imagined it could feel this... awake.

A Veris priest approached, robe trailing across the frozen ground. His face was narrow, his features sharp with age.

"You who carry the gift," he said, addressing Mira's small group, "step forward and stand upon the designated circle."

A series of glowing runes shimmered at the lake's edge. Mira's stomach dropped. The runes crackled with cold magic, a signature she knew intimately from her childhood lessons.

Frost resonance circles.

She had practiced in circles like these as a young girl, under her father's careful watch. Back when she still believed the Thornvale name meant something good. Back when she believed the kingdom valued her.

She did not want to step into one now. Not with her magic trembling beneath her skin. Not with the strange heat resonance lingering from that brief encounter.

But refusal was not an option.

Mira walked toward the circle. The other summoned villagers followed, none of them aware of the danger prickling beneath her calm expression. She positioned herself at the edge of the rune, hoping the magic would not react too strongly.

The young man from Ashrow had moved closer to the lake, though he remained behind his soldiers. He seemed drawn to the water, leaning slightly forward. His brow furrowed.

He sensed it too.

The lake pulsed with a faint glow. Frost breathed across its surface in concentric rings.

The priest began chanting softly.

"Open your senses," he instructed. "Let the Ember's call flow through you. Do not resist."

Mira swallowed hard. Her heart thudded painfully.

She braced herself.

The magic surged.

Cold flooded through her like a tide. Not painful, but powerful. It pulled at her, whispering in tones she almost remembered, like lullabies her mother used to hum.

Her vision blurred for a moment as frost spiraled across the runes.

On the other side of the gathering, Kael Ashrow felt the surge.

He stepped back abruptly, hand clutching his chest. His fire magic flared in instinctive defiance, reacting to the frost that rippled through the air.

A spark burned through his glove.

The soldiers glanced at him sharply.

"Easy," one muttered. "Do not draw attention."

Too late.

The emissary turned toward the disturbance.

Her gaze swept past Kael, landed on Mira, then darted back.

Her brows lifted. She sensed the strange ripple, even if she did not yet understand the source.

The priest's chant rose to a sharper pitch.

The lake's glow deepened.

Mira's breath hitched.

Heat slammed into the connection, but it was not her own.

The young Ashrow mage had dropped his mask for a fraction of a second. His fire magic flared instinctively, pushing back against the frost in the air, creating a strange counterpulse.

The clash of cold and heat sent a shockwave through the circle.

Mira gasped. Frost burst from her palms before she could contain it.

Kael staggered as flames rippled across his sleeve.

A collective gasp rose from the crowd.

The emissary pointed sharply. "Contain them."

Soldiers moved.

Priests advanced.

The air thickened with tension.

Mira forced her magic back, hands trembling. Kael did the same, though his fire fought him harder than hers fought her.

The priest's voice cut through the chaos. "Enough."

Silence fell like a heavy cloak.

Everyone froze.

Snow drifted quietly in the air while the frost and fire traces slowly faded.

The emissary scanned the gathered individuals before her eyes locked onto Mira with unnerving certainty.

"You," she said coldly. "You react far too strongly for an untrained villager."

Mira swallowed, unable to speak.

Kael's gaze snapped to her again. He looked equally troubled. Equally aware.

The emissary's gaze shifted to the Ashrow group. "The same reaction from you is expected. Your blood has always burned too hot."

Kael said nothing, but his jaw tightened.

Mira stared at the lake, pulse racing.

Something was deeply wrong with the Ember.

She could feel it twisting beneath the ice, alive and restless. And somehow, impossibly, her magic and Kael's were reacting to the same disturbance.

The priest turned back to the lake, concern etched into the lines of his face.

"The Rite will begin soon," he murmured. "And the Ember stirs with an unknown hunger."

Mira closed her gloved fingers around her palm.

Kael lowered his hand, heat fading beneath his skin.

Neither of them understood what had happened.

But both knew this was only the beginning.

* * *

A cold wind swept across the valley, lifting snow into thin spirals. The crowd shifted uneasily as the frost runes dimmed beneath Mira's feet. Her breath came in slow, controlled exhalations. She tried to calm the tremor in her hands, but the magic inside her remained alert, agitated by the strange pull from the lake and the heat she had felt from the Ashrow mage.

He stood only thirty paces away, yet she could feel his presence like a warm ripple in the wintry air. She did not dare look toward him again. She could not risk even the appearance of familiarity.

The emissary signaled her attendants. "Form the outer circle. Increase the warding lines. Something in the lake is disturbing the gifted."

Priests hurried to obey. They carried carved poles of ice infused with crystal, placing them around the gathering in a wide ring. Runes along the poles ignited, glowing white with rigid authority. The air tightened with their presence, pressing down on Mira's senses. Her frost magic recoiled, retreating deep inside her chest.

She took a slow breath. Now she could not feel the young man's warmth at all. The wards had severed the subtle connection between them.

Good, she told herself. She needed distance. She needed control.

But as she looked out across the lake, she knew distance would not save her from what waited beneath the ice.

The frozen surface stretched wide and glassy, reflecting the temple towers in distorted patterns. Pale blue light pulsed under the ice, rising and fading in slow waves. It should have been beautiful. It should have carried the serene breath of an ancient and sacred place.

Instead, the lake felt restless.

Predatory.

As if the Ember beneath it was pacing against its bounds.

A priest knelt at the edge of the circle and pressed his palm to the ice. His eyes widened with alarm. He whispered something to the emissary. Mira could not hear the words, but she saw the emissary's expression tighten.

A ripple passed through the gathered crowd.

One of the Ashrow observers stepped forward. His voice carried steel beneath his calm tone. "You feel it too."

The emissary stiffened. "Feel what?"

The man gestured toward the lake. "A fracture. A weakness in the central bound. Something is wrong with your Ember."

Several Veris acolytes bristled. The emissary's face hardened.

"Your people speak freely on matters you do not understand."

"Do you understand it?" the Ashrow soldier countered.

The emissary refused to answer. She turned sharply to her priests. "Strengthen the wards."

The poles flared brighter. The air grew denser. Mira clenched her jaw as the pressure increased, making her head throb. The villagers beside her gasped, overwhelmed. Frost crept across her glove, unbidden. She covered her hand in her cloak to hide it.

The Ashrow mage had moved to the very edge of his group. He stood tall despite the pressure bearing down on him. His eyes were locked on the lake. His breath came low and controlled, but the faint shimmer of heat beneath his coat betrayed the strain.

Their gazes crossed again.

Not intentionally. Not meaningfully. Just the shared pull of two people sensing the same impossible imbalance.

For a moment, her frost magic stirred in answer.

His fire flared quietly.

Two forces trying to reach one another and recoiling under the weight of the wards.

Mira looked away quickly.

The priest who had touched the ice spoke again, his voice shaking slightly. "The Ember is rising sooner than predicted. The Rite is not prepared for this."

The emissary hissed under her breath. "We take our guidance from the Ember itself. Prepare the gifted for resonance."

Another priest approached, holding a polished silver ring inscribed with ancient runes. He placed it around the Seeker's sphere, which Mira had hoped she would never see again. The sphere brightened as the ring shifted its properties.

"Resonance check," the emissary ordered. "One by one."

Mira's throat went dry.

She had already been flagged once. A second display could expose the truth of her lineage. If they recognized the Thornvale frost signature, she would never leave this place alive.

The first villager stepped forward, trembling. The sphere reacted gently, a mild swirl of pale color. The priests nodded.

The next stepped forward. Same response. Mild. Harmless.

A young fisherman approached. The sphere glowed brighter than before, recognizing potential, but not fully awakened talent. The priests accepted him with approving murmurs.

Then Mira's turn came.

She stepped forward slowly. The sphere brightened even before she reached it. Her breath hitched. She tried to calm the magic rising inside.

Remember the cold. Remember stillness. Do not feel. Do not react.

She reached the sphere with careful steps.

It pulsed.

Not wildly. Not dangerously. But definitely.

Enough to mark her.

Enough to draw the emissary's attention again.

The emissary stepped closer. "You are hiding something."

"I am no one of importance," Mira said quietly.

The emissary studied her, expression cold. "Your magic does not behave like a villager's. You have training."

Mira kept her face still.

"You will be watched closely," the emissary said. "If you show instability, you will be removed."

Mira nodded once, though her stomach knotted tightly.

A shout from the far side of the clearing interrupted the moment.

One of the Ashrow soldiers had staggered backward, nearly dropping to a knee. His hands glowed red beneath his gloves. Heat rippled through the air. Snow melted in a tiny circle around his boots.

Kael grabbed the man by the shoulder. "Contain it," he growled.

The soldier inhaled sharply, forcing his hands still. The glow dimmed.

But not fast enough.

The emissary pointed. "You bring instability here on purpose."

Kael glared at her. "We bring warnings you are too proud to hear."

"Enough," a Veris priest snapped. "Your fire disrupts the frost wards. Maintain control or be removed."

Kael held himself rigid. "Tell your Ember to stop pressing on my magic and I will obey your request."

His words struck the crowd like a spark in dry tinder. Several gasped. A few muttered threats. The emissary's eyes narrowed.

Mira felt the tension coiling between the two sides, tight as wire.

The scene reminded her of the political fractures she had glimpsed through her father's study door years ago. Quiet wars fought in words before they erupted in steel and magic.

Before anyone could speak again, the lake pulsed.

A deep, resonant thrum rolled across the surface, vibrating through the air and into the earth. Snow leapt from the ground in a fine mist. The wards flickered.

Everyone froze.

The pulse came again, stronger this time.

Mira's breath caught. Her vision spun for a heartbeat. Frost spiraled across her palm without her command.

Kael inhaled sharply. Heat flared down his arm.

Their powers had reacted at the exact same moment.

The emissary took a step back, alarm in her eyes. "What is happening?"

The priest whispered, voice trembling. "The Ember pushes outward. Something draws it."

Another pulse. Strong enough to rattle the poles anchoring the wards. Strong enough to make several villagers stumble.

Mira grabbed the edge of the rune circle to steady herself. The cold in her chest flared dangerously.

She glanced toward Kael.

He was doubled over slightly, hand pressed to his chest, fighting a flare of fire inside him.

Their eyes met for a third time.

This time, she did not look away fast enough.

For one breath, the world around them seemed to blur. Frost and fire rippled in the air between them, faint but undeniable. A current. A pull.

A connection.

Then the wards surged violently, snapping the sensation apart.

The emissary shouted. "Separate them. Now."

Soldiers on both sides stepped forward. Priests moved to increase the distance between Mira's group and the Ashrow delegates. Confusion spread like wildfire.

Mira backed up, hands trembling.

Kael straightened, breathing hard, and forced his magic down beneath the surface.

The lake pulsed again, deeper, like a heartbeat beneath glass.

Everyone stared at the frozen water. Even the emissary fell silent.

A final pulse radiated outward, so strong it sent cracks whispering across the ice in thin, jagged lines.

The crowd collectively inhaled.

Then the ice stilled.

Silence returned like a held breath.

The emissary pointed sharply to the gifted group. "Bring them into the temple. Lock the wards behind us."

The priests hurried to obey.

Mira followed, heart pounding, magic trembling inside her. She could not stop thinking about the strange current that had rippled between her and the Ashrow mage.

It was impossible.

It was forbidden.

It was dangerous.

And yet it had happened.

Kael watched her go as the Ashrow soldiers were directed to their own restricted area. He tried to look away, but something about that final pulse lingered in his mind.

Something about her frost signature.

Something that should have been impossible.

Neither of them understood what had transpired on the ice.

But both knew it was more than a coincidence.

And deep beneath the lake, the Ember stirred as if it recognized them both.

* * *

The interior causeway leading into the Temple of Glass felt colder than the valley outside. Frost traced every archway like delicate script, and thin sheets of ice shimmered across the walls in layered patterns. Lanterns glowed within protective glass spheres, their light scattering into thousands of fractured reflections.

Mira followed the emissary into a long hall where rows of tall crystalline pillars stood like frozen guardians. The summoned villagers trailed behind her, whispering nervously. She remained silent, forcing her breathing steady as the sound of the lake's last pulse echoed through her thoughts.

The emissary stopped near a raised platform. Priests hurried around her, marking runes across the floor with chalk and melting small indentations in the ice to place silver bowls of fragrant herbs.

"You will wait here until the high priest arrives," the emissary instructed. "The Ember has spoken. A stronger rite is required. Your presence will be used to stabilize the resonance."

One of the villagers asked timidly, "Will it be safe?"

The emissary barely looked at him. "Safety depends on obedience."

Mira swallowed tightly. She hated that she understood what those words truly meant. Veris did not offer safety. It offered containment. It offered control. And she had walked directly into its grasp.

A sharp chill crept across her spine. The frost spiral beneath her glove tingled faintly, as if whispering a warning she could not decipher.

She stepped to the side of the group, close enough to appear compliant but far enough that she could observe the hall. The growing hum of magic within the stone made her skin prickle.

A low voice drifted from the entrance behind her. Not loud. Not demanding. Just steady and close enough to catch her attention.

"Watch your steps. Their floors are never as stable as they look."

The tone was smooth yet edged with caution.

She turned slightly.

Kael Ashrow strode into the hall with two guards flanking him and the remaining Ashrow observers behind. His expression was controlled, but tension lingered beneath his calm surface. The heat of his presence rippled faintly, disturbing the still air.

He should not have been allowed inside this far. Ashrow delegates were usually restricted to the outer chambers.

Mira frowned.

The emissary marched toward them with narrowed eyes. "This area is restricted. You were ordered to wait near the side hall."

Kael gave a short incline of his head. "Your priests summoned me."

The nearest priest nodded reluctantly. "His fire signature reacted during the last pulse. We require him for resonance balancing."

The emissary's jaw tightened. Clearly she did not like the idea of Ashrow magic mingling with her sacred rite.

Kael stepped past her toward the edge of the platform. The air around him shimmered with subtle heat. Mira felt it like a warm breath against her cheek, even from several paces away.

She tensed.

Do not react, she warned herself.

Not again.

But her magic whispered and shifted, reaching toward the warmth instinctively.

The emissary snapped an order. "Separate the gifted groups. Keep them apart."

Priests moved quickly, dividing the hall into sections using tall ice screens carved with runic sigils. Mira was pushed toward the right side of the chamber. Kael and the Ashrow observers toward the left.

The moment a screen settled between them, Mira felt the air lose its unnatural warmth. The quiet flare inside her died away. Her magic retreated like a startled animal.

She released a shaky breath she had not realized she was holding.

The high priest entered the hall at that moment, robes sweeping across the floor like drifting snow. His presence carried weight that pressed against every breath. Fine strands of silver hair framed his face, and the intricate runes stitched into his sleeves glowed faintly.

He approached the raised platform and lifted his hands.

"Children of the Ember," he said, voice echoing across the hall. "The lake calls with a voice we have not heard for many lifetimes. It strains against the bindings that hold it. The Rite must be prepared sooner than expected."

A murmur rippled through the gathered priests.

The high priest fixed his gaze on Mira's group. "You will be placed around the outer circle to lend your resonance to the Rite."

He turned toward Kael's side of the chamber, his expression colder.

"Your presence is required for balance, though unorthodox. Your magic threatens to disrupt the frost currents. You will follow our command or face removal."

Kael bowed his head slightly. Respectful enough to avoid conflict. Unsubmissive enough to make his real stance clear.

The high priest continued. "Before we begin the preparations, each of you will undergo a personal assessment to measure your bond with the Ember. Step forward one by one."

The villagers moved nervously.

Mira waited, hoping she might be evaluated quietly. She did not want attention. She wanted invisibility.

The fisher youth stepped forward first. The high priest placed a hand on his forehead. The runes on the robe glowed. The sphere flared faintly, then dimmed.

The high priest nodded. "Minor frost affinity. Acceptable."

The next villager stepped forward. Another minor glow. Another nod.

Then the priest's gaze settled on Mira.

"You. Step forward."

Her stomach twisted. She stepped toward him, keeping her hands tight at her sides.

He lifted his hand toward her. Frost runes brightened on his sleeve. Mira braced herself.

Cold energy brushed her skin.

Her magic surged in answer.

Not violently. But sharply. Bright enough to make the frost spiral beneath her glove pulse in alarm.

The high priest inhaled sharply. "Your pattern is... unusual."

Her breath hitched. "I have simple frost magic. Nothing rare."

"Do not lie in this place," he said quietly.

His hand remained suspended above her.

Mira forced her expression still. "I am no threat."

The high priest studied her for several long seconds, eyes narrowing. He lowered his hand at last.

"You will be placed near the northern quadrant during the Rite. Your presence may be needed to stabilize a breach."

She bowed her head.

A breach.

So the lake truly was fracturing.

She stepped back into the line, heart pounding so hard she felt it in her fingertips.

On the opposite side of the hall, Kael stepped forward for his assessment. Mira should not have watched, yet her gaze flicked toward him through a narrow gap between screens.

The high priest moved toward him cautiously.

Kael stood tall, expression unreadable. His fire magic simmered beneath the surface, struggling against the cold walls and oppressive wards.

The high priest extended his hand.

The runes on his sleeve flickered.

Kael's magic rose sharply. Heat rippled across his chest and arms. He clenched his fists, forcing control.

The high priest stepped back. "Your power is volatile."

"I keep it restrained," Kael said evenly.

"For now."

The high priest turned away with a troubled expression.

"Place him in the southern quadrant," he instructed. "Far from the frost convergence."

Mira exhaled softly. At least distance would make the strange pull between their powers easier to control.

The high priest raised his arms again.

"Prepare the grounds. The Rite may begin before nightfall if the Ember continues to rise."

Priests scattered like startled birds. Bells rang deep within the temple, signaling urgency. Acolytes rushed through the hall with stacks of woven blankets, carved ritual tools and glowing orbs of light.

The floor beneath Mira trembled faintly.

Another pulse.

Quieter, but present.

She stepped back instinctively, her fingers brushing the cold wall behind her.

Kael turned sharply in the direction of the lake, even though he could not see it from inside. He pressed a hand to his chest, fire magic reacting again.

Mira clutched her cloak, trying to calm her breath.

She felt it too. The pulse. The pull. The faint magnetic tug between her frost and Kael's fire, both reacting to the same unseen force under the ice.

She closed her eyes for a brief moment.

This was not normal resonance.

This was something older.

Something hungry.

A young acolyte passed by Mira and whispered in a trembling voice, "The Ember should not be waking like this. The bindings are ancient, but they were never meant to hold forever."

Mira's breath stilled.

Not meant to hold forever.

She opened her eyes.

Across the hall, Kael stared at the floor as if listening to something deeper than sound.

For a heartbeat, Mira felt the faintest brush of warmth again, slipping past the weakened wards. Not a wave. Not a flare. Just a whisper.

A whisper that matched the rhythm of the pulse beneath the lake.

Their magic brushed.

Only an instant.

But unmistakable.

Her hand trembled.

His jaw tightened.

The emissary shouted new orders.

Priests hurried them toward separate exits leading to their assigned quadrants around the lake.

The Rite preparations had begun.

And whatever waited beneath the ice had already set its sights on both of them.

Chapter 5

The sky over the Temple of Glass shifted into shades of violet as dusk bled across the horizon. The first ribbons of northern light unfurled above the valley, shimmering in slow waves that reflected across the frozen lake. Colors deepened from lavender to cobalt, then lifted into arcs of pale green that swirled like smoke caught in a soft wind. The priests called the lights a blessing of clarity, a sign that the Ember welcomed the rite. Yet as Mira followed the acolytes to her assigned position on the northern side of the lake, the lights felt more like an omen. The air trembled with a delicate tension. Even the snow seemed to hold its breath.

The ritual grounds had transformed into a vast circle marked by etched lines of frost and columns of ice carved with ancient runes. Witnesses stood behind a secondary ring of guards and ropes, hundreds of them wrapped in heavy cloaks. Families clung together, breath clouding the air as they whispered predictions or prayers. Officials from Veris stood nearer the front, their polished attire catching the light of the lanterns. Across from them, distant but unmistakable, the Ashrow delegates waited in disciplined formation. Their expressions bore a silent challenge to the ceremony unfolding before them.

Mira was guided to a narrow platform carved into the ice. A priest touched her shoulder with a quick brush of cold fingers to anchor her in place. She steadied herself and tried to ignore the pressure that gathered at the center of her chest. The frost resonance circle beneath her feet glowed with a pale blue light. It hummed with living energy, threads of magic rising and falling like the breath of a sleeping beast. As the hum settled into a steady rhythm, small spirals of frost lifted from the surface and curled around her boots. She inhaled sharply and felt the chill crawl up her legs and into her palms.

Across the lake, Kael took his place within the fire containment circle. The southern quadrant had been carved into the ice with deep channels meant to draw heat downward so it could dissipate safely. Unlike the cool blue glow at Mira's feet, the fire quadrant pulsed with a soft amber tone. Even from a distance Mira could sense the heat trembling above the surface. Kael stood at the center with a rigid stillness that suggested enormous effort. His shoulders were set, feet wide for balance, and his hands hung close to his sides with fingers splayed slightly. The fire inside him pressed against his control. She could almost feel it, a coiled force demanding release.

The high priest stepped onto the central platform dressed in layers of shimmering cloth that trailed behind him like frostwoven mist. His voice carried across the basin, amplified by the natural acoustics of the frozen lake. He spoke the ancient invocation to waken the Ember gently and bind its rising to the will of Veris. The words echoed through the valley in rolling waves that blended with the whisper of the wind and the crackle of torches.

The crowd fell into complete stillness. Even the rustle of fabric quieted.

Mira felt the frost respond. Thin streams of icy vapor curled from her fingertips, weaving through the runes with a life of their own. She tried to guide them, but they slipped past her will, weaving into the ritual pattern as if pulled by an unseen hand. Her heart pounded at the loss of control, but the resonance held firm and did not become dangerous. The threads of magic from each participant rose together, intertwining like strands in a vast tapestry.

Kael's fire answered the call from his own quadrant. The warm glow around him shifted into brighter ribbons that circled his arms and chest. He closed his eyes, jaw tight, and forced the flames back to a controlled flicker. His circle required him to contain his power rather than release it. The fire strained toward the outer edges of the carved lines, but Kael held it steady with visible effort. Sweat glistened along his hairline despite the cold.

As the first phase of the ritual deepened, the northern lights brightened above the valley. Their colors pooled across the frozen lake, casting shimmering reflections across the ice. The surface beneath Mira's feet vibrated with a steady pulse, almost like a heartbeat. She braced herself and widened her stance to remain stable. The frost around her hands thickened until it formed delicate crystalline filaments that drifted upward in spiraling strands.

A sudden murmur spread through the crowd. Mira looked down.

Thin cracks of white light flickered beneath the frozen surface. They were faint at first, like tiny veins of illumination, but they grew with each pulse until they spread outward from the center like the branches of an intricate tree. Light gathered beneath the ice in erratic bursts that did not follow the rhythm of the chant.

The priests exchanged alarmed glances. Several tightened their grip on the long staffs used for emergency containment. The high priest raised his voice, weaving more force into the ritual words, attempting to steady the energy. Mira felt the shift instantly. The frost around her surged stronger as the Ember pressed upward.

Kael's fire roared in response.

Heat burst more sharply around him, climbing his arms in a wave that nearly spilled beyond the lines of his circle. He gritted his teeth and forced his hands downward, channeling the flames into the containment channels cut into the ice. The glow around him flickered violently. The air above his quadrant shimmered.

Mira's breath caught. Her magic strained toward the heat, reacting to it even across the large gap between them. She tried to clamp down, but a thin shard of frost rose from her palm with a sharp sound and tore through the air before dissolving.

Kael's eyes opened in that instant. He snapped his gaze toward her, even though the ritual should have held his attention entirely. For a moment their powers reacted again, drawn to the growing imbalance between fire and frost.

The ice beneath them groaned.

A deep, resonant sound rolled across the lake. The cracks of light widened into thicker streaks. Several witnesses backed away from the ropes, some clutching each other in fear. The high priest lifted both arms, summoning more of the ancient words, but the response from the lake did not follow the pattern he sought.

The Ember was waking early.

And it did not seem pleased.

Mira felt the energy gathering below, thick and impatient, like a storm trapped beneath glass. The frost threads around her fused together into sharp lines that rose toward her wrists. She fought against the pressure, but the magic pushed harder, demanding release. Her hands trembled as she tried to keep the frost contained.

On the opposite side, Kael staggered as flames erupted across his chest, bursting past his control. The heat spread into the air around him and melted a thin ring of ice despite the containment runes. One of the priests shouted at him to regain discipline, but Kael was already fighting with everything he had. His face twisted with effort as he pushed the fire back into his circle.

The lake cracked again with a hollow sound that echoed through the valley.

A jagged line of light shot across the surface, splitting one of the carved paths in Mira's quadrant. Frost vented upward in a sudden flash that forced her to throw her hands up. The blast knocked one of the villagers beside her to the ground. Mira reached out quickly, steadying the young woman before she fell over the rim of the platform. The others backed away in panic, but the ring of priests shouted for them to hold positions.

The high priest stepped forward once more, lifting his staff. The air thickened with raw power as he forced stronger spells into the ritual. The staff ignited with pale white fire that sank downward through the ice in a column of light. The cracks beneath the lake hissed and shuddered.

The Ember pushed against the pressure.

It was not supposed to rise without the completed Rite. It was not supposed to answer anyone without permission. Yet Mira felt its awareness like a cold hand pressed to her chest, heavy and intrusive. She gasped as the frost spirals along her arms lit with unfamiliar strength.

Kael felt the shift at the same moment. His fire no longer moved only with his will. For a brief instant it responded to something deeper, something that felt like a summons. The heat surged toward the lake as if trying to reach it, breaking through his grip with a violent jolt. He slammed one knee into the ice to brace himself as his magic threatened to explode.

The high priest's voice cracked with strain. He shouted for the ritual to stabilize, but the lake answered with another tremor.

A final crack of light snaked from the center of the lake to the outer edge, stopping only a few feet from Mira's boots. She stared at it with wide eyes, breath thin and fast. Her frost magic surged again, bursting across the air in jagged streaks before she forced them down. The villagers beside her cried out and covered their faces. The priests moved between groups, shouting reassurances that sounded less confident with each passing moment.

Across the lake, Kael steadied himself and looked at Mira. Their eyes met in the rising chaos. The space between them shimmered faintly as frost and fire strained toward one another, responding to the same violent heartbeat under the ice.

This time neither of them looked away.

The northern lights overhead flared brighter, casting vivid green and purple across the lake. The Ember pulsed again, stronger than before, sending thin waves of luminous energy spiraling outward from the shattered center.

The Rite had begun. But something beneath the glass had woken before its time, and its rising power did not follow the laws of any kingdom.

Chapter 6

The frozen lake convulsed beneath the gathering crowd, sending a deep vibration rolling through the valley. Mira braced herself against the surge, her fingers digging into the icy rim of the resonance circle. The cracks of white light beneath the surface widened in branching paths, glowing so brightly they illuminated the faces of the witnesses standing well beyond the safety ropes. The northern lights above swirled in restless spirals, casting moving shadows across the temple towers.

The high priest shouted for the rite to hold steady, but his voice was swallowed by the rising groan from the lake. Frost curled upward from the broken runes at Mira's feet, forming sharp spirals that wrapped around her wrists. Her magic strained like a creature pulled in two directions at once. She tried to bury the surge in her chest, but the ritual had opened a door she no longer controlled.

Across the lake, Kael fought a battle of his own. Flames erupted along his arms, climbing in streaks of fiery gold. He forced them down with sheer strength of will, but each pulse from the lake sent another wave of heat roaring through him. His breath came in ragged gasps. Sweat froze at the ends of his hair, only to be burned off again by the fire wreathing his shoulders. Around him, priests shouted frantic instructions, demanding he hold the containment lines.

The Ember pulsed again. The frozen lake flashed with a blinding burst of light.

Something tore free in the air between Mira and Kael.

A thin, shimmering arc of energy sparked above the lake, so faint at first that Mira barely noticed it. It appeared like a thread of frost, catching the last trace of sunlight. Then it thickened, brightened and shot across the lake with a swift, crackling arc. It connected two points with uncanny precision.

Her.

And him.

Mira gasped as the light struck her chest. The world tilted. Her knees buckled, and she clutched the resonance circle for support. The frost spiraling around her arms shattered into drifting white shreds that hovered in the air. Every breath she drew tasted like winter lightning.

Kael staggered as the same arc hit him squarely in the sternum. His fire exploded upward in a burst of uncontrolled heat. Flames flared around him, warping the air and melting the protective ice channels. He dropped to one knee, gripping the runes carved into the circle with shaking hands. His vision blurred with dancing sparks.

The arc of light between them pulsed once, twice, then flared so brightly the entire valley was washed in white.

Mira's scream was swallowed by the explosion.

The world evaporated.

There was no cold. No heat. No sound.

Only falling.

Only light.

She tried to inhale but found no air. Her body drifted as though suspended in deep water. Colors swirled over her vision, shifting from frost blue to molten gold. A faint warmth brushed her cheek, though she could not tell if it came from outside or from somewhere deep within her chest.

Then the vision took shape.

White mist curled around her, thickening into familiar outlines. Walls formed out of swirling frost. Crystal lanterns glowed overhead. She stood in a hall she had not seen since childhood, her breath catching at the sight of Thornvale sigils carved along the pillars. A younger version of herself ran past, laughing, hair braided in loops for a festival she remembered all too clearly. Her father's voice called from the far doorway, warm and calm.

Mira reached for the memory, her hand shaking. Her fingers passed through the ghost of her younger self like drifting smoke.

A shadow crossed the hall.

The scene twisted.

The next vision struck with sharp clarity.

She saw herself standing in the courtyard of Thornvale stronghold on the night of exile. Veris soldiers surrounded her family, torches illuminating the cold cruelty in their expressions. Her mother clutched her arm, whispering for her to stay silent. A priest in ceremonial robes pointed at Mira with disdain, announcing their disgrace.

The air brimmed with frost.

Mira tried to turn away, but the vision held her captive. She felt her father's trembling hand as he placed a final coil of frost magic around her wrist, hiding it under her sleeve. A last protection. A last act of love.

She reached for him as the memory dissolved.

The vision shattered into swirling shards of ice.

In the darkness between one breath and the next, heat surged across her back.

A new vision engulfed her.

She stood in a stone courtyard lit by flames. Sparks drifted in the air like dying stars. Young boys trained with practice blades under the harsh gaze of Ashrow elders. Among them was Kael, smaller than the others but determined, sweat streaming down his face as his fire magic flickered with uneven bursts. A young girl, slightly smaller, cheered him on while weaving strands of flame between her fingers. Lira.

Mira stepped closer without meaning to.

She saw Kael stumble during his magic drills. His power burst too strong. The elders scolded him for recklessness, accusing him of letting emotion guide the flame. She watched him clench his fists and hide the hurt in his eyes. She saw Lira slip him a quiet smile, reminding him that he was more than the elders' expectations.

The scene twisted again, harsher this time.

Kael stood in the middle of a hall filled with Veris envoys. Their voices dripped with false civility. His clan elders argued with them, their tones sharp and laced with tension. A treaty lay open on a table, ink still wet. Mira saw the moment Kael realized he was being lied to. His jaw stiffened. Heat flared beneath his skin. The vision shifted so suddenly she felt her stomach turn.

Darkness surged. Cracks of white light spiked out in all directions.

The vision dissolved into an endless storm of frost and fire.

Both forces circled her like spiraling smoke, twisting tighter and tighter. Mira's breath stuttered as she tried to push them apart. Fire licked her skin without burning. Frost curled around her fingers without chilling. The two elements collided, clashing in bursts that shook the vision.

A presence moved through the storm.

Kael.

Or the vision's reflection of him.

He approached slowly, eyes glowing with a molten light. Sparks drifted from his hands. The fire surrounding him responded to the frost around her, spiraling closer in a strange dance she could neither understand nor stop.

"Mira," he said, though she could not tell if the sound was real or imagined. His voice felt like something entering her mind rather than her ears. "What is this?"

"I do not know," she whispered.

The frost around her pulsed in panic. "I am not supposed to be here. You are not supposed to be here."

Their surroundings twisted again.

A swirl of ice. A burst of flame.

Then the vision folded inward.

The world dropped away.

For a moment Mira felt her heart pulled toward a single point of light. It felt like a thread winding around her ribs, pulling tight, binding itself into the center of her chest. The sensation was terrifying and strangely familiar at the same time. It anchored her, even as she fell deeper into the darkness.

She felt the presence of another heartbeat.

Not touching her.

Not near her.

Inside her.

Her breath broke.

Kael's voice echoed through the collapsing vision. "Something is binding us."

"I feel it too."

The thread tightened.

The storm collapsed in a blinding flash.

Reality struck like a blow.

Mira's eyes snapped open as her body collided with the frozen ground. Frost shot across the packed snow around her in jagged waves. Shouts echoed through the temple grounds, but her ears rang too loudly to decipher the words. Pain radiated across her ribs as she struggled to rise.

Across the lake, Kael slammed onto one knee, flames bursting around him in uncontrolled arcs before dying in a violent sputter. Steam rose from the ground beneath him. He gasped for air, hands braced against the ice, his eyes wide with shock.

Their eyes met across the chaos.

She felt the thread.

It pulled tight.

The air left her lungs.

Kael felt it too. His expression shifted in horror and disbelief.

A soul bond.

Uncontrolled.

Unbidden.

Impossible.

Yet undeniable.

Before either of them could react, the lake screamed.

Not with sound.

With light.

A seismic pulse erupted from beneath the frozen surface, shattering the center of the lake in a massive burst. Sheets of ice cracked like brittle glass. Priests scrambled to reinforce the wards. Witnesses shrieked as the ground trembled beneath their feet. Frost towers toppled. Fire channels burst into molten steam. Elemental energy spiraled upward in violent columns.

Mira clutched her chest, the bond burning like a second heartbeat. Her frost surged uncontrollably, spinning outward in shards that cut through the air. She fell backward as the force overwhelmed her.

Kael roared as fire erupted from his arms in violent streams that scorched the ice. He threw his hands outward to keep the flames from hitting the priests restraining the perimeter. The bond pulled tighter every time he resisted, sending a violent echo through Mira's chest.

The high priest shouted orders, but his voice was drowned in the roar of cracking ice.

The winter sky lit with spiraling arcs of frost and flame.

The Rite had failed.

The Ember had awakened.

And Mira and Kael, bound by a magic neither wanted, stood at the center of the storm that should never have existed.

* * *

The blast rolled outward from the lake with a force that Mira felt in her bones. She hit the ice hard and slid several paces, her cloak whipping behind her as the frozen surface cracked beneath her weight. The ringing in her ears made the world fade in and out in disjointed fragments. Above her, the northern lights shuddered as if struck by an unseen blow, their colors flickering in jagged bursts.

Priests scrambled around the edges of the ritual circle, shouting incantations that dissolved into the roar of splitting ice. Columns of frost crumbled and shattered. The runes meant to stabilize the rite flickered like dying embers, then went dark. A blinding jet of light shot upward from the center of the lake, illuminating the valley in stark white.

Mira pushed herself up onto shaking hands. Her limbs trembled with exhaustion, but the strange new pulse inside her chest frightened her more than the ruptured ice. The bond thrummed like a second heartbeat. Every time she drew breath, the connection pulled and twisted through her ribs.

Across the lake, Kael struggled to stand. Flames erupted along his arms and then died in sputtering waves. His body shook as if caught between two opposing currents. For a moment he faltered and dropped back to one knee, gripping the cracked ice to keep from collapsing entirely. The bond responded to his pain with a fierce tug that sent Mira gasping.

She flinched at the sensation. His breath. His pain. His pulse. All of it echoed inside her like distant thunder that somehow reached directly into her mind. She felt his fire magic flare and then collapse inward, as if crushed under the weight of the awakened Ember. The recoil slammed into her frost magic, sending a shock through every nerve.

She staggered to her feet, breath ragged. Around her, villagers and witnesses fled in panic as massive fissures carved their way across the lake. Guards shouted for people to withdraw from the ritual site. Some dragged injured acolytes toward the safety of the temple walls. Others rushed to support priests who were struggling to keep the remaining wards from collapsing entirely.

A chunk of ice the size of a wagon toppled from the lake's broken center, splashing into the churning water beneath. Steam shot upward as frost and fire collided inside the depths. The Ember glowed beneath the surface with an intensity that Mira had never imagined possible. It pulsed with unsettling consciousness, its light swirling like a restless eye searching for something.

Or someone.

Mira felt its attention like a scrape across her mind.

She recoiled and snapped her gaze to the far end of the lake.

Kael met her stare with raw fear in his eyes.

For the first time, she knew the truth with chilling certainty. The Ember was aware of them. Not separately. Not as two gifted individuals caught in the chaos of a botched rite.

As a pair.

A bond.

A contradiction that should not exist and yet now burned inside both of them.

Another pulse tore through the lake. The ice cracked beneath Mira's boots, forcing her to jump back. Her landing faltered and she stumbled, catching herself only at the last second. The ground quivered like a living creature trying to shed its frozen shell.

Kael lurched to his feet at the same moment. Flames burst from the cracks around his hands, flaring in bright spirals that shot outward before collapsing in sparks. He steadied his breathing, but Mira felt his panic through the bond as clearly as her own. The connection hummed with rising desperation.

A priest sprinted toward Mira, robes torn and stained with frost. "Do not stand near the runes," he shouted. "Your presence destabilizes the convergence. Move away from the circle at once." His voice shook with panic, and his eyes widened when he noticed the frost spirals curling around her wrists. He stepped back, fear flickering across his features.

Another acolyte ran to his side. "She is reacting the same way the fire wielder is. They cannot be near the focal points."

The priest nodded and reached for Mira's arm, intending to drag her away, but the moment his hand brushed her sleeve, a burst of frost erupted between them. He cried out and stumbled, shaking his numbed hand.

Mira jerked back. "I did not mean to. I cannot control it."

"Stay back," the priest warned, retreating. "Your magic is tangled with something beyond you."

She knew what he meant.

Or at least she feared she did.

Kael had finally regained enough balance to stand upright. He glanced down at his hands, his expression twisting between dread and disbelief. Flames flickered across his palms without his permission, leaping higher with every rapid breath he took. He pressed his fists against his chest in a desperate attempt to control the magic, but the bond magnified every surge.

Mira felt another tug.

His breath hitched. His heart raced.

Her own pulse followed, rising in perfect rhythm.

She squeezed her eyes shut, trying to break the connection, but it held tight, woven deeper than anything she had ever felt. Not even childhood training had described something like this. A soul bond was considered nearly mythical, a rare alignment seen only in legends about great catastrophes or unions forged by ancient magic.

It was not supposed to happen by accident.

It was not supposed to happen between frost and fire.

A shout erupted across the lake. Mira opened her eyes in time to see three Veris guards charging toward Kael. One held a restraint collar carved from enchanted ice. The containment tools shimmered with dangerous intent.

Kael tried to step back, but the ice cracked beneath him, forcing him to shift his weight. The guards closed in quickly. Mira felt his pulse spike in alarm. Her own breath caught, the panic flowing through the bond like lightning.

Her magic surged.

Frost spiraled out from her again, curling upward in a bright arc of shimmering white. It shot across the lake in a thin, uncontrolled streak that matched his earlier flare. Kael's flames burst in mirror reaction, erupting into a shield of golden heat. The combined energies collided in a violent flash that forced the guards to retreat.

The crowd screamed.

The high priest shouted orders at the top of his lungs. "Contain the gifted! Separate them at once. They are amplifying each other."

Another priest struggled to form a barrier of frost, but the ground ruptured beneath him, toppling him into the snow.

A column of light shot upward from the lake's center, spiraling into the sky. It twisted violently, then collapsed back inward, slamming into the broken ice with a deafening roar. Waves of blinding white washed across the valley.

Mira shielded her face with her arms. Her vision went white for several seconds. When she lowered her hands, she saw the impossible.

The lake was no longer flat.

The ice had risen.

Jagged peaks of crystalline frost pushed upward like the ribs of a great beast. Between them swirled molten light from the awakened Ember, glowing with unnatural intensity. Water hissed as frost and fire collided with each new pulse.

Priests scrambled to form a barrier around the largest fissure, but each incantation broke under the turbulent magic. Some of the acolytes fell to their knees, overwhelmed by the sheer pressure in the air.

Mira stumbled backward as the bond pulled again.

Kael gasped, clutching his chest. "Stop. Do not move."

"I am not moving," she snapped, breath shaking. "It is pulling us together."

"Fight it."

"I am trying."

The bond tightened.

Mira felt his fire raging in her veins. Kael felt her frost spiraling through his lungs. Their magic tangled in the air, drawn toward the same rupture in the lake. She pushed against the force with everything she had, but the bond coiled tighter.

A group of Ashrow delegates surged toward Kael, shouting for him to withdraw. Their attempts to reach him faltered each time his fire erupted in desperate bursts. Mira could feel his panic rising, and the bond echoed it brutally through her own mind.

Her legs buckled.

Not from fear.

From the strain of holding back something she had no training for, no understanding of, and no way to control.

The high priest raised his staff, shouting an incantation meant to sever magical interference. The runes along the staff glowed white and erupted outward in a circular wave intended to push back rogue magic.

The wave hit Mira and Kael at the same moment.

Both screamed.

The bond snapped tight, then pulled harder, as if the Ember itself refused to let go. Their magic surged wildly, smashing into the priest's spell and sending it rebounding in a burst of shattered runes.

The priest stumbled backward, horrified. "The bond is resisting. The Ember has recognized it."

Gasps rippled across the crowd.

A soul bond was rare.

An uncontrolled soul bond was dangerous.

A soul bond forged in the presence of the Ember was unheard of.

The lake pulsed again.

The cracks widened.

The bond held.

Mira dropped to her knees, clutching her chest. Kael did the same, both of them trembling as their magic spiraled in violent circles.

The Ember rose beneath them in a blinding swell of frost and flame.

The chapter ends on the brink of everything breaking.

* * *

The ground lurched beneath Mira as another violent pulse tore through the lake. Cracks shot across the frozen surface like lightning, splintering in branching paths that reached for the outer rings of the ritual grounds. The ice groaned in long, aching tones that vibrated through her ribs. The bond inside her tightened in a wrenching pull that forced a gasp from her throat.

She pressed a hand against her chest, trying to hold herself steady. Frost spiraled outward from her palm in thin, frantic lines. Every breath she drew felt as though it tugged on Kael's lungs as well as her own. The sensation jarred her, disorienting and intrusive, as if she were being dragged into another life with each pulse.

Across the shattered span of the lake, Kael was fighting a losing battle against his own magic. Flames burst from his shoulders and back in uncontrolled waves that warped the air and made the ice beneath him hiss. He crouched low, one hand braced on the fractured surface, the other pressed against his sternum. His face was pale with strain. Sweat mingled with melting frost along his temples.

Mira felt the heat surging inside him. She felt the tremor of his muscles as he forced himself upright. She felt the fear he buried beneath anger. The bond echoed every sensation, binding them tighter than she could comprehend.

Priests converged on the central platform in a frantic attempt to restore control. Ice staffs clattered against the shaking ground as they formed a circle and began to chant. Their voices blended into a single rising pitch. Runes flared beneath their feet, burning with frantic light. Yet the Ember pushed back against their efforts. The lake trembled with a growing fury.

The high priest shouted over the roar of the collapsing ice. "We must seal the breach. Focus the frost lines. Contain the fire. Stabilize the convergence."

His commands did little to calm the rising terror. Witnesses rushed away from the ropes in a scattering of footsteps. Some slipped on the frozen ground in their haste to escape. Others cried out as the icy ridge of the lake buckled, sending jagged shards rising upright like the teeth of a massive beast.

One of the younger priests lost his footing and fell forward, sliding dangerously near the edge of a widening fissure. Mira darted toward him without thinking, catching his arm and pulling him back from the brink. Her frost flared sharply at the contact, freezing the fabric of his sleeve. He stumbled away from her with wide, terrified eyes.

"Stay back," he stammered. "You are feeding the imbalance."

She pulled her hand to her chest, clutching it as if she could cage her magic by force. Her heart thudded painfully against her ribs. The frost spirals along her arms pulsed with each beat. The bond made her feel Kael's fire just as clearly, a second rhythm fighting against the cold.

The high priest raised his staff again. Light gathered at its tip, swirling in chaotic spirals. He slammed the base of the staff into the ice. A shockwave rippled outward, splitting the surface in several sweeping arcs.

Kael flinched violently as the wave hit him. Mira felt the impact through the bond as though it struck her own chest. The shock stole her breath. She cried out, staggering backward. The frost within her surged in response, spiraling out of control.

Kael lifted his head sharply, breathing hard through clenched teeth. His flames snapped around him like angry serpents. When he forced them down, Mira felt her own magic pulse in pained sympathy.

"Stop fighting it," he shouted across the chaos. His voice cracked with strain, but the words carried with unexpected force. "You are making it worse. I feel every time you force it back."

"I am trying not to lose control," she shouted back. Her throat burned with cold. "You are feeding it too."

"I am barely holding on," he threw back. "The bond keeps pulling."

"We have to resist it together."

"Then stop resisting alone."

The ground shook. A massive fissure split the lake in a booming crack, dividing the central platform in half. The priests rushed to stabilize it with a binding spell, but the spell collapsed under the Ember's pressure, scattering the casters across the ice.

A swell of molten gold glowed beneath the broken surface. Mira pressed a hand to her chest again as the Ember pulsed upward, its consciousness pressing against her mind like a cold and ancient whisper. She had never felt anything so vast. The presence was heavy, searching, curious. It brushed across her magic with invasive interest.

Kael jerked as if struck. He felt it too.

Mira stumbled closer to the edge of her broken circle. Her boots slid across the unstable surface. She righted herself quickly, but the bond pulled harder. Each step she took toward the center of the lake tightened the connection between them. Fire flared faintly across Kael's arms in response.

Priests yelled warnings, but their words blurred under the roar of the awakening Ember.

A jagged ridge of ice rose between Mira and the central breach, then split open in a shower of frost. The shards lifted into the air, suspended by a force she could not see. A swirl of golden steam twisted upward through the gap. It rose in spiraling currents that glowed brighter than any flame she had witnessed.

The Ember surged again.

Mira felt the pulse slam into her chest. She dropped to one knee, digging her nails into the ice. The cold wind whipped her hair across her face. She tasted blood on her lip from biting back a cry. The bond lashed out violently, pulling at her ribs, her spine, her heart.

She forced herself upright, trembling.

Across the lake, Kael did the same. His fire flickered and roared, barely held in check.

Their eyes met through the rising chaos.

The pull between them intensified.

Priests tried desperately to force a barrier between the two gifted. Several raised ice walls that shot upward in tall spires, but the walls cracked immediately under the mixed force of frost and fire bound across the lake. The bond pushed through any separation like water through shattered stone.

The high priest's face twisted in fury and fear. "They are anchored to each other," he shouted. "Remove one from the grounds before the bond strengthens."

Guards rushed toward Mira.

The moment they approached, frost burst from her arms in a wave, pushing them back. She gasped as the magic ripped free involuntarily. The bond amplified the surge. Kael staggered as heat flared violently, forcing him to brace his hands against the ice.

"Enough," Kael growled. "This thing will tear us apart if they keep pushing against it."

Mira's vision blurred. She felt dizzy, overwhelmed by cold and heat spiraling in equal force. The bond throbbed with a rhythm she could not stop. It pulled her forward again, toward the broken center of the lake.

Another swell of energy erupted beneath the surface.

The ice buckled upward, forming a jagged ridge that forced everyone back. Priests scrambled to maintain footing. Witnesses screamed as the outer edges of the lake cracked, spilling ice into the churning water below.

Kael stepped back from the widening fissure. His fire lashed outward in a frantic burst. He clenched his teeth and forced his hands downward, pushing the flames back into himself. Mira felt the effort as a spike of pain in her ribs.

She pressed a hand against the lake, steadying her balance, and forced her magic inward. She closed her eyes, searching for calm in the storm, but the bond pulsed again. She felt Kael's exhaustion as if it were her own.

The Ember rose beneath them in a luminous swell.

A column of white gold light shot upward, piercing the sky with an anguished brilliance. The heat and cold of it hit Mira's body all at once, knocking her backward. She collided with the ice, breath torn from her lungs.

Kael was thrown several paces by the same blast. He hit the ground with a harsh grunt, sliding across the fractured surface. The bond yanked at both of them, forcing their magic to spill out in jagged bursts.

The high priest raised his staff again and shouted for the wards to be reinforced, but the staff cracked down the middle under the strain. The sound echoed across the valley, hollow and final.

A final rupture tore open the center of the lake.

Mira dropped to her knees and felt her consciousness blur at the edges. The bond surged again, drawing her and Kael toward each other across the widening breach. The ice between them shattered, sending chunks tumbling into the glowing water.

Kael struggled to stand, one hand reaching for balance. Mira felt the pull dragging her toward him. She clawed at the broken edge of her circle to anchor herself, but her fingers slipped. Her body pitched forward.

Kael lunged in instinctive response.

The bond snapped tight.

Frost and fire spiraled upward in a violent convergence that drowned out every sound. The magic slammed into both of them with overwhelming force. Mira felt her vision distort as the world twisted and folded around her. Kael shouted something, but the words dissolved in the blinding glare.

The Ember flared one final time.

The blast tore through the valley.

Mira felt herself falling.

Kael felt himself torn from the ice.

Their hands reached toward each other through the blinding light.

Then everything went dark.

Their bodies hit the frozen ground at almost the same moment. The ice beneath them hissed as frost and flame collided once more in sharp, dying flashes.

Silence crashed over the valley as the light faded.

The lake stilled.

Priests froze in place, staring in paralyzed horror.

Witnesses dropped to their knees, breath shallow and uneven.

The high priest clutched the broken staff in shaking hands.

At the center of the wreckage, Mira and Kael lay unconscious, bound by a soul link that now pulsed faintly between them with undeniable certainty.

The Ember had awakened.

And its first act had been to fuse two strangers into a single, volatile destiny neither had chosen.

Chapter 7

The world returned to Mira in fragments. Cold air pricked her skin. Voices swelled and fractured like distant echoes. The scent of scorched ice burned in her nose. When she forced her eyes open, the sky above her rippled with fading remnants of the broken Rite, threads of pale green and purple trembling across the northern lights. The lake lay in ruins. Great jagged plates of ice leaned at precarious angles, surrounding a crater of molten glow where the Ember had surged before sinking once more into restless silence.

Her pulse throbbed painfully in her ribs. Not a single pulse. Two. Her own, and Kael's echoing faintly through the bond. The realization sent a fresh chill down her spine.

She tried to move. A sharp flare of pain raced through her limbs as if her magic had been stretched too far and torn. Her body shook with exhaustion, but she forced herself onto her elbows. Every shift, every breath carried a whisper of someone else's pain.

Across the shattered ground, Kael stirred.

Mira felt his movement before she saw it. The bond tugged sharply, painful in her chest, as if warning her not to drift too far. She pushed to her knees, steadying herself.

Chaos swelled on all sides of the lake. Priests circled the high priest, who looked shaken for the first time Mira had ever seen. His staff lay broken on the ice beside him. Guards yelled conflicting orders. Witnesses pressed against the outer ropes, frantic and pale.

Amid the confusion, voices rose in heated accusations.

A Veris officer pointed at the Ashrow delegates. "This would never have happened if your people had not interfered. The fire signatures disrupted the frost balance."

One of the Ashrow soldiers stepped forward, eyes blazing. "Your Rite failed long before we arrived. The Ember was unstable. You masked it with arrogance."

Several Veris guards stepped between them, hands on their weapons. Snow whipped between the two groups as a fierce wind surged over the lake. The tension thickened like storm clouds gathering over a battlefield.

The emissary appeared at the edge of the chaos, hair disheveled, eyes sharp with fury. She pointed to the center of the ruined ritual ground. "The Ember reacted to them. Both of them. They did something to the Rite."

Mira's breath caught. Faces turned toward her and Kael with accusations etched into their frost chilled features.

Kael pushed himself upright and looked around with wary eyes. His breath came in uneven pulls. The echo of it thudded against Mira's ribs. He clenched his jaw when he saw the Veris soldiers advancing toward him with restraint tools. Steam curled from his shoulders as his fire trembled dangerously near the surface.

Mira rose to her feet just as the emissary turned her pointed accusation on her. "And you. You hid your true magic. You hid your lineage. That alone is treason."

Mira stepped back, heart pounding. The pain behind her sternum sharpened as the bond tightened again. Each time Kael moved or braced for impact, she felt a ghost of the same motion. She forced her expression calm even as panic fluttered beneath her ribs.

Kael's eyes snapped toward her. He felt it too. She could see the realization crossing his face like a storm. He scanned the distance between them, perhaps intending to move closer, but three Veris guards closed in around him with weapons raised.

"We must separate them," one priest shouted. "The bond is still unstable. It could trigger another surge."

Another priest answered with trembling certainty. "If they separate too far, the bond will destabilize the lake again. We cannot risk it."

Their conflicting orders added to the rising frenzy.

The emissary raised her voice, slicing through the arguments. "Take them both. Bring them to the inner cells until we understand the bond. They will be studied and restricted until this danger is contained."

Mira's stomach twisted. She had seen what Veris did to those deemed magically dangerous. Her father's memory flashed behind her eyes. Her family's exile. Her own near capture. She would not survive imprisonment. Neither would Kael. Not with their bond tying every breath, every heartbeat, every flare of magic together.

A guard grabbed Mira's arm.

Pain shot through her chest, sharp and sudden. Kael staggered as if struck. He fell to one knee, gripping the ice. Mira gasped and shoved the guard away on instinct. Frost erupted from her palm, coating the man's gauntlet in a sheath of ice. He recoiled with a cry.

Pandemonium erupted.

More guards rushed toward them. Ashrow soldiers surged forward in defense of their envoy. Veris priests shouted to reinforce the wards while others screamed to open containment channels.

Mira stumbled backward toward Kael because the bond yanked her in that direction. Each step she took eased the pain behind her ribs, and each step she took sent a jolt of warmth through Kael's limbs.

He rose slowly, fire flickering unevenly beneath his skin. "The bond. It wants proximity."

"It hurts when we are apart," Mira whispered, unable to hide the fear in her voice.

"It will hurt worse if they drag us in opposite directions," he said, though his breath came in ragged pulls. "We cannot let them take us."

Guards pushed through the priests and charged toward them. Mira grabbed Kael's arm to steady herself, and a sharp shock of heat and cold sparked between them where their skin touched through the fabric. The bond pulsed fiercely. The ground beneath them cracked.

A priest shrieked. "They are destabilizing the ice again. Separate them now."

"Separate them and the entire lake will rupture," another argued.

"What do you suggest. Bind them together?"

"We do not have time. Stop arguing and act."

The contradictory orders drove the crowd into deeper frenzy.

Kael scanned the surrounding chaos with quick, decisive movements. His gaze snapped to the northern slope leading into the forest, far from the temple, far from Veris control. The path was steep but accessible, and the stormy lights above cast enough glow to guide their escape.

He moved closer to Mira. The bond hummed in relief. "We need to run."

Mira's pulse spiked. "If we run, they will shoot us with binding spells."

"If we stay, they will imprison us until the bond consumes us or the Ember ruptures." His voice dropped, intense and steady even through the shaking of his limbs. "Pick the danger we can actually survive."

Guards began to circle them with precision, forming a tightening ring.

Mira looked into Kael's eyes and saw the same truth she felt in the bond. They had no allies here. No safety in the temple. No control over their magic. If they allowed Veris to cage them, they would die or spark another explosion.

She nodded once, breath sharp. "Run."

Kael grabbed her hand.

The bond surged with heat and frost in a dizzying whirl. Pain vanished. The pull steadied.

Then the two of them sprinted.

Shouts erupted across the ritual grounds. Priests thrust their staffs forward, but the disruption of the Rite had weakened their powers. Runes flickered out before spells could form. Veris guards lunged to intercept them, only to be blocked by Ashrow soldiers who shouted accusations of treachery.

Wind sliced across the lake as Mira and Kael leapt broken slabs of ice and dodged fissures that still smoldered with the afterglow of the Ember. Light shone beneath the cracks like a warning, yet the bond guided their feet almost eerily, tugging them away from the most dangerous paths.

A bolt of frost shot across the ice from the high priest, aimed at Mira's back. Kael yanked her sideways at the last second. The spell shattered into shards against the ground.

They reached the northern bank and scrambled up the slope toward the forest. Snow and ice slipped beneath their boots. Mira's breath burned in her chest. Kael's fire flared along his arms in sharp bursts that melted through branches as they pushed into the trees.

Behind them, chaos continued to swell.

"Stop them," the emissary screamed. "They cannot leave the grounds."

"Do not strike the lake again," a priest protested. "The bond will collapse."

"They will destabilize the Ember if they are not contained."

"Then catch them without magic. Move."

The sounds faded as Mira and Kael ran deeper into the forest, branches closing behind them like sheltering arms. Snow fell in small drifting spirals that muffled the frantic shouts. The wind carried the distant groans of the ruptured lake, but the valley's lights dimmed as they moved out of sight.

Only when they reached a narrow clearing surrounded by pine did they stop, chests heaving, legs shaking.

Mira released Kael's hand instinctively.

A sharp bolt of pain stabbed her ribs.

Kael grunted and stumbled, pressing a hand to his sternum. His expression twisted in shock. "That pain. It is worse at distance."

Mira took a step closer, and the pain eased immediately. Her breathing steadied. "The bond punishes separation."

Kael nodded, face pale. "It forces proximity. It is designed to keep bonded pairs aligned."

"This is unnatural," she whispered. "This was never meant to happen. Not between frost and fire. Not between strangers."

Kael leaned against a pine trunk and closed his eyes. "Whatever happened at that lake changed everything."

Mira scanned the dark forest, her pulse still trembling from the run. "Veris will hunt us. Ashrow will do the same. They will not let a bond like this exist."

Kael opened his eyes and looked at her, firelight flickering faintly in his gaze. "Then we figure out what this is before they catch us."

"And if we do not?" she asked quietly.

Kael exhaled slowly. The bond pulsed between them like a living thread. "Then we survive long enough to try again."

Mira lifted her hand to her chest, fingers trembling over the place where the bond throbbed like a second heart.

They were tied together.

Magically. Physically. Fatefully.

And separating too far could trigger another disaster on the scale of the Rite.

The cold forest wind swept around them.

Somewhere behind the trees, Veris horns sounded in pursuit.

Mira met Kael's gaze with a mixture of fear and reluctant understanding. "We have no choice. We stay together."

His jaw tightened. "Until we figure out how to stop this bond from destroying us."

The horns grew louder.

The bond pulsed.

And with that unsteady heartbeat echoing between their chests, Mira and Kael vanished deeper into the winter night.

Learning the Bond and Uncovering the Truth

Chapter 8

Snow drifted in soft spirals through the trees as Mira and Kael pushed deeper into the forest, the cold air thick with silence. The chaos of the failed Rite still echoed faintly behind them, but the deeper they moved into the Frostwood, the more the sounds of pursuit faded into distant murmurs swallowed by the dark. Their boots crunched through the fresh snow in uneven rhythm. Neither spoke. Neither dared to.

The bond pulsed with every step.

It felt like a thread stitched beneath Mira's ribs, tugging each time she drifted even a little too far from Kael. The pressure was dull at first, a faint tightness in her chest, but the moment she stepped behind a cluster of trees and put a handful of paces between them, the pain sharpened so abruptly it stole her breath. She pressed a hand over her heart, grimacing.

Kael stiffened and sucked in a sharp breath. He turned toward her quickly, eyes narrowing as the shared spike hit him.

"Again," he muttered through clenched teeth. "It pulls when you stray."

"It pulls when you do as well," Mira said, trying to steady her breathing. "We cannot pretend it is only reacting to me."

He ran a hand through his hair, the motion irritated. "I am not pretending anything." He took a cautious step backward, testing. Mira felt the tug immediately. Her ribs burned. Kael hissed in pain and stopped. "There. That is the limit."

Mira exhaled shakily. "A dozen paces. Maybe less."

Kael paced in a narrow circle, still panting softly from the last surge. The faint glow of fire flickered beneath the skin of his hands, betraying his fraying control. He tried to suppress it, but the flames answered the bond instead of him, flaring each time his breath hitched.

Mira folded her arms tightly. "We cannot keep testing the boundary. The feedback is too strong."

"You think I enjoy this?" Kael snapped, then bit off the rest of the sentence. The sharpness in his voice softened into something weary. "I am not your enemy, Mira."

She flinched. Her name on his lips startled her for reasons she did not fully understand. "You are right," she said quietly. "But we do not know what we are to each other now."

They stood in silence beneath towering pines. Frost gathered on the branches above them, ready to fall at the slightest disturbance. The forest air carried a faint metallic scent from the broken Rite, as if the magic still lingered here in scattered fragments.

Mira glanced toward the valley behind them. Smoke rose from the temple grounds in thin streaks. Torches shifted like restless fireflies at the border of the forest. "They are still searching," she whispered. "If they find us now, we will not get another chance."

Kael followed her gaze. His jaw tensed. "The priests will blame us for everything. Veris will want to study us. Ashrow will want to contain me. Neither side will care what the bond does."

Mira wrapped her cloak tighter around her shoulders. The memory of the high priest's fear flickered behind her eyes, sharp and unmistakable. "They will not try to help us. They will try to control us."

Kael nodded grimly. "Or use us."

A cold tremor ran down Mira's spine. She stepped closer without thinking, drawn by the bond's steady pull. The pain eased slightly in her chest. Kael noticed but said nothing. His silence spoke enough. Neither of them liked the dependence, but they had no choice.

They walked again, slower this time, matching each other's pace without speaking. The forest felt endless. The sky dimmed as night settled around them, turning the snow into a pale silver sheet that glowed beneath the moonlight. Their breaths formed soft clouds that drifted upward like quiet ghosts.

At a narrow ravine, Mira paused to examine a fallen log covered in a thick layer of frost. "We should stop for a moment," she said softly. "Just long enough to decide our next direction."

Kael scanned the area with restless eyes, his hand flickering faintly with fire. "We cannot stay out in the open."

"We are not," Mira said. "Not entirely."

He did not argue, but his tension did not ease either. He perched on a low rock beside her, stretching his aching legs. Mira sank onto the log, shuddering as exhaustion crept through her limbs.

A moment passed before Kael spoke again. "We need a plan."

Mira let out a tired laugh. "I had a plan this morning. Live quietly. Stay hidden. Avoid Veris forever." She gestured at the surrounding forest, at the snow, at the faint glow of the northern lights still lingering through the trees. "Now we are fugitives with a bond we cannot control."

Kael stared at the ground. "I planned to reach the Rite and find answers for my sister. Instead I helped destroy it." He looked up at her, eyes serious. "We both lost our futures tonight."

Mira's throat tightened. She had no answer for that.

The silence between them thickened. The bond pulsed again, not painful this time, just present, like a steady tap against the edges of her thoughts. She hated how it felt, how invasive and intimate. She hated even more the realization that she was growing accustomed to its constant presence.

Kael drew a slow breath. "We need to understand how it works. At least enough to avoid another surge."

"Do you feel it now?" Mira asked softly.

He nodded. "A pressure. Like heat trapped under stone."

"And mine feels like frost spread too thin," she said. "Always on the edge of cracking."

They exchanged a cautious look.

"We try again," Mira said reluctantly, "but slower. We test the boundary with intent, not panic."

Kael rose to his feet. Mira followed, though her legs trembled with fatigue. They stood about five paces apart. The bond hummed in warning.

Kael took one step backward.

Mira inhaled sharply as the pain sharpened. "Stop."

He froze.

"It reacts instantly," she said, pressing a hand against her ribs. "Even to hesitation."

Kael stepped forward until the pain eased for both of them. His breath came out in a frustrated sigh. "If distance is lethal, then travel is impossible."

"It is possible," Mira said quietly. "Just not alone."

Kael met her gaze, and she felt the intensity of his focus ripple through the bond. "So we keep moving together."

"For now," she answered.

"For survival," he corrected.

Mira did not argue.

Kael settled against the rock again, rubbing his temples. "If we try to suppress the bond, it reacts. If we separate, it punishes us. If we resist its magic, it spikes. That leaves only one truth."

Mira braced herself.

"We must follow it," he said.

Her pulse jumped. "Follow it where?"

"I do not know," Kael admitted. "But it has a direction. I can feel it. A pull not just toward you. Something else. Something beyond the forest."

Mira swallowed. She felt it too. A distant tug beneath the constant pressure. Like a thread leading somewhere neither of them could see yet.

"We follow the pull," Kael said again, as if convincing himself as much as her. "At least until we understand what it wants."

Mira closed her eyes for a long moment.

"We follow," she said.

But inside her chest, fear stirred like distant thunder.

This bond had already ruined one Rite.

It could destroy far more if they chose wrong.

* * *

They walked until the sky grew thick with cloud and the last color bled out of the world. The trees stood close together, their trunks dark and silent, branches heavy with snow that occasionally slid free in soft showers. Each time a cluster of snow fell, Mira flinched, braced for another surge of magic, another crack of light, another punishment from the bond. For a while, nothing happened except the steady rhythm of their steps and the sound of their breaths misting the air.

By the time full night settled over the forest, fatigue pressed on them both. Mira's legs ached with every step. Her fingers felt numb even beneath her gloves. The bond pulsed with dull insistence, no longer sharp but never letting her forget it was there. When she glanced at Kael, she saw the same strain etched into the tight line of his mouth and the stiffness of his shoulders.

"We should stop," she said at last. "If we go much farther in the dark, we risk breaking an ankle or falling into a ravine."

Kael paused, listening to the forest. For a moment she thought he would insist they keep moving, but eventually he nodded. "We camp. Just until dawn. Then we keep moving away from the temple."

"Not too far," she reminded him. "The bond may not like it."

"For once, we agree," he said.

They found a shallow hollow in the roots of a fallen tree, partly sheltered from the wind by a curtain of hanging branches. Mira brushed snow aside with her boots to make a level spot. Kael gathered a small pile of dead wood from nearby, his movements efficient but careful. When he knelt to light the fire, his hands trembled.

"Do you want me to do that?" Mira asked, kneeling opposite him. "My magic will freeze the wood. Yours may burn the forest."

He almost smiled, but the exhaustion in his eyes dulled the expression. "I will use flint, not flame." He produced a small kit from his cloak and began striking sparks onto the kindling. After a half dozen careful attempts, a thin tongue of flame caught. He coaxed it gently until the wood began to crackle. "There. No bond flare. No priests. No collapsing lakes."

Mira exhaled slowly, grateful for the small pocket of warmth. The fire's glow painted their faces in shifting gold. She sat back against the old tree trunk, drawing her cloak around herself, and watched the sparks drift toward the dark canopy. For a few breaths, they simply sat there, listening to the wind.

The bond throbbed quietly in her chest, not painful, but present. She realized with an uncomfortable start that she could sense more than just Kael's movement now. She could feel the heaviness in his limbs, the ache in his muscles, the way his fire lay coiled low in his core, exhausted yet restless. The recognition made her feel unsteady, like a door had opened in the wrong wall inside her own mind.

She cleared her throat. "You said you came to the Rite for your sister." Her voice sounded oddly soft in the hushed forest. "What did you hope to find?"

Kael stared into the fire for a long moment before answering. "She is sick. Her magic started to glow in strange ways at night. Not the usual ember glow. Something thinner. Sharper. The elders said it was an old curse. One tied to the original pact with the Ember. They had no answers." He drew a line in the snow with his boot. "The temple has records, secrets, rites they never share with anyone else. I thought if I could get close enough, I might find something."

"Something to break the curse," Mira said.

He nodded once. The bond vibrated faintly with the force of his worry when he spoke of her. The sensation unsettled Mira. It was like feeling someone else's grief brushing against her own.

She hesitated before offering anything in return. Her past felt like a door best left closed, but the forest, the fire and the strange link between them had already torn away so many layers of safety that withholding every truth seemed pointless. "My family was exiled over a treaty as well. Thornvale was accused of letting Ashrow diplomats escape before a negotiation could be sealed. The charge was treason." Her jaw tightened. "We never received a chance to defend ourselves."

Kael's gaze lifted from the fire. "That was your house."

"Yes," she said. "That was my house."

The bond stirred, picking up the old hurt hidden beneath her flat tone. For a second, she felt his reaction flicker through the connection, a mixture of surprise, caution and something close to guilt. She suspected the Ashrow version of that story was very different from the one told by Veris.

"I remember the talk," he said carefully. "From my side, the story was that Thornvale turned on us in a negotiating hall and tried to trap our envoy. We barely escaped."

Mira's fingers curled into the fabric of her cloak. "That is not what happened."

"Then someone lied," he said simply.

"Yes," she replied. "Someone did."

The fire crackled between them, the only sound for several heartbeats. Neither pushed further. The old wound of their kingdoms sat between them like another presence, as real as the bond threading through their chests.

Without warning, the bond tightened.

Mira jerked slightly. "Did you feel that?"

"Yes," Kael said. "What changed?"

She glanced around, heart thudding faster. Her fear had risen, sharp and sudden, as she spoke of exile and betrayal. The bond had answered as if emotion itself were fuel. The magic in her chest began to vibrate, the frost along her veins prickling as though it wanted to bloom outward.

"It reacts to feelings," she said slowly. "Not just distance."

Kael frowned. "So if one of us loses control, the other pays the price?"

"More than that," Mira said. She pressed her fingers against her sternum, wincing as another tight pulse ran through her. "If we slip too far into fear or anger, the bond pushes our magic outward. That could cause another surge."

Kael swore under his breath. "So we must stay calm while being hunted by two kingdoms. That is a good plan."

"Do you have a better one?" she asked.

He was silent for a beat. Then he shook his head. "No."

He shifted closer to the fire and sat with his back against the tree, legs stretched toward the warmth. Mira watched him in the flickering light. He looked older than he had at the temple, though she guessed only a day had passed. The strain on his face matched the heaviness she felt echoing through the bond.

"Try something," he said quietly. "Breathe with me."

"What?"

"If emotion amplifies it, perhaps shared rhythm calms it." His eyes met hers, steady and focused. "Inhale when I do. Exhale when I do. See if it steadies."

She opened her mouth to argue, but the memory of the Rite's collapse flashed before her and closed it again. Anything that might help was worth an attempt. She nodded reluctantly.

They sat facing each other, the fire between them. Kael drew a slow breath. Mira forced her lungs to mirror his pace. At first it felt awkward, like trying to walk in step with someone whose stride did not match hers. The bond pulsed with irregular beats, some sharp, some dull.

"Again," he said.

They inhaled together. Exhaled together. Once, twice, three times.

The pain in her chest eased slightly.

The frost that had been prickling beneath her skin calmed. She sensed his fire settle as well, no longer pushing against his ribs quite so fiercely. The bond's pulse shifted from a frantic tapping to a slower, heavier thud.

"It is working," she murmured.

"For now," he said. "We cannot breathe in unison every moment we are alive."

"No," she agreed. "But at least we know there is a way to pull it back from the edge."

They continued the shared breathing until the bond's pressure receded to a tolerable ache. Only then did they allow normal rhythm to return. The magic did not vanish, but it no longer scraped at their nerves.

Exhaustion crept in, heavy as snow.

"We should sleep," Mira said. "In turns. One watches, one rests."

"Agreed," Kael answered. "You sleep first. You kept your head while I nearly set the lake on fire. That earns you an hour."

She almost smiled at the rough attempt at humor. "Wake me at the slightest hint of trouble."

"The bond will do that anyway," he said.

She could not argue with that.

Mira curled close to the fire, cloak wrapped tight, one hand still pressed lightly against her chest. Her eyes drifted shut despite her effort to remain alert. The last thing she felt before sleep pulled her under was the quiet throb of the bond and the distant echo of Kael's weariness threading through it.

Sleep did not bring peace.

She dreamed of the lake, of ice cracking in shards of white and light swallowing the sky. She saw her younger self standing in the courtyard of Thornvale and, a breath later, saw

Lira in a similar courtyard, doubled over in a coughing fit as sparks flew from her hands. The images twisted together until she could not tell which memory belonged to whom. Frost curled around one set of fingers. Fire around another. Somewhere in the middle, the Ember watched with a gaze she could feel but not see.

She woke with a jolt.

The bond surged with sudden heat. For a heartbeat she felt not her own body, but Kael's, lungs straining, shoulders stiff, hand reaching for balance. Her eyes flew open.

The fire had burned low. Ash glowed like scattered coals. Kael stood at the edge of the clearing, head tilted toward the distant trees, one hand lifted slightly as if he had sensed something in the air.

"Why are you so far?" Mira demanded, scrambling to her feet. Pain stabbed her chest, sharp and immediate.

He flinched. "I am barely ten paces away."

"That is enough," she said, pressing a hand against her ribs as the bond tightened. "Come closer."

He hesitated for half a breath, then stepped back toward her. The pain eased. His posture relaxed, if only slightly.

"I heard something," he said. "Voices, faint. To the south."

Mira tasted fear in the back of her throat. The bond amplified it before she could smother it. She felt his fire stir in response. "Searchers?"

"Most likely," he said. "Veris patrols. Perhaps Ashrow scouts as well. They will follow the path of the Rite's collapse."

"Then we need to move," she said.

"Agreed," he replied. "But now we know one more thing."

"What is that?" she asked, gathering her pack.

"The bond does not care if we are awake or asleep," he said. "If one of us wanders too far, both will pay the price."

Mira swallowed, throat dry. "So we stay close. Always."

"Always," Kael said quietly.

They stamped out the rest of the fire and stepped into the darkness together. The bond thrummed between them with every step, a constant reminder that survival now meant moving as one, no matter how little they trusted each other, and no matter how much they wished they could walk away.

* * *

They moved through the dark as if walking on the edge of a knife. Every step away from the temple felt like stolen time. The trees closed in above them, black branches clawing at the sky. The snow underfoot glowed faintly in the dim light from the distant aurora. Their breaths came in steady rhythm, but their hearts did not. The bond pushed each beat into the other, creating a strange, shared cadence that unsettled them both.

After an hour of slow progress, Mira's legs burned with fatigue. Her thoughts felt sluggish, yet the tight ache in her chest would not let her drift into the numbness that sometimes came with exhaustion. The bond kept her too aware of every flicker of Kael's movement, every shift in his breathing. Even when neither of them spoke, his presence throbbed against her senses.

Eventually Kael raised a hand. "Here," he said quietly. "We rest again. Not long. Just enough to think."

Mira sank onto a fallen trunk with a grateful exhale. The bark dug cold ridges into the back of her legs, but she did not care. She let her head fall back against the rough wood and closed her eyes for a moment, though she did not dare relax completely.

"You feel it too," Kael said, leaning against a nearby tree, arms folded. "Not just the pain when we separate. Something else."

Mira opened her eyes and turned her head toward him. "You mean the pull."

"Yes. But it is more than that," he said. He spoke slowly, as though choosing each word with care. "When we pushed the bond away at the camp, the magic lashed back. When we tried to stretch its limit, it punished our bodies. This is not simple resonance. It behaves like the bindings around the lake."

Mira frowned. "You think the bond is connected to the Ember's bindings."

"I think the Ember recognized us when the Rite collapsed," Kael replied. "It formed something through us. Or around us. Or both."

She did not like the direction of his thoughts, but her own instincts mirrored them too closely to dismiss. "If the bond is tied to the Ember, then careless pressure could affect more than just us."

Kael nodded. "Which is why we need to stop prodding at it as if it were a bruise and we were children with nothing better to do."

"We still have to understand it," Mira said stubbornly. "If we do nothing, we risk another surge without warning."

He studied her for a moment, then sighed. "Then we test it one more time. Carefully. And not with distance."

Mira sat up straighter. "What do you suggest?"

"We try to suppress our magic together rather than separately," Kael said. "If emotion feeds it, perhaps shared intent can drain it. We saw a hint of that with the breathing exercise. That was the first time it loosened."

Mira considered his words. "If we are wrong, we might send another flare into the sky that guides every patrol straight to us."

"If we are right, we learn control," he countered.

She grimaced, but she could not argue with the logic. "All right. What do we do?"

Kael stepped closer until they were only a few paces apart. The bond eased at the shorter distance, the pain receding into a heavy pressure rather than a sharp ache. He sat on the same fallen trunk, leaving a careful space between them, and rested his forearms on his knees.

"Close your eyes," he said.

Mira obeyed, though every instinct told her to keep them open in a forest that might be crawling with enemies. The bond hummed at the decision, picking up the edge of her unease.

"Find your magic," Kael said quietly. His voice carried a low steadiness that she had not heard in the chaos of the Rite. "Not the bond. Not mine. Yours. The frost that was there long before all of this."

She focused inward, tasting the familiar cold that had lived in her veins since childhood. Her magic felt strained, frayed at the edges, but it was still hers. It coiled like a silver river beneath her skin.

"I see it," she said. "Or feel it."

"I feel the fire," he answered. "It is tired. Angry. But mine." He exhaled slowly. "Now imagine it shrinking. Not in fear. In choice. Like banked coals. Like frost that settles instead of cutting."

Mira pictured snow falling slowly over a frozen river, softening its sharp edges. She imagined her magic resting beneath that gentle layer. Not trapped. Not crushed. Only still.

The bond stirred.

Heat and cold brushed against each other, the proximity inside her chest both unnerving and strangely soothing.

"Now," Kael said, voice barely above a whisper. "We ask it together."

"How?" she murmured.

"Silently," he replied. "Tell your magic to step back from the bond without fighting it. I will do the same."

Mira inhaled and shaped her thoughts carefully. She did not push the frost away. She did not try to sever the connection.

She only asked it to move a fraction aside, to loosen from the bond's tight grip.

For a heartbeat, nothing changed.

Then the pressure in her chest eased.

She heard Kael's breath catch softly.

"The fire is pulling back," he said.

"The frost as well," she answered.

Hope flickered through her, but she was afraid to feed it in case the bond interpreted the feeling as another surge. They stayed there, eyes closed, breathing in the same slow rhythm they had discovered by accident. The bond's pulse throbbed with less force. It did not vanish, but the edges softened, like a rope loosened around a railing.

Mira opened her eyes cautiously. Kael did the same. Their gazes met.

"Still there," she said quietly, pressing a hand to her sternum. "Just not as sharp."

"I feel it too," he replied. "We did not break anything. That is a start."

Before she could reply, the ground trembled very softly, almost imperceptibly. Snow slid from branches in delicate sheets. The breeze shifted direction with a whisper that carried the faint scent of smoke.

Mira stiffened. "Did you feel that?"

"Once you have seen a lake split in half, it is hard not to

imagine tremors," Kael said, though his eyes narrowed in caution. "What did you sense?"

"It felt like a faint echo of the pulses at the temple," Mira said slowly. "Muted. Far away. But the same pattern."

Kael straightened. "Perhaps the Ember flared again."

"Or perhaps our attempt to loosen the bond sent a ripple back along whatever tether it shares with the Ember," Mira countered.

The idea hung between them, heavy and unwelcome.

She pushed herself to her feet, suddenly restless. "We cannot keep doing this in the dark without knowing what happens to the world around us every time we experiment."

"We cannot stop either," Kael said. "If we leave the bond completely unchecked, we might unleash something worse by accident."

"What if both choices are dangerous?" she asked.

"Then we choose the danger that gives us a chance to learn," he said. "And we stay ready to run when the ground starts to break under our feet."

A faint glow flickered between the trees to the south, no more than a distant suggestion of light. It disappeared almost as soon as Mira spotted it, but her nerves jumped.

"Did you see that?" she whispered.

Kael nodded. "Faint. Like a campfire smothered quickly. Or a patrol covering its lanterns."

Fear tightened her chest. The bond responded instantly, pulsing sharper. Kael winced as the pain hit him too.

"Calm," he said quickly. "Breathe."

She forced herself to inhale slowly, then exhale. The pain receded. "They are closer than I wanted to believe."

"Then we move again," he said. "We follow that distant pull you felt earlier rather than stumble in circles."

Mira closed her eyes briefly, searching for the subtle direction they had spoken about before sleep. Beneath the constant pressure of the bond, she sensed a faint tug toward the north, away from the temple and away from the glow in the trees. It felt like the echo of a road she had never walked, yet somehow knew existed.

"There," she said, lifting her chin. "North."

Kael studied her. "You are certain."

"No," she answered honestly. "But the bond settles when I think of walking that way."

"The same for me," he admitted. "Then we trust it for now."

They resumed their trek, feet crunching through snow that grew deeper as they climbed a gradual rise. The trees thinned, then thickened again as the land dipped. The pull in Mira's chest guided them like a compass that had no patience for hesitation.

After another span of time that might have been an hour or several, her legs felt like lead. Yet each time she imagined stopping for too long, the bond tensed with wordless disapproval. It did not hurt, but the sense of urgency grew.

"You feel that change," she said quietly.

"Yes," Kael replied. "It wants us moving. It is ridiculous that a bond can have opinions."

"Perhaps it is not the bond," Mira said slowly. "Perhaps the Ember is tugging the thread."

Kael exhaled sharply. "I liked that idea even less when you said it aloud."

They topped a small ridge, and the forest opened into a narrow clearing streaked with moonlight. The snow here was smoother, less disturbed by animal tracks. The air felt strangely thin, as though sound would not travel as far. For a moment, the bond quieted to its lowest hum since the Rite.

Mira halted. "Here. It feels different."

Kael scanned the clearing with wary eyes. "Different how?"

"Less strained," she said. "As if the bond is no longer pulling against the land beneath us."

He stepped to the edge of the clearing and touched his hand lightly to the snow. His fire did not flare. It rested. "There is old magic here," he said. "Not Ember, but something older than the temple's wards. It feels like a place that remembers."

Mira shivered. "You said no new troubles. This sounds like a new trouble."

"Or a starting point," Kael said. "Somewhere to breathe without the bond clawing at us every step."

They moved toward the center of the clearing, staying close enough that the bond remained calm. Mira sank to her knees and brushed a thin layer of snow aside. Beneath it, faint lines of worn runes etched into stone appeared. The markings were nearly erased by time, but she recognized the rhythm of their structure.

"These are not temple runes," she murmured. "They are older."

Kael crouched beside her. "Can you read them?"

"Not entirely," she said. "But I understand enough to see the purpose. This is a place of balance. A place where opposing forces were once joined for a time instead of forced apart."

He glanced at her sharply. "Frost and fire."

"Possibly," she answered. "Or something like it."

The bond pulsed again, but gently this time. The sensation felt almost like relief.

Mira sat back on her heels, heart still pounding from the long walk and the steady fear, yet for the first time since the Rite, the bond did not scrape at her nerves. It still tied her to Kael, still wove his breath into hers, but here it did not rage against its own existence.

Kael looked around slowly. "This does not solve anything."

"No," she agreed. "But it tells us something important."

He waited, eyes on her.

Mira drew a deep breath. "If distance can cause pain and uncontrolled magic, and if our attempts to suppress the bond send ripples through the land, then we cannot risk separating too far. Not just for our own sake. For everyone's."

Kael nodded reluctantly. "Survival is tied to staying together."

"And to learning what this bond really is," she added. "Somewhere, someone must have known. Long before Veris tried to shape everything. Long before Ashrow and Thornvale argued over borders. The answer will not be found in a prison cell."

He tipped his head back, studying the small patch of sky visible between the branches. "Then Act Two of our misfortune begins here. We run. We learn. We do not let either kingdom use us as a weapon."

Mira did not smile, but something in her steadied. "Agreed."

The bond pulsed once more, quiet and firm.

In that frozen clearing, under the thin wash of moonlight, Mira and Kael accepted the truth neither of them wanted. The path ahead would be dangerous, uncertain and full of old secrets, but from this moment forward, there would be no safe way to walk it apart.

Chapter 9

The abandoned hut emerged from the darkness like a forgotten skeleton of wood and frost. Its roof sagged under decades of winter weight, and the shutters hung at odd angles, barely clinging to the walls. Snow had piled against one side in a soft drift, leaving only a narrow doorway exposed beneath a crooked overhang. Mira felt the bond ease slightly as they approached, as if the land itself recognized the place and quieted in response.

Kael brushed a hand along the frostbitten frame of the door. His fingertips left faint scorch marks that disappeared almost immediately beneath a whisper of cold. "No footprints," he murmured. "No fire pits. No signs of life."

"Good," Mira said, pulling her cloak more tightly around her shoulders. The forest wind had sharpened since they left the clearing, and the weight of exhaustion settled heavily in her limbs. "We need shelter."

Kael pushed the door open. The hinges groaned in protest, and a cascade of snow slipped from the roof, falling past Mira's boots. Inside, the hut was a single room lined with warped wooden shelves. A collapsed table leaned near the back wall, buried under a thin crust of frost. The air smelled of old pine and cold stone. Despite the abandonment, the space felt strangely intact, as though it had been waiting for them.

A single narrow cot stood in one corner, its wool blanket stiff with age. Mira tested the edge with her fingers. The fabric crackled softly but held. "Better than the ground," she said, though her voice was uncertain. The hut had a quiet weight to it, a heaviness she could not place.

Kael knelt near the center of the room and cleared a space for a small fire. "We will not sleep long," he said, arranging the kindling. "Just until our bodies stop threatening to collapse."

Mira sat near the wall and rested her head against the timber. "You keep watch first. I will take over later."

"We should sleep at the same time," Kael said without looking at her. "The bond reacts too strongly when one of us wakes alone. That moment at the camp proved it."

She hesitated. "Then we take turns only if the bond permits it."

Kael struck the flint. Sparks flew, catching the tinder in a low crackle. The fire blossomed slowly, throwing a faint glow through the room. Shadows stretched across the walls in soft, wavering shapes.

Mira's eyes drifted toward the door. The wind sighed through the gaps in the hut's exterior, carrying the muffled howl of distant wolves. Her body shivered involuntarily, but the bond warmed slightly, faint as a heartbeat through layers of cloth and air. Kael's fire pulsed in sync, responding to her tension without conscious effort.

"Sit," Mira said quietly. "You are swaying. If you fall over, the bond will wake me anyway."

Kael smirked weakly but obeyed. He lowered himself beside the fire, his elbows resting on his knees. In the flickering light, his face looked thinner than it had earlier, worn by fatigue and strain. Mira could feel threads of his exhaustion curling into her own mind.

She shifted onto the cot, drawing her knees closer. "If something happens while we sleep, the bond will warn us."

He nodded, though his expression flickered with hesitation. "I hope so."

Silence settled between them. The fire crackled softly. Mira felt the weight of her eyelids pull downward, and her breath slowed. The bond began to hum with a faint, rhythmic warmth that made her chest loosen. Kael shifted beside the fire, stretching out on the floor near enough that the link remained calm.

She let sleep reach her.

But the moment she drifted into darkness, the world changed.

She was standing not in the hut, nor in the forest, but on an expanse of frozen ground beneath a sky streaked with pale light. The northern lights pulsed above her in long, swirling ribbons that dipped close to the earth. The air felt sharper, colder, charged with a strange energy that prickled against her skin.

Mira shivered and looked down.

Her boots stood on ancient ice, thick and clear enough that she could see faint shapes moving in the depths. Shadows. Light. Broken fragments of something that glowed like dying embers.

A figure appeared beside her.

Kael.

He blinked in confusion, and Mira felt the same shock echo through the bond. His fire flickered faintly along his hands, casting a pale glow across the ice.

"Are you seeing this?" he asked, voice soft with disbelief.

"Yes," Mira whispered. "This is not a dream."

The bond vibrated sharply, as if agreeing.

The frozen landscape around them stretched endlessly in all directions. No forest. No mountains. Only ice and sky. Yet the world did not feel empty. The air carried the weight of presence, invisible and vast.

Mira stepped forward. The ice beneath her feet shifted with a sound like distant chimes. Kael followed, though he moved with greater caution. The bond pulled them onward, guiding their steps across the ancient expanse.

A distant wind began to rise. It carried a low hum that grew louder with each step, blending with the pulse of the bond in a strange harmony.

Then the ice beneath them glowed.

Not with the soft flicker of the lake near the temple, but with a harsh, brilliant white that seared through the surface. The hum turned into a sharp tone that vibrated through their bones. Mira shielded her eyes, breath quickening.

Shapes formed beneath the ice.

Two figures.

Tall. Cloaked in garments woven from frost and fire.

Mira felt her pulse stumble. "Who are they?"

Kael stepped closer. The vision sharpened, drawing the figures into clarity. Their forms were ghostlike yet solid enough to cast shadows across the ice. One radiated cold that shimmered like crystal. The other burned with a golden glow that flickered along the edges of its outline.

"Frost and fire," Kael whispered. "A pair. Bound."

The figures moved closer, their steps sending ripples through the ice. The frost-bound figure lifted its hand, trailing a long ribbon of cold light. The fire-bound figure mirrored the gesture, shaping heat into a narrow arc.

Their hands touched.

A blaze of brilliant white erupted between them.

Mira cried out as the world exploded in a flare of light. The bond surged violently, pulling her forward with such force that she stumbled. Kael reached for her, but his hand passed through her arm in a swirl of mist.

The two ancient figures fused their light into a single burst that shot straight upward, piercing the sky and splitting the aurora into fractured rivers of color. The ice beneath them cracked in glowing lines. The hum deepened, turning into a low thunder that rolled through the air like the heartbeat of a waking titan.

Then a voice filled the frozen expanse.

Not words. Not sound.

A presence.

Vast. Old. Watching.

The vision twisted.

The two figures collapsed into the ice, their forms dissolving into shards of frost and fire. A new shape rose in their place. A swirling sphere of white gold light, pulsing with the same rhythm as the Ember beneath the lake.

Mira staggered backward. "This is a memory."

Kael shook his head. "Or a warning."

The sphere pulsed again. The bond surged in response, nearly dragging them to their knees.

The world shattered into darkness.

And both Mira and Kael woke at the same time.

Their breaths tore through the hut in harsh gasps. The fire had burned low, glowing faintly against the stone floor. Frost climbed the walls in delicate patterns, while small sparks drifted from Kael's fingertips, rising and fading like dying fireflies.

Mira pressed her hand to her chest, heart pounding wildly. "That was not a dream."

"No," Kael said, voice rough. "The bond pulled us together into it."

"And the figures," she whispered. "They were like us. Frost and fire."

Kael's gaze darkened. "Which means we are not the first."

The bond throbbed once, heavy and cold.

Mira felt her breath catch in her throat.

They had not stumbled into an accident.

They had stepped into the echo of a pattern older than either kingdom.

* * *

The air inside the hut felt too still, too tight, as if the vision had not truly ended but lingered in the corners like a shadow waiting to reform. Mira pulled her cloak tighter around herself, trying to shake the cold that clung to her skin. The frost on the walls gleamed faintly in the dying firelight, the delicate patterns almost beautiful, but the sight made her stomach twist. She had seen similar frost in the vision, etched along the cloak of the figure who had stood across from the fire wielder.

She rubbed her arms, trying to anchor herself in reality. "They did not speak," she murmured. "Not one word. But I felt something in the air. A presence watching them. The same presence that watched us."

Kael sat heavily on the floorboards, bracing his elbows against his knees. His hair clung damply to his forehead, and his skin glowed faintly from the remnants of his magic. "It felt older than the lake," he said. "Older than Veris. Older than Ashrow. Something that does not need words to make itself understood."

Mira nodded slowly. "I felt it press against my mind when the two figures touched. As if it was testing us."

"Testing," Kael repeated, rolling the word in his mouth as if weighing it. "I do not know if that makes me want to run or fight."

"Both seem appropriate," Mira said, breath trembling. She looked down at her hands, half expecting them to glow. "I have never shared a dream with anyone. Let alone a vision. This was not my magic."

"It was the bond," Kael said. His eyes drifted to her face, then to the fading fire. "It reached out for us. It wanted us to see that."

Mira was silent for a long moment. The memory of the vision pulsed in her mind like a heartbeat. Two figures. Frost and fire. Bound by a single blinding convergence. Shapes collapsing into each other. A sphere of ancient light rising in their place.

A fragment of creation or destruction. She could not tell which.

Her voice felt small when she finally spoke. "Do you think they were destroyed?"

Kael lifted his head. His expression was grim. "Maybe. Or maybe they became something else. Something the Ember remembers."

Mira shivered. Images flickered across her vision. Ice cracking in thin lines beneath ancient feet. Flames spilling like liquid light. A sphere rising from their merging forms. "If the Ember remembers them," she said, "then the bond may not be new. It may be something the Ember once understood."

"And we stepped into its path," Kael finished.

She swallowed. "We need to know who those two were. What they were meant to become."

Kael pushed himself to his feet and paced slowly around the narrow room. The firelight danced across his eyes. "If we find the truth," he said, "we might find a way to break this bond before it becomes what we saw."

"Or a way to control it," she said before she could stop herself.

Kael stopped midstride. "You want to control it?"

Mira lowered her gaze. "I want to survive it."

He studied her for a long moment, then nodded. "Then we agree."

The wind howled outside the hut. Snow shifted against the wood. Mira felt the temperature drop a few degrees, and she pulled her cloak more tightly around herself. The fire sputtered as if in sympathy.

She watched the flames for a while before speaking again. "In the vision, the two figures moved toward each other willingly. They were not pulled together like we were. They chose it."

Kael shook his head. "Or they accepted it. That is not the same as wanting it."

"Do you think they knew what would happen?" Mira asked.

Kael rubbed the back of his neck, the firelight catching on the faint shimmer of heat beneath his skin. "I think they were prepared for something. The way they moved felt deliberate. As if they had trained for that moment."

Mira considered this. "Then the bond might have a purpose. A ritual. A path."

"And we have no idea what it is or why it chose us," Kael finished.

The bond pulsed between them, steady and firm, as if reminding them that purpose or not, it existed all the same.

Mira pushed herself to her feet, knees trembling. "We should write down everything we remember before it fades."

Kael nodded. "Agreed. The details matter."

She crossed to the shelves along the back wall and brushed dust from a warped wooden box. Inside sat a bundle of brittle parchment, wrapped in cloth that had once been red but had faded to brown. Mira unwrapped it gently and found a few blank sheets free of mold. She carried them to the fire and set them carefully near Kael.

He reached into his satchel and withdrew a small charcoal stub. "This will do," he said.

Mira crouched beside him and began to speak slowly, dredging every detail from the vision.

"The two figures stood on ancient ice. The sky looked different, thicker with light. The aurora pulsed as though alive. The ground glowed from beneath."

Kael wrote quickly, jaw clenched in concentration.

"They approached each other without hesitation," she continued. "Their magics were visible, not hidden. Frost and fire meeting at the hands. When they touched, the light changed. It was not violent at first. More like recognition."

Kael paused. "Recognition," he repeated. "As if their magic knew each other."

"Yes." She nodded. "That is exactly how it felt."

He made another mark on the parchment.

"And when the light grew too strong to look at," she said, "what rose between them was the same color as the Ember beneath the lake."

Kael set the charcoal down.

Mira frowned. "What is it?"

He lifted his head and looked at her directly. "That light was not new. The Ember did not react to us at random. It knew us. Or it knew what we represent."

Mira's stomach twisted. "We are not the first."

"No," Kael said quietly. "But we might be the first in a very long time."

The fire crackled loudly, sending sparks drifting up the chimney gap. Outside, the wind grew fiercer. Snow and frost battered the walls like whispered warnings.

Kael leaned back against the wall and shut his eyes for a moment. "The bond is still active. It feels stronger after the vision, not weaker."

Mira pressed a hand to her chest. "Same for me."

"It did not take energy from us," he said. "It gained something."

Mira felt dread claw through her. "Knowledge."

"Or direction," Kael replied. "Like we were a door it passed through."

She felt cold settle in her bones. "Then the vision was not for us alone."

"No," he said. "We were shown something because the bond wanted us to see it. Or because the Ember wants something from us."

Mira wrapped her arms around herself. "What if the vision was not a memory of the past? What if it was the beginning of something that intends to repeat?"

Kael opened his eyes. His expression was sober. "Then we need to decide if we are running from it or running toward it."

Mira turned to the window. Snow swept past in white sheets. The air outside glowed faintly, illuminated by distant moonlight. The world felt poised on the edge of a precipice.

She whispered, "We are already in the middle of it."

Kael did not argue. The truth hung too heavily between them.

The bond pulsed again, a slow, steady beat.

Mira sat beside him and rested her back against the wall. The room felt colder than before. The fire flickered weakly. Her limbs ached, yet she felt too shaken to close her eyes.

Kael watched her quietly for a moment. "Sleep if you can. I will stay awake until the storm quiets."

She gave a small shake of her head. "If either of us sleeps alone, the bond will pull us back together the moment danger rises."

"So we sleep together," Kael said simply, shifting to make space beside him. "Not touching. But near enough that the bond stays calm."

The simplicity of the suggestion startled her.

Then she nodded.

They rested side by side, bodies a breath apart, the fire dimming slowly as the storm outside raged. The bond hummed with a deep, ancient rhythm. Mira felt the tremor of it in her bones.

She closed her eyes, letting the exhaustion pull her under once more. No vision rose to meet her this time. Only the steady presence of Kael near her, and the unsettling truth that their path was no longer their own.

Before sleep claimed her, she whispered into the darkness.

"We need answers before the bond decides our fate for us."

Kael did not respond. But the bond did.

It pulsed once, firm and inevitable.

As if agreeing.

Chapter 10

The storm rolled in without warning. One moment the forest lay in a fragile stillness, branches dusted with soft white powder, the wind a gentle sigh through the trees. The next, the sky darkened in a bruised curtain of cloud, and snow began to lash sideways in a furious dance. Mira pulled her hood low and tightened her cloak around her neck. The cold bit at any exposed skin with sharp teeth, and the wind carried a faint hiss that sounded too much like warning.

Kael scanned the trees behind them with growing tension. His eyes narrowed, and heat began to flicker faintly beneath his skin. Mira felt the rise of his magic through the bond even before she saw it, a flare of fire answering the spike of adrenaline inside him.

"You sense something," Mira said, already tightening her grip on her satchel. "Tell me."

Kael tilted his head, listening through the storm. "Footsteps.

Light ones. Trained. They are trying to stay downwind, but they are not far."

"Veris?" Mira whispered.

"Veris," Kael confirmed. "Trackers. I hear at least two. Possibly three."

Mira felt her stomach drop. "They should not have found us this quickly."

"They followed the collapse at the Rite," Kael said. "They know this part of the forest better than we do. And we left traces."

"You created false heat prints twice," Mira countered. "I covered our trail with frost."

His jaw tightened. "Not well enough."

The bond pulsed sharply at his frustration. Mira winced but steadied herself. "Then we focus. We keep moving. The storm will hide us if we use it well."

Kael exhaled and nodded. "Northward. The land slopes down toward a river. Trackers will have trouble moving quietly on ice."

They pushed forward into the storm.

Snow gathered on Mira's hood so quickly she had to shake it off every few steps. The wind stung her cheeks and turned her breath into sharp, icy crystals. Her legs ached from the relentless climb, and her fingers felt stiff even inside her gloves. The forest seemed to huddle close against the storm, branches bending low as if trying to shelter themselves.

Kael kept slightly ahead, reading the terrain with an instinctive caution that Mira had come to trust. Despite the storm, he moved with surprising steadiness, his fire simmering low and warm in his core. Mira sensed it through the bond, a quiet ember keeping exhaustion at bay.

After nearly an hour of trudging through deepening drifts, Kael suddenly raised a hand. Mira halted. The bond hummed with his tension, and she pressed her back against the trunk of a thick pine, squinting into the swirling white.

He leaned close enough that she could hear his breath. "I saw a flicker of movement to the south. Too steady to be wind," he murmured. "They are gaining."

"How many?"

"Hard to tell. But they are not giving up."

The storm howled louder, drowning the crack of branches, yet Mira sensed the truth in Kael's voice. The trackers were close. Close enough that the bond prickled with instinctive warning.

Kael turned to her, eyes sharp. "I will cast another false heat trail. But this time I have to make it strong enough to confuse trained trackers. That will be risky."

Mira frowned. "Risky how?"

"The fire cannot flare too high," he said. "If it does, the bond might react. Or the snow might melt too fast and give us away."

Mira nodded. "And while you do that?"

"You watch the ridge. If you see movement, tell me."

She hesitated, then reached out and gripped his arm. The warmth under his sleeve was startling. "Do it carefully," she said softly.

His expression flickered with something like surprise. Then he nodded once and stepped away.

Kael knelt in the snow and pressed both palms to the ground. Mira sensed his magic coil inward, then flare outward in a slow, controlled pulse. Heat rippled along the surface in a faint shimmer. The surrounding snow glowed red for a heartbeat before settling.

Mira felt the bond stretch with the effort, a tight pull in her chest that mirrored his exertion. She steadied her breathing, focusing on keeping her mind calm so the bond would not spike.

Kael's energy seeped into the snow, leaving behind a trail of faint warmth that curved southward, leading toward a cluster of old game paths. It was subtle enough to avoid suspicion but strong enough that a trained tracker would follow the heat signature first.

Finally he let out a shaky exhale and lifted his hands. "That will have to do."

Mira nodded and gestured for him to follow. "Come on. The river cannot be far."

They moved again, the storm fighting them with every step.

By the time they reached the riverbank, the water had frozen into a thick white sheet that curved through the forest like a pale ribbon. Snow draped its edges, and the ice shimmered faintly beneath a thin layer of frost.

"Careful," Kael warned, stepping lightly onto the frozen surface. "This time of year the ice is stable, but the storm may hide weak spots."

Mira stepped after him, testing each placement carefully. Their breath fogged the air in small clouds. The wind roared behind them, driving the snow sideways.

Halfway across the river, the ice groaned sharply.

Mira froze.

Kael turned instantly. The bond tightened in alarm. "Do not move," he said. "The ice shifts with the weight."

Mira swallowed, her heartbeat loud in her ears. "We chose this route because it is safer than the ridge."

"Safer," Kael said, "not safe."

The ice groaned again.

A hairline crack zigzagged beneath Mira's boots.

Her breath caught. "Kael."

He stepped toward her, but the bond pulsed hard, as if warning him not to move too quickly.

Carefully, Kael raised his hands and pressed them against the ice. He let out a soft breath, guiding a low, steady wave of heat into the cracks. The warmth spread under the surface, melting the thin web of fractures just enough that the larger sheets settled together.

Mira felt the strain through the bond as though it were her own magic weakening. She pressed her palm lightly against the ice as well, calling frost to reinforce the cooling edges of the melted seam.

The bond vibrated sharply, then steadied.

The ice held.

Mira exhaled shakily. "That was close."

"Too close," Kael said. "We need to get off this river before the storm worsens."

They moved again, faster now, both of them alert and tense. Mira's magic burned cold along her arms. Kael's fire simmered steadily beneath his skin. The bond hummed in uneasy rhythm between them.

By the time they reached the opposite bank, Mira's legs felt like they could barely carry her. The storm had grown even more violent. Snow slashed across the clearing in thick waves, burying their tracks almost as soon as they made them.

Kael shielded his eyes and scanned the area. "We need shelter. Something that will hold against this wind."

Mira's teeth chattered. "A cave or a hunting post. Something with a roof."

He nodded and led them along the base of a ridge. The trees here grew closer together, their branches forming a rough canopy that blocked some of the storm. After several minutes of searching, they found a narrow crevasse in the rock face, just wide enough to squeeze through.

Inside, the small cave was barely large enough for two people, its floor uneven and cold. But it blocked the wind, and that alone felt like salvation.

Mira collapsed onto the ground with a soft groan. "I cannot walk another step. Not in this storm."

Kael sank beside her, breathing hard. "We stay here until it settles."

The cramped space forced them close together, their shoulders nearly touching. Mira felt the bond ease in a strange, warm pulse. The two of them breathing in the same small pocket of air made the connection feel calmer, steadier.

Mira rested her head against the stone wall, exhaustion washing over her. "For once, the bond is not fighting us."

Kael exhaled softly. "Perhaps it likes the cold."

She almost smiled. "Or it likes that you cannot wander off and start trouble."

Kael gave a tired laugh. The sound startled her. It was the first time she had heard genuine humor from him since the Rite.

The warmth of the bond deepened.

Mira closed her eyes, letting the exhaustion sink into her bones. "I never thought I would say this," she murmured, "but I am grateful you are here."

Kael shifted slightly. The movement brushed his shoulder against hers. "Do not worry," he said quietly. "I am not going anywhere."

For the first time since the bond formed, Mira felt something gentle beneath the constant pressure. Not comfort. Not trust. But something close.

A beginning.

* * *

The storm thickened as the night deepened. Snow hammered the rocks outside the cave with such force that it sounded like distant drums. The air in the cramped shelter grew damp and chilled, but the small space at least kept the wind from stealing their breath. Mira pulled her knees closer to her chest and pressed her back against the stone, feeling every shallow rise and fall of her lungs. The bond vibrated faintly as Kael shifted beside her, adjusting his position to ease a cramp in his leg.

She could feel his discomfort as clearly as her own. The shared ache in his thigh, the pinch at his shoulder, the bone deep fatigue. It should have made her feel trapped. Instead, in this miserable little pocket of shelter, it made her feel less alone.

"How far do you think the trackers are?" she asked quietly, more to distract herself from the cold than from any real hope of a reassuring answer.

Kael tilted his head, listening with his eyes closed. "The storm hides their steps, but if they kept moving during the worst of it, they will be close to the river by now."

"Do you think the false heat trail worked?" she asked.

"For a little while," he said. "Someone trained will know a natural signature from a crafted one, but the storm may have blurred the difference. It will at least slow them."

Mira glanced toward the narrow crack that served as the cave entrance. Snow had piled along its edges, turning it into a dim frame of white. "They will check every hollow while they search. Huts, caves, even the spaces beneath fallen trees."

"Then we leave before dawn," Kael said. "We move as soon as the wind shifts."

A shiver ran along the bond as he spoke. Mira sensed something beneath the words that he did not say aloud. He was not just worried about discovery. He was worried about what would happen if the trackers tried to separate them by force. The bond would not take that kindly. Neither would the Ember, still restless under its fractured lake.

She felt the same fear, deep and cold. "We will not let them take us," she said softly.

"We may not have that choice," Kael replied, but his voice had a quiet resolve beneath the realism. "They will expect panic and disarray after such a failure. If we stay collected, we keep some power."

Mira watched the small fire sputter and die. "Collected is not the same as unafraid."

"No," he agreed. "But it is what we can manage."

Silence settled again, thicker this time. The storm's roar muffled the world beyond the cave, turning everything outside into an indistinct rush. Inside, the only sounds were their breathing and the occasional drip of melted snow seeping through a crack in the stone and freezing again.

Mira's head drooped forward as exhaustion tried to drag her down. The bond throbbed with the weight of Kael's fatigue as well. She could feel his mind slipping toward the edge of sleep. The shared pull made it harder to resist.

"Do not go fully asleep," she murmured. "If one of us drops too deep, the bond might pull the other in."

He huffed a soft, humorless breath. "You think the bond is hungry for dreams now."

"It already took us into one vision," she said. "I would rather not give it another chance while trackers are nearby."

"That is fair," he conceded.

They hovered in that half waking state for what felt like a long time. Mira's thoughts drifted between memories of Thornvale and flashes of the Rite. Each echo of her past tugged at the bond, but she kept her emotions as steady as she could. Kael did the same, focusing on the rhythm of his breath.

Eventually, the pitch of the wind outside began to change. The harsh, relentless rush softened into a lower murmur. The storm was loosening its grip.

Kael straightened slowly. "The worst has passed."

Mira swallowed the dryness in her throat. "Then we move."

They crawled out of the cave into a world reshaped by snow. Drifts lay piled in strange hills against the trees. The sky had lightened to a muted gray, hinting that dawn was only a few hours away. The air still tasted sharp and cold, but the wind no longer screamed in their ears.

Mira looked at the ground. The storm had erased almost every sign of their presence. Only a faint depression near the cave mouth hinted that anyone had sheltered there. She exhaled in relief.

Kael's eyes swept the forest beyond. He stilled, his body tensing. "Do not speak," he whispered.

Mira followed his gaze.

Far down the slope, barely visible through the lingering curtain of snow, three shadowed figures moved with deliberate care. They were spread in a loose line, each scanning a different portion of the landscape. One paused and knelt, touching the ground. The others rallied toward that point.

"Trackers," Kael breathed.

Mira's heart hammered against her ribs. The bond surged with her fear, then tightened with his response. "They are on the far side of the river," she whispered. "The false trail still holds them there."

"Not for much longer," Kael said. "We have to move while their focus is elsewhere."

They skirted the upper side of the ridge, staying low and using the snow laden bushes as cover. Every step felt louder than it should, but the wind carried enough leftover sound that Mira hoped it would blur their passage. The bond thrummed steadily, uneasy but not panicked.

As they climbed, the forest thinned and the ground dropped away suddenly.

Mira pulled up short at the edge of a steep ravine. She peered down into a narrow gulch where jagged rocks jutted through the snow. A frozen stream glimmered faintly beneath the uneven surface.

Kael joined her at the edge and swore under his breath. "We cannot go around without passing into clear sight."

"Is there another way?" Mira asked.

He pointed across the ravine. "There."

A natural snow bridge arched from one side of the ravine to the other. It had formed where heavy drifts had built up over a fallen tree. The snow was packed tight and pale, stretching like a narrow white ribbon. It looked just strong enough to bear their weight, but faint fissures ran along the sides where the storm had gnawed at its edges.

Mira's stomach twisted. "That is not a bridge. That is a promise to break."

"We do not have time to be cautious," Kael said. "If the trackers crest the ridge behind us, they will have a clear line of sight. The ravine is a bottleneck. If we cross first, then collapse the bridge, it might buy us time."

"And if it collapses while we are on it?" she asked.

He looked at her, eyes steady. "Then we do not let it."

The bond pulsed between them like a steady drumbeat.

Mira drew a deep breath and nodded. "All right. But I go second."

"Why?" he asked.

"Because you can melt the ice in front of you if you slip," she said. "I can freeze the cracks behind us. It is the only way both of us can help."

He studied her for a beat, then inclined his head. "Fine. Stay close."

Kael stepped onto the snow bridge first. The packed snow compressed slightly under his weight, emitting a faint creak. He moved with extreme care, placing each foot deliberately. Mira followed, heart in her throat, the bond tightening with every shift of his balance.

The snow bridge was only wide enough for one person. Mira kept her eyes on the back of Kael's boots, ready to react if he stumbled. The ravine yawned beneath them. Wind funneled through the narrow space, lifting powdery snow around their ankles.

Halfway across, the bridge groaned.

Mira froze. A thin crack shot along the edge beside her. Snow crumbled away, exposing a glimpse of empty air.

"Keep moving," Kael said, voice tight. "We are almost there."

"The bridge is weakening," she warned.

"Then hold it," he said. "You are frost. This is your element."

His trust startled her almost as much as the command itself.

She pressed her palm against the packed snow at her feet and called her magic. Cold surged through her arm, an instinctive rush that answered the bond's rising urgency. The fissures along the bridge's sides began to crystallize, thin veins of ice knitting the cracked layers together.

The bridge steadied.

Kael continued forward, but as he placed his next step, a chunk of snow collapsed beneath his heel. He lurched, arms flailing for balance. Mira felt the jolt hit through the bond like a blow to her chest.

Without thinking, she slammed both hands onto the snow and forced her frost outward.

The bridge hardened in a rapid wave, freezing the damaged section just long enough for Kael to regain his footing. He stumbled, then righted himself, breathing hard. "Do not stop," he said through gritted teeth. "We are almost across."

Mira pushed herself upright, legs shaking. The edge of the ravine below swam in her peripheral vision, but she kept her focus on the path directly ahead of her.

They reached the far side just as another groan echoed through the snow bridge. A large fracture split along its underside. The structure sagged dangerously.

"Now," Kael said, voice urgent. "Break it. Slow them down."

Mira turned back toward the bridge and raised her hands. Her frost flared along the surface, not to repair it this time, but to control how it fell. She traced the cracks with quick, precise bursts of cold, guiding the breakage so that the central span would collapse first.

The bridge shuddered, then dropped in two chunks, falling into the ravine in a roar of cascading snow. A cloud of powder rose from the depths and swept upward, obscuring their trail.

Mira staggered backward, panting. Her vision blurred for a moment as the bond flared in reaction to the strain.

Kael grabbed her elbow to steady her. "Are you all right?"

"Yes," she managed. "Just drained."

"You held a collapsing bridge together long enough to save us," he said. "Drained is reasonable."

She did not answer, but something in his tone settled the tremor in her chest.

In the distance, a faint shout rose from the far side of the ravine. The trackers had reached the ridge and discovered the broken bridge. Their angry voices carried thinly through the air.

"They know we crossed," Mira whispered.

"But they cannot follow without losing more time," Kael replied. "That is all we needed."

Snow swirled around them, softer now but still steady. The sky brightened slightly, hinting that dawn was not far away. The bond beat sharply between them in a rhythm that felt more alive than ever.

"We need shelter again," Mira said. "Somewhere the storm and the terrain work for us, not against us."

Kael scanned the slopes ahead. "There are overhangs in cliffs like these. We find one and ride out the rest of the night, then decide where to move next."

They moved along the ridge, keeping the ravine to their right as a natural barrier. The snow grew deeper, but the land sloped gently upward, making the walking easier than the steep descent had been. Their breaths came in visible puffs. The bond pulsed with shared exhaustion.

At last they found a shallow recess in the rock, shielded by a cluster of bent pines whose branches formed a partial roof. It was not a true cave, more a pocket in the stone, but it broke the wind and offered enough cover that a small fire would not be easily spotted.

Mira slumped against the inner wall with a tired groan. "This will do."

Kael sank beside her, shoulders brushing hers as he settled. "Better than the last shelter. At least we can straighten our legs."

The space was small enough that their knees nearly touched when they sat facing the entrance. Mira could feel the warmth of Kael's body through both layers of cloth when he shifted closer to make room for his boots. The bond hummed in quiet satisfaction at their nearness.

For once, she did not fight it.

They were alive. The bridge had held long enough. The trackers were behind them. The storm had lost some of its teeth. For the first time since the Rite, the world outside their bond did not feel immediately poised to break.

She let herself breathe.

And for the first time, she wondered not only how they would survive each day together, but who this man beside her had been before the Ember decided to tangle their fates.

* * *

The wind softened as the sky shifted from storm gray to a thin, pale lavender that hinted at the coming dawn. The faint glow seeped through the tree branches above their shelter, casting long shadows across the snow packed ground. Mira blew gently into her hands, trying to coax warmth back into her fingers. The cold had settled into her bones, but exhaustion weighed even heavier.

Kael knelt near the back of the recess, gathering what little dry wood he had managed to collect from the crevices in the stone. It was barely enough for a handful of small flames, but any heat was better than none. The moment he coaxed the first ember to life, Mira felt the bond loosen, as if the warmth soothed not only her body but the connection itself.

She watched him in the firelight as he fed the flames. His movements were slower than usual, his exhaustion clear in every gesture. Fire magic responded to emotion, yet his flames tonight were calm and steady. It was the most controlled she had ever seen him.

"You are quieter than normal," he said without looking at her.

"I am listening," she replied softly.

"To what?"

She hesitated. "Everything."

Kael sat back on his heels and looked at her directly. "Tell me."

Mira drew her cloak tighter. "The storm is fading, but the forest still feels tense. The trackers are frustrated. Angry. They are not close, but not far either. The bond... it mirrors emotion sometimes. If we let fear run wild, it could spark another reaction."

Kael nodded. "So we stay calm."

The simplicity of his answer steadied her more than she expected.

She shifted, the stone wall rough against her back. "Does your fire always quiet like that when you are tired?"

He looked down at his hands, where faint gold lines glowed beneath the skin. "Not always. Usually it lashes out. It blames me for being weak. But tonight..." He paused, frowning as if surprised. "Tonight it feels no need to fight."

Mira felt a soft rise in the bond that mirrored his calm. "Because you are not alone."

Kael looked away, jaw tightening. "Do not give the bond credit for your pity."

"That is not what I said."

He sighed and sank down beside her, back resting against the stone. The space was small enough that their shoulders brushed. The bond hummed warmly at the contact, but neither of them shifted away.

For a long moment they sat in silence, watching the small flames flicker. Mira felt her heartbeat slow to match the rhythm of Kael's breathing. The tension in her shoulders eased. The bond's pressure softened to something almost gentle, like a steady pulse warming her ribs.

At last, Kael spoke again, voice quiet. "I have never trusted the cold."

She blinked. "You fear it?"

"I respect it," he said. "Fire can be shaped. Fire listens. Cold does not. Cold simply is."

Mira let out a soft breath. "I have always felt the opposite. Fire is unpredictable. It seems one moment away from destroying everything. Frost... frost holds. It preserves. It is constant."

Kael turned his head slightly. "You think frost is gentle?"

"No," she said. "But it is honest."

His gaze lingered on her face longer than she expected. "Perhaps that is what frightens me."

She held his stare for a heartbeat longer than she meant to. The air between them shifted.

A pulse rippled through the bond, slow and warm. Mira inhaled sharply. Kael felt it too. His expression flickered with recognition, and something unspoken passed between them.

She looked quickly at the fire. "We should talk about the trackers."

"Yes," he said, his voice steadier now, though there was an undercurrent in it she could not ignore. "We should."

But they did not.

The silence that settled over them was not the strained, brittle quiet of their earlier days. It felt different. Cautious, but not hostile. Mira felt the warmth of Kael's presence through the bond, and for the first time she did not tense at the sensation.

After several minutes, Kael drew a deep breath. "There is something I should say."

Mira glanced at him. "What is it?"

"You saved my life on that bridge," he said simply. "Without hesitation. Without thinking about what you risked."

Mira's pulse stumbled. "You saved mine first."

"That is different," he said. "If the ice collapsed under me, you would have fallen too. The bond would have pulled you with me. But when your magic surged to hold the bridge, you acted despite the risk. That was your choice. Not the bond's."

His words landed with surprising weight. Mira stared at the fire, unsure how to respond. "I did what I had to do."

"No," he said softly. "You did more."

She felt heat rise in her cheeks, though the cave was cold. "You would have done the same."

Kael gave a tired, crooked smile. "I already have done the same. Twice. Whether I like it or not."

The honesty in his tone disarmed her.

The bond pulsed again, gently this time, like a small wave rolling against the shore. Mira felt a soft pressure under her ribs, the sense of his emotions brushing against her own. There was no panic. No anger. Only a quiet thread of something she could not name.

She drew her knees closer. "This bond... it changes things. It pulls emotions together. I do not know where yours end and mine begin sometimes."

Kael nodded. "Neither do I."

"But I know one thing," she said. "What happened back there on the bridge, in the storm, in the cave… none of that was the bond alone."

Kael lowered his eyes. "No. It was not."

She felt the truth echo through the bond.

He cleared his throat softly. "We should rest. At least a little. Dawn is coming."

"And we will need our strength," Mira agreed.

Kael raked snow against the cave entrance, creating a partial barrier that let light through but blocked the worst of the wind. When he returned, he settled beside her again, closer than before. The warmth of his fire radiated through his cloak and into her shoulder. Mira leaned slightly into the heat before she could stop herself.

Kael stiffened for a moment.

Then relaxed.

They sat like that for a while, their shoulders touching, the bond calm and steady. The storm had left the world muted and pale. Dawn crept slowly toward them.

Mira spoke first, voice quiet. "When we first ran from the temple, I thought surviving with you would be impossible."

Kael let out a soft laugh. "Believe me, the feeling was mutual."

"And now," she said slowly, "I no longer think it is impossible."

He turned his head slightly toward her. "No," he said. "Neither do I."

The warmth of their shared breath mingled in the small space. The bond pulsed once, deep and resonant.

It felt like acknowledgment.

Outside, the sky brightened. The storm had passed, leaving the world wrapped in soft white silence. A new day waited beyond the ridge, full of danger and uncertainty, but for the first time since the Rite, Mira and Kael faced it together not as strangers forced into an unwilling bond, but as allies beginning to understand each other.

The silence in the shelter was no longer cold or strained.

It was peaceful.

And something in the bond curled around that peace as if memorizing it.

Mira closed her eyes, letting the warmth of Kael's presence steady her.

"Rest," he murmured beside her.

And for the first time since her exile, she did.

Chapter 11

Morning settled over the forest in a muted veil of pale light. Snow clung to every branch, weighing the pines into slow bows. The storm had left the world washed clean and silent, as if all sound had been brushed away during the night. Mira stepped carefully through the deep drifts, her boots crunching softly, each footprint swallowed almost instantly by drifting flakes. Her breath formed small clouds that drifted behind her as she walked.

Kael followed just a step behind. The bond rested between them in a strange stillness. It had been calm since the moments in the cave, almost watchful, and that quiet made Mira uneasy. Silence in the bond felt like silence in her own chest, as though her heart had slowed to match its rhythm.

She kept her hood low and her thoughts guarded. The shared vision still troubled her. The fire figure and frost figure. The collapsing shapes. The rising sphere. She had not expected to see anything again so soon, yet the bond carried an undercurrent that felt like a glass surface stretched too thin. Ready to crack.

Kael seemed deep in thought as well. She sensed the flicker of questions he had not voiced, waves of curiosity brushing the edges of her mind. His silence today was not simple restraint but pressure held tight. He wanted answers. He wanted to understand the memory the Ember had shown them. And deeper than that, he wanted to understand her.

The realization made her tense.

Kael glanced at her, sensing the shift. She kept walking, but her fingers curled inside her gloves.

They descended a long slope where the wind had carved ridges into the snow. At the base of the hill, half buried beneath a fallen spruce, Mira found a cluster of frozen berries. She plucked them from the branch and tucked them into her satchel. A small meal, barely enough to steady them, but better than nothing.

Kael watched the sky. "The storm will break fully by midday. Once the sun rises a little more, the trackers will move faster."

Mira nodded, trying to focus on the practical urgency of their journey rather than the unease in her mind. "We will need to travel along the ridge to avoid the open fields. The snow there is too shallow to hide our prints."

Kael agreed with a quiet sound. But beneath that agreement, she felt it again. Pressure. Questions bracing against the bond like someone leaning against a locked door.

She hardened her thoughts instinctively, trying to form a barrier.

The bond pushed back.

Just a little. Enough to make her wince.

Kael stopped walking. "Mira."

Her breath caught. "Not now."

"We cannot keep pretending the bond is not shifting." His voice was calm but edged with tension. "Something changed after the vision. It is different today."

"I feel it," she said softly. "But letting it pull us further is not safe. We need to focus on surviving."

Kael took a careful step closer. The bond eased at the nearness, but Mira's chest tightened in a different way. "This silence between us," he said, "is not helping. Something is pressing through the bond. Something you are holding back."

She turned her face away, jaw clenched. "Do not try to push inside my thoughts."

"I am not pushing," he said. "But the bond is listening even if I am not trying. You know that."

His voice held no threat, no anger. Just unvarnished honesty. That honesty made her pulse jump in discomfort.

Mira closed her eyes. "Kael. Please. Leave it."

He hesitated. The bond shifted, tight with conflict. And that tension, mixed with her fear, pushed too hard against the fragile equilibrium they had kept since dawn.

Something in the connection slipped.

Not through her choice. Not through his.

A sudden, sharp pulse shot through both of them.

Mira gasped. Kael staggered backward, clutching his head, as the world around him blurred and melted away.

The forest dissolved.

Snow vanished.

The sound of wind disappeared in a breath.

Kael found himself standing in a stone courtyard bathed in pale winter sunlight.

He blinked, dazed.

A banner of frost blue fabric rippled overhead. Children's laughter echoed faintly from beyond the gates. Ice clung to the railings in delicate crystalline patterns.

It was not his memory.

He knew immediately.

Mira's breath hitched behind him, though she was not physically present. He felt her panic vibrate through the bond like a struck chord.

Kael turned slowly.

A younger Mira stood near the center of the courtyard. Her hair was longer, braided neatly. She wore a silver trimmed cape, her eyes bright with hope. She looked no older than seventeen.

Her mother stood beside her. A tall woman with clever eyes and calm grace. Her father paced near the fountain, his expression tight with worry. Veris soldiers lined the far side of the yard. Their armor gleamed coldly in the pale sunlight.

Diplomats from Ashrow waited near the steps. They wore heavy cloaks and stiff expressions.

Kael felt his stomach drop.

He recognized the insignia on one cloak. A spiral of black and gold. The mark of a high Ashrow emissary.

A man stepped forward from that group.

Tall. Severe. His voice deep and cold.

Kael's father.

The one he had not seen in more than a year. The man whose expectations had once shaped every decision he made. Until the day Kael walked away.

Kael felt the shock reverberate through the bond like a scream. Mira tried to pull the memory back, to force the connection closed, but her panic only strengthened it.

The scene sharpened.

Her father addressed the diplomat. "We have upheld our portion of the treaty. The artifacts were delivered. The delegation was prepared with every formality requested. Why has Veris accused us of misconduct?"

Kael's father responded with chilling calm. "Your daughter attempted to manipulate the ritual flame. She risked igniting a false reading. That is grounds for immediate inquiry."

Young Mira flinched. "I did nothing. My hands never touched the flame."

The Veris priest barked, "The magic surged because of your presence."

Mira's mother stepped in front of her. "The flame surged because you failed to stabilize the circle. Do not blame my child for your incompetence."

Kael's father raised a hand, silencing them. He exchanged a knowing glance with the Veris priest. "The Thornvale family will be taken for questioning. Until guilt or innocence is proven, they are exiled from the court."

Mira's father's voice broke slightly. "You cannot do this."

But Kael had heard enough.

He suddenly felt as if the ground opened beneath him. His father had been there. Had supported the accusations. Had allowed the Thornvale family to be cast out. Not for justice. Not for truth.

For politics.

For power.

Kael reached for the edges of the memory, desperate to withdraw. The bond thrashed between them, reacting to Mira's spiraling anguish.

Her younger self was crying silently as soldiers escorted her family out of the courtyard. Snow fell softly on her shoulders as her life unraveled.

Then the memory shattered like ice broken underfoot.

Kael hit the snow covered ground of the real forest with a harsh gasp, clutching his chest.

Mira fell to her knees beside him, breath ragged, tears streaking the frost on her cheeks. Her face was pale with horror and shame.

"What did you see?" she whispered.

Kael lifted his head slowly. "Everything."

* * *

The forest returned slowly, as if reality had to thaw its way back into place. The gray sky, the hush of snow, the dark rise of the trees. Mira's breath came in sharp, unsteady pulls, each one dragging a fresh ache through her chest. The bond still buzzed with the echo of the memory, raw and electric.

Kael knelt in the snow, hands dug into the frozen crust as if he needed to feel something solid. His head throbbed. His heart hammered in a rhythm that was not entirely his. His father's voice still rang in his ears, calm and cold, ordering exile with the same tone he once used to correct a sword stance.

He shut his eyes and swallowed hard.

Mira's voice trembled. "You were not supposed to see that."

He looked up at her. Tears glistened along her lashes, already beginning to freeze at the edges. The shame in her expression cut him deeper than the memory itself.

"I did not choose it," he said, voice rough. "The bond slipped. It forced the memory open."

"You were pushing," she said, though her accusation sounded more like self defense than certainty. "You kept pressing with your questions."

"Maybe," Kael admitted. "But I did not mean to pry that far." He drew a breath that felt like swallowing broken glass. "I would never have chosen that memory for you."

Her jaw clenched. "And now you know why I wanted it buried."

He did not deny it. The scene in the courtyard had stripped away whatever composed dignity she allowed others to see. In that moment she had been a frightened girl watching her family's life crumble under the weight of a sentence they could not appeal. He understood why she had built walls since then, why she hid behind a false name in a remote village.

And why his presence in her story hurt so much.

Because he was not merely another mage caught in the same disaster.

His father had been there.

Ashrow had stood beside Veris and helped turn the blade.

Kael rose slowly, snow crackling under his boots. The bond pulsed with each movement, picking up Mira's fear, his anger, their combined confusion until his stomach churned.

He took a cautious step nearer. "The man speaking beside the Veris priest. The one with the Ashrow crest. That was my father."

Mira's eyes darkened. "I know."

"Why did you not tell me?" he asked quietly.

Her laugh came out brittle. "Tell the son of the man who helped ruin my family that his father might be responsible? Before we were tied by whatever cursed ritual the Ember chose to show us?" She shook her head, snow scattering from her hood. "I did not owe you that pain. Or myself that risk."

"Risk," he repeated. "You thought I would defend him."

"I thought you might turn on me," she said softly. "Or walk away. Or decide the bond was a mistake to be fixed by removing the problem on my side."

The words hit him harder than the memory.

He stepped back, as if distance could soften the blow.

Pain flared in his chest at once, sharp and punishing. The bond yanked tight. Mira gasped, clutching her ribs. He forced himself forward again, kneeling in the snow in front of her to stop the pain from growing worse.

"We do not get to walk away," he said, breathing hard. "Not from the bond. Not from the truth."

She looked at him as if she wanted to believe him and could not yet allow herself to.

He held her gaze anyway. "Mira. My version of that history was different."

"Of course it was," she whispered. "Victors always rewrite the story."

"Not victors," he said. "Just those who survived the argument loudest." He drew a slow breath. "I was told Thornvale attempted to tamper with the ritual flame to twist the reading in Ashrow's favor. That your father tried to pressure our delegation into signing the treaty with false auspices. Ashrow claimed the treaty would have been cursed if we accepted it."

Mira's eyes flashed. "That is a lie."

"I know that now," he said quietly.

She froze.

Kael continued, his voice steady despite the churn in his chest. "In your memory, the flame surged before you touched it. The circle was flawed. The Veris priest panicked. And my father... he sided with Veris instead of allowing time to correct the mistake. He let them scapegoat your family because it removed a potential complication."

Mira swallowed. "You saw all that."

"Yes," he said. "And I will not pretend I did not."

The bond eased a fraction, responding to his honesty. Mira blinked rapidly, as if that tiny shift startled her.

She dropped her gaze to her gloves, clenching them until the leather creaked. "My father believed Ashrow would speak for us. That if anyone knew the truth of unstable circles and faulty rites, it would be those who honored the Ember's earlier pacts." Her lips twisted. "Instead, your father watched and said nothing when Veris called for exile."

Kael heard his own breath rasp in the cold air. He could see his father's face in his mind, stern and unyielding. A man who believed sacrifice was necessary for strength. A man who would not lose sleep over one family's disgrace if it maintained political advantage.

"He has always served Ashrow first," Kael said, more to himself than to her. "But I did not know how far he was willing to go to keep our leverage."

Mira lifted her eyes, and he saw the hurt beneath the anger. "My father died in exile," she said. "Without clearing our name. Without ever seeing justice. I do not know if your father wielded the blade or simply handed it to Veris, but he was there. He could have spoken. He did not."

Kael swallowed against the tightness in his throat. "You think I bear that guilt with him."

Her shoulders rose and fell in a slow, shaky breath. "I think you carry his name. His fire. His expectations. You came to the Rite as his son, even if you walked away from his house. That is enough to make me wonder whose side you will choose when it matters."

The bond throbbed, heavy as a hammer blow.

For a moment, Kael said nothing. Snowflakes settled on his lashes and melted slowly from the residual heat in his skin.

Then he spoke, each word deliberate. "If I chose his side, I would still be in Ashrow's hall, obeying orders, not standing on a ruined lake with a foreign kingdom blaming me for crimes I did not commit." His pulse spiked at the memory of the Rite, and the bond echoed it, but he kept his tone steady. "I left because I could not stomach the way he twisted protection into control. The way he measured people in terms of usefulness."

Mira watched him, eyes searching.

He met her gaze fully. "If I had known your family's name at the Rite, if I had known the truth of that day in your courtyard, I would have made a different choice."

Her laugh was soft and bitter. "You could not have stopped an exile."

"No," he admitted. "But I could have confronted him sooner. Refused sooner. Broken from him sooner. Maybe then I would not be standing here, hearing how long his shadow has been cast over your life."

Silence fell between them, thick but not empty. The bond hummed with a tension that felt less like anger and more like grief layered on grief.

"I do not blame you," Mira said at last, voice hoarse. "Not for what he did. But now you know why I could not trust quickly. Why I flinched each time Ashrow entered the story."

He nodded slowly. "And now you know why I will not defend him."

She studied him, eyes narrowing slightly as if testing the solidity of his words. "You saw the moment he chose. He could have told Veris to pause. To recheck the circle. He did not."

"No," Kael said. The admission tasted like ash. "He chose convenience over truth."

"Is that who you will become?" she asked quietly.

The question pierced more deeply than any accusation.

He shook his head. "If that was who I wanted to be, I would not be here at all."

The bond pulsed in agreement, surprising them both.

Mira's shoulders sagged as the tension in her frame slowly unwound. She drew a breath that seemed to come from somewhere deep in her chest. "Then we live with this truth between us. I will not pretend it does not cut. But I will try not to use it like a knife against you."

Kael let out a breath he had not realized he was holding. "That is more grace than I expected."

"Do not mistake it for forgiveness," she said, though there was no venom in the words. "Forgiveness is for the dead, and I am not ready to grant it."

"I would not ask you to," he replied.

They stood there in the snow, facing each other, the ghosts of their families stretching long shadows behind them. The forest remained silent, the wind barely a whisper through the branches. Somewhere far off, a raven called, the sound thin and distant.

Mira wrapped her arms around herself. "The memory you saw. That was only one piece. There were hearings afterward. Quieter rooms. Closed doors. More chances for Ashrow to speak up and more decisions not to."

Kael's hands curled into fists. "Then the rot is deeper than him alone. And I have more to unlearn than I thought."

Her gaze softened, just a little. "You cannot carry all of Ashrow's crimes."

"No," he agreed. "But I can refuse to repeat them."

The bond steadied at that promise. It did not fade, but the frantic edge of its earlier pulse eased.

Mira sensed it too. "It reacts to truth," she said quietly. "I felt it settle when you spoke plainly."

"Maybe that is its only rule," Kael answered. "No lies between bonded souls."

She almost smiled, though the expression was weak. "That would make it a very demanding judge."

"Then we should stop giving it reasons to tighten," he said.

She nodded, and some of the stiffness in her posture finally relaxed.

Wind ruffled the edges of their cloaks. The moment stretched until it felt fragile enough to break if either of them spoke too carelessly.

At last Mira broke the silence. "We cannot stay here. The bond may be calmer, but the trackers will not stop simply because our emotions have."

He huffed a faint, tired sound. "A shame. It would be easier if they did."

She turned, her boots crunching through the snow as she set off once more toward the north. Kael fell into step beside her, not too close, not too far. The bond pulsed with a quiet ache that felt almost like the soreness left after a healed wound.

After a while, she spoke again, more softly. "When this is done, when we have found answers about the bond and the Ember, you will return to Ashrow."

It was not a question.

Kael stared ahead. "I will return," he said. "But not as the son who left."

"You will confront him," she said.

"Yes," he replied. "About you. About Thornvale. About everything he withheld."

She nodded once. "Then perhaps the bond has chosen its bearer well."

He glanced at her, startled. "That sounded suspiciously like trust."

"Do not let it go to your head," she said, though there was the ghost of a smile in her eyes. "I am still deciding."

"That is fair," he said softly.

They walked on, the forest stretching around them in endless white. The weight of the shared memory remained, but it no longer pressed quite so sharply against Mira's ribs. Kael's fire felt different in the bond now, less like an invading force and more like a second heartbeat that had chosen to stand beside hers instead of over it.

For the first time since her exile, Mira allowed herself a small, fragile thought.

Maybe the truth, even when it hurt, could be the beginning of something rather than the end.

The bond stirred, almost in agreement.

Ahead, the land sloped downward toward deeper forest and the possibility of new answers. Behind them, the past did not vanish, but it no longer dragged at their heels with the same merciless grip.

They kept moving.

Not just away from the trackers.

But toward the tangled heart of the story that had bound them long before they ever met.

Chapter 12

The light filtered through the forest in thin streaks, softened by drifting flurries that made the world feel dreamlike and distant. Mira walked in silence beside Kael, her thoughts tangled like winter roots beneath frost. The memory they had shared the day before still echoed in her chest, cold and sharp, but something had shifted since then. The truth between them, painful as it had been, had settled into the bond like a stone dropped into deep water. The ripples had not vanished, but the immediate storm of emotion had faded.

For a while, their journey north passed without a word. The forest felt tight around them, not threatening, only dense, full of the cold hush that followed snowfall. The bond hummed quietly, neither strained nor calm, simply present.

Kael walked with his hands tucked into his cloak. His steps were measured, almost too careful, as if he feared any misstep would jostle the fragile steadiness they had found. His fire simmered under his skin in a muted glow, less restless than usual, but weighed with something heavy. It was not anger. It was not fear.

It was guilt.

Mira sensed it before she understood why. The emotion did not spike the bond, but it lingered like smoke in the air, curling at the edges of her awareness.

She tried not to pry. The memory of her own vulnerability, exposed without her consent, was still raw. But the bond did not respect intention. It responded to emotion, to truth, to the weight of unspoken things.

And Kael was holding something heavy enough that the bond reacted.

As they crossed a narrow stream that had frozen in a perfect glassy sheet, Mira felt a sudden tug under her ribs. Sharp. Sudden. Deep. She stumbled, catching herself against the trunk of a birch.

Kael turned instantly. "Are you hurt?"

"No," she gasped, clutching her chest. "I think... the bond is slipping again."

Kael's expression tightened. "It feels unstable on my side as well."

The air around them changed. A faint hum resonated through the ground, similar to the one that had preceded the earlier vision, but softer, almost hesitant. Mira backed away instinctively, but the bond tightened so sharply that a cry escaped her lips.

"Mira?" Kael reached for her.

Too late.

The world tipped.

Snow blurred. Trees twisted into streaks of shadow. Mira felt her breath ripped from her lungs as she was pulled through the bond, the connection flaring hot and cold all at once.

Then everything stilled.

She stood in a stone chamber lit only by the flicker of fire. The walls were carved with Ashrow runes. Heavy tapestries hung in deep red and gold. A wide window looked out over a volcanic landscape of black rock and glowing vents.

Mira's breath caught.

This was Ashrow.

Not as she imagined it in maps or whispered stories, but as Kael had seen it. The air smelled of heated stone and ember smoke. The walls radiated warmth. And somewhere far below, the ground thrummed with the low, constant vibration of fire magic.

Then she saw him.

A younger Kael stood near a low bed. His shoulders were tense, his jaw set, his eyes full of fear he tried to hide. He looked barely older than sixteen. His hair was shorter, his frame leaner, but the fire in him was the same. Burning. Restless.

The girl on the bed caught Mira's breath.

Dark hair tangled across a pale pillow. A slight frame curled under thick blankets. Hands trembling faintly. Her skin glowed with fever that had nothing to do with normal illness. Her breath came in short, uneven gasps. Her cheeks streaked with heat lines only a mage's eye could see.

Fire poisoning.

Mira stepped closer without thinking. "Is that your sister?"

Kael's voice came from beside her, though she knew his physical body still stood in the waking world. "Yes."

In the memory, the younger Kael took the girl's hand. "Arin," he whispered. "Stay awake. Please."

Arin stirred weakly, her voice a thin thread. "Tell me another story."

He forced a smile that did not reach his eyes. "The one about the Ember river?"

She nodded.

He began speaking softly, describing a river of molten gold that ran through the heart of ancient Ashrow. His voice trembled. Mira could see the truth beneath the story. This was not distraction. This was desperation.

A shadow fell across the doorway.

Their father.

Taller in the memory than Kael remembered him, dressed in ceremonial Ashrow robes lined with fire woven thread. His presence filled the chamber like a second heat source, commanding, unwavering, cold despite the flames.

He surveyed the room with a single sweeping glance. "She worsens."

Kael rose quickly. "We need another healer. The last one said she needed rest, but she grows weaker every day. She needs—"

"She needs discipline," his father cut in. "Her fire must be trained to align, not treated like a broken bone."

Kael's hands curled into fists. "She is not weak because she lacks discipline. She is cursed."

His father's gaze sharpened. "Do not repeat that word."

"It is the truth," Kael snapped. "Something touched her magic during the Ember Rite. Something from beneath the stone. She has been burning from the inside since the day I—"

He cut himself off, face paling.

Mira felt the bond twist.

In the memory, Arin whimpered softly.

Her father stepped forward with icy authority. "There was no curse. The Rite revealed instability. The girl's flame is fractured. If she fails to master it, she will die. That is her burden."

Kael stepped in front of Arin, fire rising unconsciously in his palms. "Then help her."

"I have," their father said. "By bringing tutors. By arranging tests. By pushing her magic to grow."

"You pushed her until she broke," Kael hissed. "She was fine before the Rite. Something went wrong."

Mira held her breath.

She knew Ashrow rituals. She knew the Ember's old paths. And she recognized what Kael was not saying.

"Kael," she whispered. "What happened at the Rite?"

He did not answer, but the memory did.

The room blurred with a rush of firelight.

Now Mira stood in a crowded ceremonial chamber, its walls shimmering with heat. A younger Kael stood in the center, surrounded by robed masters. Arin stood beside him, small and excited, her fingers gripping his sleeve.

The Ember flames in the chamber pulsed with dangerous strength.

Kael whispered, "She was supposed to watch. Only watch."

The memory surged.

Arin stepped too close.

Kael reached to pull her back.

His fire flared.

Her flame answered.

Two lights collided.

A crackle of Ember energy ripped through the circle in a sudden violent spike, throwing everyone backward. Arin collapsed. Fire seeped under her skin like molten veins.

Mira gasped.

The vision snapped back to the sickroom. Arin lay trembling

in her bed. Kael knelt beside her, his younger face ravaged with guilt.

His father stood stiffly by the window, refusing to look at them.

"You did this," younger Kael whispered to himself. "I lost control. I hurt her."

Mira felt the grief through the bond like a cold wave.

The memory trembled, beginning to dissolve.

Kael's father spoke again, voice cold as ash. "If she dies, it will be because she failed to strengthen her flame."

Younger Kael looked up sharply. "If she dies, it will be because I failed to protect her."

The memory shattered.

Mira was hurled back into the freezing forest, knees hitting the snow hard. She gasped, clutching her ribs. Kael stumbled beside her, bracing a hand against a tree trunk.

The bond throbbed, thick with open grief.

Mira's breath rushed out in a cold cloud. "Kael... your sister..."

He did not look at her. His jaw clenched tight enough that the muscles trembled. "She is dying."

Mira swallowed hard. "Because of what happened in the Rite."

"Because of me," he said quietly.

She felt the truth ripple through the bond like a deep wound pulled open.

"No," she said, reaching for steadiness she barely felt. "You were a child. She stepped forward. You only reacted."

His voice cracked. "My fire harmed her. If I had controlled it better, if I had not panicked, she would be well. She would be happy. My father reminded me every day that her weakness was my fault."

Mira's heart ached. "Your father lied to you."

Kael finally turned. His eyes shone with raw pain, unshielded and devastating. "I believed him."

Mira drew a slow breath, the cold burning her lungs. "Kael. That was not a curse you caused. That was a surge. A bond spark. She was touched by the Ember's raw current. You were both too young."

He stared at her, stunned.

And the bond softened in a way Mira had never felt before.

Not warm.

Not calm.

But open.

Kael whispered, "I did not want you to see that."

She stepped closer despite herself. "Now I understand why you chase answers. Why you risked everything to reach the Rite."

His breath shook. "Because if I do nothing, she will die. And I will have her death in my hands."

Mira shook her head. "You carry guilt that was never yours."

The bond pulsed.

Gentle.

Firm.

Quiet.

For the first time, it did not push or pull.

It simply held.

Their eyes met.

Something fragile formed between them.

Not forgiveness.

Not trust.

Understanding.

* * *

Snow drifted around them in quiet spirals, softening the shapes of trees and stones, wrapping the forest in a muted hush. The world felt distant, as if it had taken a step back to allow this moment to exist without interruption. Mira stood close enough to feel the heat of Kael's presence, the bond humming low between them, dense with grief and something new.

She drew in a breath that trembled faintly. "How long has she been like this?"

Kael looked past her, to a point somewhere far beyond the trees. "Three years. It began as fevers and fainting spells. Then the flickering light under her skin. The healers said it was Ember echo. A residue from the Rite. They tried treatments. Rituals. Infusions. Nothing worked."

His throat tightened as he spoke, but he did not look away this time. "Every time she woke, she smiled anyway. Said she did not want me to worry. But I could feel it. Her flame was shrinking. Each season took a piece of her."

Mira listened quietly, her heart aching with each word. Through the bond, she felt the weight behind his voice, the hollow guilt that had settled into his chest and refused to leave. It was like a stone wrapped in heat, pressing against his ribs.

"What did your father do?" she asked softly.

"Trained me harder," Kael said, a bitter twist at the edge of his mouth. "He said if my flame was stronger, I could lend her more power, keep her stable. So he pushed. And pushed. Until I could barely stand. Until my own magic turned sharp from too much strain."

Mira's hands curled at her sides. "He used your guilt as a tool."

Kael almost laughed, but the sound broke halfway. "He called it purpose."

"And you believed him."

"I needed to," Kael said. "If I stopped believing I could fix it, what was left except watching her fade?"

The bond pulsed with the shadow of that helplessness, echoing like a memory of standing at someone's bedside with no way to help. Mira felt it slice through her, familiar in a way she did not want to admit. She had watched her father die in exile. She had listened to him blame himself for failing his house, though the fault had never been his.

Guilt was a cruel inheritance.

She stepped another half pace closer, until their boots nearly touched. The bond stilled, holding its breath. "Listen to me," she said. "I have spent years carrying the weight of my family's exile. The shame. The anger. The need to prove something to a kingdom that had already decided we were guilty. It cuts in circles. It never ends. But none of it brought them back. None of it changed the past."

His gaze flicked to hers, sharp and searching. "So you stopped carrying it?"

"No," she said. "I learned to carry it differently."

He frowned. "What does that even mean?"

"It means I stopped blaming my younger self for not seeing the trap coming," she answered. "I stopped reciting every little thing I could have said or done differently. The past is a locked door. I cannot pry it open without losing my hands. So I stand in front of it and remember, but I do not bleed there anymore."

Her voice softened. "You were a boy in that chamber, Kael. Just as I was a girl in that courtyard. We were not the ones holding power. We were simply close enough to feel its fallout."

His eyes darkened with pain. "But my hand touched hers when the flames collided."

"Yes," she said. "Your hand did. In a moment of fear, not malice. If you had done nothing, the surge still might have hit her. Or worse. You were both inside a circle that should never have exposed you to such raw force."

He swallowed hard. "You are saying the fault lies with the ritual, not with me."

"I am saying responsibility lies with those who built the ritual and decided children belonged inside it," Mira replied. "Not with the brother who tried to pull his sister back when the fire flared."

The bond responded to her words with a slow, deep ripple. The harsh edge of his guilt softened, just a fraction, but the shift was clear. It felt like a band loosening around his chest.

Kael let out a breath he had been holding for years. "If I accept that... if I let the blame go... what is left of me?"

"You," Mira said simply. "Without the lie your father wrapped around you."

He looked at her as if he had never seen her before. The bond carried the weight of that stare. Curiosity. Hurt. A cautious, fragile trust.

"You sound very certain," he said quietly.

"I am not," she replied. "I am simply tired of watching both of us drown in things neither of us can change."

He huffed out a breath that might have been the beginning of a laugh. "You think I am drowning."

"I know you are," she said. "Because I recognize the look. I have worn it."

Silence settled again, but it no longer pressed down on them with the same crushing weight. The forest around them seemed to exhale. A patch of brighter light slipped through the clouds above, casting faint silver across the snow.

After a while, Kael spoke again. "There is something else you did not see. In the memory."

Mira tilted her head. "What is that?"

"I was supposed to travel with my father to the Ember conclave when Arin first began to worsen," he said. "It was an honor. A place in the circle of decisions. I turned it down."

"Why?" Mira asked.

"Because she was scared," he said. "She clung to my sleeve and begged me not to leave. She said the fever always spiked when I was gone." He swallowed. "So I stayed. I missed the conclave. My father never forgave me for that."

Mira's chest ached. "You chose her over advancement."

"I chose her," he echoed. "And she still got worse. So in his eyes, I failed twice." He smiled without mirth. "You asked earlier what side I would choose when it matters. I already answered that once. I just did not recognize it for what it was."

Mira met his gaze, and this time there was no anger there, only raw, unguarded honesty. "Then do not let him rewrite that choice. Not in your memory, and not in mine."

The bond pulsed again, steady and strong. It felt almost approving.

Kael's shoulders sagged, as if something inside him had finally let go. "I do not know how to carry this without guilt. But I can try to carry it without lies."

"That is enough," Mira said. "For now."

They stood there until the cold seeped through their boots, reminding them that the world still required movement. The trackers still existed. The Ember still stirred beneath its broken lake. The bond still connected them in ways they did not fully understand.

But something fundamental had shifted between them.

Mira no longer saw only the son of the man who had helped condemn her house. She saw the boy who had stood beside his sister's bed and told stories while the world around them argued about treaties and power. The boy who had turned his back on advancement to stay with someone he loved. The man who now walked beside her, carrying a weight he had never deserved.

And Kael no longer saw only the exile with frost behind her eyes. He saw the girl in the courtyard, standing straight despite fear, watching soldiers cut her life in two. The woman who now used that same frost to hold collapsing bridges and stitch broken ice under his feet.

Their histories were no longer distant, separate tragedies.

They were threads in the same knot.

"Come on," Mira said quietly, shouldering her pack. "We should keep moving before the light fades."

Kael nodded. "North?"

She felt for the faint pull beneath the bond, the same subtle direction that had guided them before. "North," she confirmed. "Toward wherever this bond thinks we belong next."

They walked side by side through the snow, their steps falling into unplanned rhythm. The bond hummed between them, no longer clawing, no longer fraying at the edges.

It felt bruised.

It felt tired.

But it also felt aligned.

After a while, Mira spoke again, her tone almost hesitant. "When we find a way to help Arin, and to understand this… connection… you will still go back to her."

"Yes," Kael said. "And you?"

"I will return to Thornvale's legacy," she answered. "Whether that means clearing the name or burying it."

He glanced at her. "We will have to face both our pasts."

"Not alone," she said.

The words slipped out before she could check them. The bond responded with a warm, surprised pulse.

Kael did not question it. He only nodded. "Not alone."

The forest closed around them, branches dusted in silver, the sky a dull, wintry blue. Their breath steamed in front of them. Their hearts beat in echoes.

And for the first time since the bond ignited, the space between those echoes did not feel like something trying to tear them apart.

It felt like a fragile bridge being built plank by plank.

They walked on.

Chapter 13

The wind shifted as the forest began to thin. Mira felt the change first in the bond, a faint prickling like frost forming across her thoughts. Kael felt it as well, his steps slowing as he scanned the terrain ahead. The trees opened into a valley carved by time and weather, and beyond it rose the crumbling silhouette of an old structure half swallowed by vines and snowfall.

It did not look like a ruin built by Veris. The stonework was older, darker, worn in ways that suggested long abandonment. Thick roots cracked through the walls, and sections of the roof had collapsed under decades of winter storms. Yet despite its decay, the place carried a hum of magic beneath the surface. Subtle. Waiting.

Mira exhaled slowly. "We found it."

Kael narrowed his eyes. "This is where he lives? In a ruin?"

"He prefers the word retreat," Mira said, though her voice lacked certainty.

Kael arched a brow. "And this… retreat… was close to your mother?"

A soft pang stirred in her chest. Memories flickered, faint but warm. "He was her mentor at the university. She said he knew more about the Ember's old lore than any scholar alive. When the exile happened, he protested. Publicly. Loudly."

"That explains why he is hiding," Kael murmured.

"It is more complicated," Mira said, though she did not explain further. Not yet.

They made their way down the slope, crunching through layers of untouched snow. The air grew colder as they approached the ruin, as if the stone itself rejected warmth. Kael tightened his cloak around him and let a faint thread of fire warm his core.

Mira felt his discomfort through the bond, a subtle itch at the edge of her thoughts. "Do not let your flame flare," she warned softly. "He is sensitive to fire magic."

Kael grimaced. "Sensitive how?"

"Sensitive in the way that once made him throw an entire library table out a window when a student lit a candle too close to an old scroll."

Kael blinked at her. "Charming."

"He is not charming," Mira said. "He is brilliant. And insufferable."

Kael huffed a quiet laugh. "I am beginning to understand why he and your mother got along."

They reached the threshold of the ruin. A large archway stood crooked and half buried. Mira stepped forward and raised her hand, letting her frost shimmer against her palm in greeting.

"Master Ovrin," she called. "It is Mira Thornvale."

Kael tensed. "You are revealing your name?"

"He will already know," she said. "He knew the moment the bond pulled us toward him. He feels shifts in the Ember's current the way others feel shifts in the wind."

Kael opened his mouth as if to argue, but then the air shuddered.

A wave of ancient magic rolled through the ruin, vibrating through the stones. Kael stiffened, grabbing Mira's arm instinctively. She felt the bond jolt in response, pulling them closer.

Footsteps echoed from within.

They were slow, uneven, accompanied by the scrape of wood against stone.

A figure emerged from the shadows of a collapsed hallway. At first Mira saw only the outline of a walking stick, then a long, heavy coat patched with pieces of different fabrics, then a mess of silver hair tangled around a thin, sharp face. His eyes were pale as frost crystal, bright and filled with restless energy.

"Mira Thornvale," he said, voice rough with age but steady. "You arrive at last."

Mira felt her throat tighten. "Master Ovrin."

He studied her with unsettling intensity. Then his gaze snapped to Kael. His eyes narrowed. "And this one. Fire in his bones. Ashrow flame taught by iron discipline. I smell that training a mile away."

Kael straightened. "Kael Ashrow."

Ovrin's expression darkened with recognition. "Ashrow. The boy from the embassy fires. I remember you. Loud magic. Louder temper."

Kael bristled. "I did not set those tapestries ablaze intentionally."

"Few do," Ovrin said with a dismissive wave. "Your fire was young. Unfiltered. I warned your father to let you rest more during those summits, but he insisted on pushing you like a cracked hammer."

Mira looked sharply at Kael. He shrugged. "There is a reason I do not attend politics anymore."

Ovrin snorted. "A reason that walks around behind your eyes like an untrained storm."

Kael's jaw tightened, but Mira shot him a warning glance. Argue with Ovrin and the old man would never stop.

Ovrin turned back to Mira. His gaze softened, though only slightly. "You carry your mother's eyes," he said quietly. "And her talent for attracting trouble."

"Trouble found us," Mira said.

"No," he corrected sharply. "Trouble sensed what you carry. The bond is not subtle, child. It screams across the ley lines like a bell hammered too hard."

Mira's stomach clenched. "You knew we were coming."

"I knew something unstable was coming," Ovrin said. "When you added your name at the door, the rest fell into place. And when the fire boy stepped into my threshold, the bond howled."

Kael frowned. "Howled?"

"Like a predator denied a meal," Ovrin said. "And like a child demanding guidance."

Mira swallowed. "Then you know what it is."

Ovrin's sharp gaze settled on her. "I know more than you wish I did."

He gestured toward the interior of the ruin. A narrow path had been cleared between fallen stones and shelves overflowing with books, scrolls, and strange metal instruments.

"Come," he said. "The bond is unstable. If we linger in the doorway, it may try to anchor itself to the stone and collapse half the ruin."

Kael raised a brow. "That can happen?"

"With your particular version?" Ovrin said. "It can do far worse."

Mira exchanged a worried glance with Kael, then stepped inside.

The ruin was larger than it appeared from the outside. Hallways extended into shadow. Pockets of old magic clung to the corners like cobwebs. Every shelf sagged under the weight of knowledge Ovrin had refused to abandon when he went into hiding.

A single hearth burned low in the center chamber. The flames danced across ancient carvings on the walls that Mira had never seen before. Runes shaped like spirals, lines crossing in patterns that represented elemental balance.

Ovrin motioned for them to sit. Mira lowered herself onto a faded cushion. Kael remained standing until the bond tugged sharply at his chest and he reluctantly dropped beside her.

Ovrin watched them both.

His gaze flicked between their chests, where the bond pulsed like two matching heartbeats.

"Frost and fire," he said softly. "Joined by an Ember surge. This is not a simple soulbind. Not a ritual tether. Not even a resonance match."

Kael leaned forward. "Then what is it?"

Ovrin's pale eyes sharpened. "A forgotten bond. Born in an age before the kingdoms learned fear. Created to stabilize the Ember when it began to shift."

Mira felt her heart stop. "So this has happened before."

"Yes," Ovrin said. "Long ago. Before records were scrubbed. Before Veris controlled the rites. Before Ashrow began weaponizing flame."

Kael's voice dropped. "The vision we saw. The two figures on the ice."

Ovrin nodded. "The first recorded pair. Frost and fire. United to carry the Ember's burden."

Mira swallowed hard. "Why us?"

Ovrin turned toward her, his expression grim. "Because the Ember woke again. And it reached for the nearest compatible vessels."

Kael stiffened. "You make it sound intentional."

"It was," Ovrin said.

The room fell silent.

The fire crackled.

Mira felt a chill deep in her bones. "Our bond is unstable. You said so."

Ovrin exhaled, long and weary. "Your version is incomplete. Damaged by the failed Rite. The Ember forced the connection before the ritual framework could guide it. That instability is dangerous."

Kael frowned. "How dangerous?"

Ovrin's voice dropped to a near whisper.

"If you two fall out of harmony, the Ember may react. And the next surge will not stay contained to a frozen lake."

Mira felt the bond pulse hard enough to steal her breath.

Kael's fire flared under his skin in alarm.

Ovrin gazed at them with stark seriousness.

"Your bond could trigger a chain of magical collapses across both kingdoms," he said. "Avalanches, storm fractures, elemental ruptures, even faults in the ley lines."

Mira's stomach twisted. "You are saying we could destroy half the world by accident."

"No," Ovrin said calmly.

They both froze.

Then he added, "You could destroy two worlds."

* * *

For a moment Mira thought she had misheard him. The room seemed to shrink around them, the shelves looming, the hearthlight sharpening every hollow in Ovrin's face. The bond gave a single hard throb, like a heart skipping a beat, then settled into a tense, watchful rhythm.

Kael was the first to find his voice. "Two worlds," he repeated. "What does that mean exactly?"

Ovrin tapped the end of his walking stick against the stone floor, the sound echoing faintly. "You live in the surface world of snow and fire and human kingdoms," he said. "But beneath that lies the Ember lattice, the network of energy lines that carry magic through stone and air. For most people, the second world is only a rumor. For you, it is a living thing threading through your bones."

Mira swallowed, throat dry. "The Ember beneath the lake. The pulses we felt. That was the lattice."

"Part of it," Ovrin said. "A nexus. A knot. A place where power gathers and asks for structure. When the first great shifts began, long before Veris, the Ember became chaotic. Storms rose unseasonably. Earth cracked where it should have held. Someone realized the Ember needed anchors, living conduits who could steady its flow."

Kael leaned forward, eyes intent. "The first bonded pair."

Ovrin inclined his head. "They stood in the place between worlds. Their bond was forged with care, guided by ritual lines and old agreements. They shared power, memory, even breath, but they had time to prepare, to be trained, to understand that their purpose was not personal comfort but global balance."

Mira's hands tightened in her lap. "We had none of that. The Rite failed. The Ember grabbed us and forced the bond."

"Exactly," Ovrin said. "Your connection skips steps. It burned through safeguards, tearing fabric without mending it. The Ember got its anchors, but the pattern is wrong. The bond is strong in the wrong places, fragile in the right ones. It is like building a bridge with missing supports and then trusting caravans to cross without falling."

Kael's jaw clenched. "You said if we fall out of harmony, the Ember reacts. How direct is that link?"

Ovrin gave him a long, measuring look. "When you fought each other in fear and suspicion, what happened to the lake?"

"It shattered," Mira said quietly. "Our magic spiraled. The Ember surged."

"Now imagine that same dissonance magnified through ley lines that stretch beneath both kingdoms," Ovrin said. "Imagine a cascade of reactions. Lakes cracking, riverbeds boiling, ice shelves collapsing, volcanic vents opening where they should stay sealed. The physical world would suffer, but so would the lattice itself. Once the network destabilizes beyond a certain point, magic becomes unpredictable everywhere."

Mira felt the blood drain from her face. "Spells failing. Wards breaking. Rites collapsing."

"Children born with magic that burns too bright or not at all," Ovrin added. "Frost where there should be harvest. Fire where there should be sea. Two worlds, the seen and the unseen, both twisted beyond what your kingdoms know how to fix."

The room seemed colder despite the fire. Mira pressed her palm against her chest, as if steady pressure could hold the bond in place. "You are saying our bond is a fault line."

"I am saying it is a key in a crumbling lock," Ovrin replied. "Turned carefully, it can stabilize what has begun to fracture. Turned carelessly, it can break what little structure remains."

Kael's voice came low and steady. "How do we keep from breaking it?"

Ovrin studied them for a long moment. The lines at the corners of his eyes softened, and when he spoke again his tone was less sharp, more like an old teacher facing students who had already been through too much. "The original bond was built on three pillars," he said. "Proximity, emotional alignment and shared purpose. You have the first by necessity.

The second you are only beginning to learn. The third you have not yet claimed."

Mira frowned. "Emotional alignment. You mean the way the bond reacts when we lie or lash out."

"Yes," Ovrin said. "This type of bond cannot tolerate deception between its bearers. It is not a moral lecture, it is structural. If one of you hides too deep, the connection strains, and the Ember pushes. It seeks clarity. Without it, power snarls."

Kael nodded slowly, as if pieces of the last few days were sliding into place. "When we told the truth about Thornvale and my father, the bond eased. When we pushed against each other with fear, it hurt us both."

Mira thought of how the bond had softened when she spoke plainly about exile, and again when she saw Kael's guilt and refused to accept the lie he had been fed. "So if we keep secrets from each other, the bond becomes more unstable."

"Exactly," Ovrin said. "You may lie to yourselves, to your kingdoms, to me, but not to each other. The bond will not allow it. That is why the original pairs trained together for years before they carried the Ember's weight."

Kael exhaled. "We have had days."

"And those days have already shaken a lake," Ovrin said with pointed calm. "Which brings us to shared purpose. Right now your goal is simple survival. That is necessary, but not enough. You must choose something beyond yourselves, something the Ember can latch onto as an anchor."

Mira's voice dropped. "What else can we choose besides survival while half the world is hunting us?"

Ovrin's gaze softened further. "You can choose to stop running only from danger and start moving toward a solution. The Ember offered you that vision, the one you told me of, not as a threat, but as a reminder. The first pair did not flee their task. They walked into it."

Kael's eyes flicked to Mira, then back to Ovrin. "You mean we need to accept what we are. Not fight it."

"I mean you need to decide what you will do with what you are," Ovrin said. "The bond exists. You did not ask for it, but you carry it now. Even if we could sever it, which we cannot, the act of doing so might tear the lattice. So the question is no longer whether you want it. The question is how you will shape it."

Silence settled for a moment. The fire popped, sending a few sparks into the air.

Mira forced herself to breathe slowly. "You said the original bond type was designed to stabilize the Ember. Can ours still do that, even damaged?"

Ovrin's answer came after a thoughtful pause. "Possibly. But not as you are. The pattern is incomplete. There are fractures in the link that could twist stability into something else. You need training, structure, guidance. And I am only one old man with a ruined house and a pile of banned books."

Kael's jaw tightened. "Then where do we go?"

Ovrin turned toward a shelf tucked into a shadowed alcove. He rummaged through stacks of parchment until he found a rolled scroll bound with dark blue cord. When he unwrapped it and spread it across the low table, Mira saw a map etched in faded ink. The central lines marked known territories. Veris. Ashrow. Smaller regions in between. But layered over those borders were thin, curving lines that did not match any political map she had ever studied.

"The ley lines," she whispered.

"Exactly," Ovrin said. "This is not a map of kingdoms. It is a map of the Ember's pathways."

Kael leaned closer, eyes tracing the delicate curves. "What is that?" he asked, pointing to a cluster of lines converging near the edge of the page, far from both Veris and Ashrow.

"That," Ovrin said, tapping the mark with one long finger, "is the Sanctuary of Embers. Or what remains of it. Before Veris and Ashrow fractured the rituals, before politics turned every rite into an argument, there were neutral places where magic itself was studied, apart from crowns. Sanctuaries. This was the largest."

Mira felt a tingling behind her ribs, like the bond pressing toward the mark. "You want us to go there."

"I do not want anything for you except that you stop breaking the world by accident," Ovrin said dryly. "But yes. If any place still holds the knowledge of the original bond, it is that Sanctuary. Its archives, if they have not all been looted, may contain the missing structure your bond needs."

Kael's brow furrowed. "If it is so important, why have neither kingdom reclaimed it?"

"Because both kingdoms fear what they cannot control," Ovrin said. "They prefer broken pieces they can own over whole patterns they must respect. The Sanctuary does not answer to

Veris or Ashrow. It answers to the Ember. That makes it dangerous to rulers."

Mira studied the map, then lifted her eyes to Ovrin. "You said our bond could trigger a chain of disasters. If we do nothing, what happens?"

Ovrin's expression grew grave. "The Ember will continue to strain against its cracked bindings. It will keep searching for equilibrium. You two are now part of its attempt to find that balance. If you refuse that role, the pressure will find another path, through earthquakes, storms, unexpected blights. The bond will grow more erratic. Distance will hurt more. Emotion will spark more surges. Eventually something will give."

Kael's voice was quiet, but steady. "And if we go to the Sanctuary?"

"You may learn why the first pair were chosen, how they lived with their bond and what they did to keep the lattice from collapsing," Ovrin said. "You may find rituals that can patch the fractures in your pattern. Or at least reduce the risk that every argument you have creates a new crater."

Mira almost smiled despite the dread curling in her stomach. "That would be an improvement."

Kael glanced at her, a faint glimmer of wry humor in his eyes. "We could try a world where our disagreements do not cause geological events."

Ovrin snorted. "I recommend it."

Mira sobered. "If we leave, what happens to you? Veris will suspect you if they realize we came here."

"They already suspect me of everything," Ovrin said with a shrug. "It is one of the few benefits of a long life spent insulting important people. There is only so much more trouble they can imagine I cause." His gaze softened as he looked at her. "Your mother once said I enjoyed dancing on the edge of exile. She was right. But when they turned on her house, I discovered the edge cuts on both sides."

Mira's chest tightened. "She spoke of you often. She said you taught her to question everything, including the people she loved."

"She was better at listening to that advice than I was," Ovrin said quietly. "Which is partly why we are here."

He turned back to both of them, his expression sharpening once more. "Listen to me. You are not here to fix old mistakes for the sake of my conscience, or your parents', or your kingdoms'. You are here because the Ember chose you and will not release you. You can either let that choice drag you behind it or you can decide how you will walk."

Kael straightened. "We go to the Sanctuary."

Mira nodded slowly, feeling the bond respond with a subtle pulse that felt almost like agreement. "We go," she said. "Not just to save ourselves. To keep the Ember from tearing two worlds apart."

"For Arin," Kael added softly. "For Thornvale," Mira answered.

Ovrin watched them both, something like pride flickering in his pale eyes. "Then you have your shared purpose," he murmured. "It is a fragile thing, but it is a start."

He rolled the map and pressed it into Mira's hands. The parchment felt old, edges worn, but the lines drawn upon it remained clear. "Follow the ley lines when roads fail you," he said. "The bond will help you feel where they run. The Sanctuary lies beyond the old borders, in the place your maps mark as wilderness. It is not as empty as they claim."

Mira tucked the scroll carefully into her satchel. "Will we see you again?"

"If the world does not break first," Ovrin said. "And if it does, then I will be far too busy yelling at the sky to entertain visitors."

Kael gave a tired huff of laughter. "You sound like someone the Ember would argue with."

"The Ember and I have been arguing for decades," Ovrin replied. "You two are simply its newest point of punctuation."

They stood to leave. The bond thrummed warmer near the threshold, as if eager to follow the path marked on Ovrin's map. Outside, the sky had brightened, clouds thinning to reveal a hard, pale blue. Snow still glittered across the valley, but the worst of the storm had passed.

At the doorway, Ovrin called after them. "One last warning."

They turned.

"Do not assume the Sanctuary will welcome you," he said. "Old places have long memories. And your bond shines like a beacon. Some will see salvation in it. Others will see a weapon."

Mira nodded, the weight of his words settling beside the map in her thoughts. "We will be careful."

"Careful is good," Ovrin said. "Alive is better."

They stepped out into the cold.

The ruin behind them hummed with quiet magic. The world ahead stretched wide and uncertain. Between those two points, Mira felt the bond pulsing in her chest, not gentle, not harsh, but resolute.

Kael fell into step beside her. "North and east," he said. "Along the lines."

"Into the wilderness that is not empty," she added.

"And toward answers that may ruin us as much as they save us."

She glanced at him, and his faint half smile met hers. "At least," she said, "we will ruin or save things together."

The bond warmed at that.

They walked on, leaving the ruin and the hermit scholar behind, carrying with them a map, a warning and the knowledge that their bond was not a mistake, but a choice waiting to be made.

Chapter 14

Snow swept across the valley in thin spirals as Mira and Kael paused at the edge of the ruin. The cold bit at their cheeks, but neither moved. The air between them felt charged, not with anger or fear, but with the heavy knowledge of what Ovrin had revealed.

Mira stared at the distant treeline where the ley lines shimmered faintly under her skin. "There has to be another way," she said quietly. "Some method to sever the bond without tearing the world apart."

Kael shook his head. The bond pulsed in agreement with him, painful and sharp. "Even entertaining that thought hurts it. Ovrin was right. The Ember fused us too deeply. A sever would be a rupture."

"So we are trapped," she said, voice thin.

"No," he answered. "Not trapped. Bound."

She let out a cold breath that misted between them. "That is not better."

Kael stepped closer, careful not to startle her. "If we spend our lives searching for a way to break this, we will fracture everything around us. The bond hates uncertainty. You feel that as clearly as I do."

Mira closed her eyes. "It is not uncertainty. It is fear."

"Then call it fear," he said. "I am not ashamed of it. But we cannot let fear guide the Ember."

Silence settled, made heavier by the weight of a choice neither wanted to face.

Behind them, the ruin groaned as a gust of wind swept through its broken halls. Ovrin appeared in the archway, leaning on his walking stick, gaze sharp as frost. "Indecision is the most dangerous state for your kind," he called. "Stand still long enough, and the bond will choose for you."

Mira turned. "If we walk away from each other, does the bond pull us back?"

"It either pulls you together," Ovrin said, "or it rips you both apart. There is no gentle version."

Kael inhaled slowly. "Then severing it is not an option."

Ovrin gave a curt nod. "Severing would be catastrophic. Control is your only chance. And control lies at the original binding site. The Sanctuary is the only place where the old patterns survive."

Mira's heart squeezed. "And if we reach it? If the knowledge is still there?"

"Then you may learn to shape the bond rather than be shaped by it," Ovrin said. His gaze softened, though it did not lose its edge. "But do not pretend the path is safe. The Sanctuary has its own laws. Its own defenses. Its own opinions about what the Ember chooses."

Mira exchanged a long look with Kael.

He gave a faint nod, almost invisible. A gesture not of command, but of offering.

Her voice trembled when she spoke. "If we try to control it, we are stepping into danger with no certainty of success."

Kael's answer was quiet but steady. "If we run from it, we guarantee disaster."

The bond pulsed, strong enough that they both felt it in their bones. It wanted direction. It wanted alignment.

Mira turned back to Ovrin. "If we choose the Sanctuary, is there any turning back?"

"Not the way you came," Ovrin said. "Once you step onto that path, the Ember will draw you deeper. You will not be the same by the time you return. If you return."

Kael looked to Mira again. "Then we choose now."

The world felt still. Even the wind paused, as if waiting.

Mira breathed in the cold air, let it fill her lungs, and met Kael's gaze without flinching. "We choose control. We go to the Sanctuary. Together."

The bond surged, not painfully this time, but with fierce, rising strength. A spark of warmth shot through Mira's chest. Kael's eyes widened as he felt the same pulse.

Ovrin nodded once, satisfied. "Then your road begins. Follow the ley lines and do not look back. The Ember will test you. The world will resist you. But this," he tapped the space between them with the tip of his staff, "this is your only chance to keep the worlds from breaking."

Kael stepped to Mira's side, their shoulders close but not touching. "Then we walk."

Mira lifted her chin toward the pale horizon. "And we do not stop."

Side by side, they stepped away from the ruin and toward the distant lines of power thrumming beneath the snow. The wind rose behind them, swirling through the broken archway as if sealing the choice they had made.

The Scholar watched them go, eyes full of worry and something like hope.

The bond thrummed with new rhythm as they crossed the valley.

One choice.

One path.

One dangerous purpose.

Together.

Chapter 15

The journey eastward carried them into harsher country. Snow drifts climbed almost to Mira's waist, forcing them to carve a path through windswept valleys that glittered under pale sunlight. The world felt stripped down to bone and breath, endless white stretching toward serrated ridges of black volcanic stone in the distance.

The ley lines pulsed faintly beneath the surface, guiding them. Mira felt each shift like a subtle tug under her ribs. Kael sensed it differently, through a warming of his core, an instinctive recognition of where the Ember wanted them to step next. They learned to follow both signals, weaving a path that kept them balanced between frost and flame.

Days blurred into a rhythm. Walking. Watching. Listening for the faint hum of the Ember's deeper world beneath the one they crossed. Nights brought thin shelter and the quiet ache of exhaustion.

But something else lived beneath that exhaustion.

Something that grew each time they shared a look a moment too long, a silence too charged or a breath that fell in unintentional sync.

Mira tried to ignore it. Kael did too. The bond did not.

The morning after they left Ovrin's ruin, they climbed a narrow ridge where the snow thinned enough to reveal streaks of dark stone. The frost air felt sharp in Mira's lungs. She tightened her scarf and glanced at Kael. He walked ahead, shoulders tense, as if his magic strained against the cold.

"You are overheating again," she said.

He slowed slightly. "Trying not to. The cold bites harder up here."

She reached out, letting her frost settle around her fingers before gently touching his arm. "Here."

The bond flared. His fire nudged her frost. For a moment, the elements coiled around each other like a breath drawn by two lungs at once.

Kael sucked in a sharp inhale. "Mira."

She pulled her hand away quickly. The magic withdrew with a faint hiss. "You were burning too hot. I was only fading the excess."

He nodded, though the tension in his jaw did not fade. "Thank you."

She stepped back to a safer distance, aware of how fragile the bond felt when their magic brushed too closely. It was like handling a cracked crystal. Beautiful. Luminous. And one wrong touch could split it down the center.

They crossed the ridge in silence, each step sending soft puffs of snow into the air.

Just before dusk, they stopped at a narrow overlook where the valley dropped sharply into a basin of frozen lakes and jagged volcanic vents. Steam rose in curling threads from the dark fissures, drifting through the twilight like ghosts.

Mira's breath caught. "I have never seen a landscape like this."

Kael's expression softened. "Ashrow has places like this. Fissures where the Ember rises close to the surface. We call them breathing lands."

"They look alive."

"They are."

They stood shoulder to shoulder, the cold wind tugging at their cloaks. Mira could feel his warmth just inches away. More than warmth. Something steadier. Something that reached through the bond and brushed against her thoughts with subtle, unspoken care.

She exhaled slowly and stepped back. "We should find shelter before the wind worsens."

Kael nodded and followed as they descended into the basin.

Darkness gathered fast. The temperature dropped with it. The first flakes began to fall again, thin and silver, swirling like pieces of broken moonlight.

By the time they reached the base of the valley, a full storm had taken shape. The wind shoved them sideways, and snow clung to their lashes. Mira's fingers stiffened despite the magic she cycled through them to keep the cold at bay.

Kael shouted over the rising gale. "We need cover. Now."

"There." Mira pointed to a mound of rock half buried in snow. Faint steam rose from one side. Not volcanic enough to burn them, but warm enough to melt a hollow.

Kael nodded and they hurried toward it, hands over their faces as the wind cut like glass.

Under the shelter of the stone slope, the storm dulled to a rumble. Kael drew his blade and chipped away at the frozen crust until a narrow cave hollowed out before them. The cave glowed faintly from geothermal warmth. Mira stepped inside first, her breath slowing as her body adjusted to the mild heat.

Kael ducked in after her and shook the snow from his cloak.

For a moment, neither spoke.

The cave was small. Too small. They would have to sit close. Closer than was wise. The bond stirred with cautious interest, sensing proximity and potential.

Mira set her pack on the ground and removed her gloves, flexing her stiff fingers. "I will gather snow to melt. We need water."

Kael reached out, stopping her with a gentle grasp around her wrist. "You are freezing. Sit. I will do it."

His touch sent a spark up her arm that she felt all the way through her chest. The bond brightened with a soft hum.

Mira withdrew her hand slowly. "All right. But be quick."

He stepped outside while she arranged their supplies. The warmth of the cavern was misleading. Beyond its shelter, the storm screamed.

When Kael returned with an armful of snow, his face was flushed from the cold. Mira guided the frost into a thin weave around the snow and watched as Kael coaxed a gentle flame over his palms. Frost and flame worked in careful harmony, melting the snow into clean water without boiling it or freezing it back into shards.

"Better," Kael said quietly as the water warmed in the metal cup he held.

Mira nodded, though her gaze lingered on his hands. "Your control is improving."

"That is because the bond is quieter tonight."

She paused. "Quieter?"

Kael settled beside her, close enough that the heat from his body washed over her skin. "It feels less strained. More aligned. Whatever Ovrin said about purpose, it matters. It steadies the connection."

Mira looked away. "Alignment is not the same as peace."

"No," he said. "But it is a step."

He handed her the cup. Their fingers brushed. She inhaled sharply.

The bond surged like a sudden intake of breath.

Mira froze.

Kael did too.

The cave seemed suddenly smaller. The warmth heavier. Her heart thudded painfully in her chest as the bond tangled with emotion neither of them named aloud.

Kael's voice came low, roughened by something more than exhaustion. "Mira."

She looked up.

Their faces were close. Too close. His breath mingled with hers in the narrow space. His eyes glimmered in the dim light, warm and uncertain. The bond leaned between them like a hand on their backs, urging, coaxing, wanting.

Her pulse hammered.

He moved a fraction closer.

The cave air tightened. The bond brightened.

Mira's lips parted.

Kael's gaze dropped to her mouth.

The world held its breath.

She felt the moment forming, delicate and dangerous, balanced on the edge of something that would change everything if they let it fall.

Then she pulled back.

Not all the way. Just enough.

Enough to break the line between them.

Enough to send the bond fluttering in a confused pulse.

Kael exhaled sharply, closing his eyes for a moment before looking away. "If we... if we lose control of this, the bond will react."

Mira pressed her trembling hands against her thighs. "I know."

"And we cannot risk a surge," he said.

"I know that too."

Silence enclosed them, heavy and complicated.

Neither spoke for a long time.

The storm howled outside, but inside the cave, the louder storm lived between them, fragile and unspoken.

The near kiss hung in the air like a suspended spark that refused to fade.

* * *

Mira stared at the rough stone wall opposite her, heat still burning in her cheeks despite the chill that seeped around the edges of the cave. Her heart had not yet slowed. The echo of almost still tugged at her thoughts, soft and intrusive, replaying those inches between them on a loop.

Kael shifted beside her, the slight scrape of his boot on stone loud in the narrow space. The bond pulsed once, awkward and unsettled, as if even it was not sure whether it had been denied or spared.

She cleared her throat. "We should sleep in turns."

Kael let out a breath that was almost a laugh and almost not. "If you like. But the bond will drag us both awake if anything happens."

"Then we at least pretend to be sensible," she said.

"Pretending counts for something," he murmured.

She risked a glance at him. His face was turned away, the lower half in shadow, but she could see the tension in his jaw. He was trying to give her space in a place that offered none.

She drew her cloak tighter. "Take the first rest. You are still burning too warm. If you stay awake, your magic will creep higher."

"And if I sleep, it will settle," he said.

"Exactly."

He hesitated, then nodded. "Fine. But wake me the moment you feel the bond twitch in a way you do not like."

"That suggests there are ways I do like," she said before she thought.

His lips twitched, then smoothed quickly. "Go to sleep, Mira."

She muttered something under her breath and turned slightly onto her side, facing the curved stone of the cave rather than him. The floor was not comfortable, but her muscles were too tired to care. She stretched out as much as the narrow space allowed, acutely aware of the warmth at her back where his presence filled the air.

She tried to steady her breathing. Not to sync with his. Not intentionally. But her body kept matching his rhythm, chest rising and falling in time with the familiar pattern she had come to know through the bond.

Her eyelids grew heavy.

The last thing she thought before sleep pulled her under was a single, treacherous truth.

If there had been no Ember and no bond, she might have wanted that almost to become something real.

Sleep did not bring visions this time. No ancient figures. No collapsing ice. Only a vague sense of warmth at her back and a faint, steady pulse under her ribs that never let her forget she was not alone.

When she woke, the storm had quieted to a whisper.

The air in the cave was dim and cool. The geothermal warmth kept the worst of the cold at bay, but the fire in Kael had sunk low. She could feel its embers banked inside him, calm for once.

He was awake.

She knew it even before she opened her eyes. The bond hummed with awareness, alert but not alarmed.

"Pretending to sleep longer will not work," he said quietly. "I can feel you thinking."

She blinked and rolled onto her back, squinting at the faint glow at the cave mouth. "You are not supposed to feel my thoughts."

"Not clearly," he said. "But the bond picks up when your mind starts running circles around itself."

She grimaced. "Does it broadcast when yours does the same?"

"Unfortunately," he said.

She pushed herself up slowly, muscles protesting. "How long was I asleep?"

"Long enough," he replied. "The storm has weakened. We can move soon."

She swallowed, then forced herself to address the thing hovering between them. "About last night."

He went very still.

"We were tired," she said. "Cold. In a cramped space. The bond... amplifies everything. It pulled at us. Hard."

"That is one way to describe it," he said dryly.

She ignored that. "We cannot afford to let it push us like that again. Not until we know how to stop a surge before it starts."

He nodded once. "I agree."

The lack of argument surprised her.

"You do?" she asked.

"Yes." He turned his head to look at her. His gaze was steady, but there was something raw in it. "Because whatever almost happened did not feel small. And the bond rejoiced. It was not quiet. It leaned into it. If we give it that kind of leverage without understanding the structure, it could tear through both of us."

Her chest tightened. The memory of the surge at the lake flickered across her mind. "So we avoid…"

"The cliff's edge," he finished.

She nodded, pretending the answer did not sting.

Kael's voice softened. "It is not a rejection."

"Feels like one," she muttered.

"For me too," he said.

The bond flared in brief, startled recognition, then settled.

Mira blinked. "You…"

"Care?" he said. "Yes, Mira. I care. That is part of the problem."

The cave's air felt thin.

He continued, words low and precise. "I care that you freeze your own hands trying to save strangers. I care that you still flinch in your sleep when the memory of exile catches you by surprise. I care that you will throw yourself into the path of unstable magic to keep me from falling through a cracked bridge. The bond might be amplifying it, yes, but there is plenty that is mine as well."

Her throat went dry.

"I am not afraid of that," he said. "I am afraid of what happens if we let it run unchecked while the Ember is watching."

She let that sink in. It bruised and steadied her at the same time.

Then she nodded slowly. "All right. We walk carefully."

"Together," he said.

She forced a small smile. "Always, apparently."

He huffed a soft breath, then pushed himself to his feet and moved toward the cave mouth. "Come on. Before the storm changes its mind."

They stepped out into a world remade by snow and quiet. The storm had left smooth drifts and sculpted ridges across the valley. The vents still steamed in the distance, sending faint curls of warmth into the air. The sky above was a pale, washed out blue, clouds thin and high.

They climbed out of the basin, following the faint tug of the ley lines. The day passed in long stretches of walking and short exchanges that gradually smoothed the sharp edges left by the night.

It was in the small things that their growing closeness revealed itself.

When the wind picked up, Mira moved slightly ahead to cut the worst of it with her body and her magic, letting the frost harden the air around them so it deflected the sharpest gusts.

When her steps dragged, Kael slowed his pace without remark, adjusting unconsciously to her rhythm.

They shared water and dried provisions without ceremony, passing the flask and the ration packets back and forth like people who had been doing so for years rather than days.

When a patch of ice cracked unexpectedly beneath Mira's foot, Kael's hand closed around her arm almost before the sound reached her ears. She steadied herself and he let go, but the imprint of his fingers stayed with her.

The bond thrummed in quiet approval each time they moved in sync.

By late afternoon, clouds began to gather again, thick and gray along the horizon.

Mira glanced up. "Another storm."

"We cannot outrun every one of them," Kael said. "But there may be shelter ahead. The ley lines have shifted slightly upward. That often means rock formations. Caverns."

She nodded, senses tuning to the subtle pull in her chest. He was right. The flow of the Ember's undercurrent angled toward higher ground. They followed it.

Dusk was beginning to seep into the snow when they found the cave.

It was narrow at the entrance, just wide enough for one person at a time, but when they squeezed through the gap, the interior opened into a rounded chamber with a low ceiling, smooth walls and a floor free of debris. Faint warmth radiated from the stone itself, as if the Ember's blood ran somewhere deep in the rock.

Mira let out a tired sound that was almost a laugh. "The world has fewer comforts than I remember, but this... this is something."

Kael examined the ceiling and edges with a soldier's caution, checking for weaknesses. "No loose stone. No overhangs that look ready to collapse. This will hold."

They arranged themselves much as they had in the previous cave, packs against the walls, cloaks spread to add layers between them and the ground. The storm rolled in outside, its distant roar muffled by the rock.

Night settled, thick and dark.

They lit no fire. The natural warmth of the stone was enough, and firelight could leak through cracks. Instead they sat close, shoulders brushing, sharing heat in a way that had become both necessary and dangerous.

Mira rested her head back against the wall, letting her eyes close for a moment. "I never thought I would feel grateful for volcanic stone."

"Do not say that too loud," Kael murmured. "It might start asking for offerings."

She smiled, small but real. "You have a strange sense of humor."

"It was worse before the bond," he said. "You are benefiting from the improved version."

She laughed quietly, the sound echoing softly off the curved stone.

They fell into a companionable silence. Mira listened to the rhythm of their breaths, the distant rush of wind and the faint, pulsing hum of the ley lines beneath them.

"You know," she said at last, eyes still closed. "When Ovrin spoke of shared purpose, I thought it would feel like a burden. Another weight on top of exile and guilt and responsibility. But it does not."

"How does it feel?" Kael asked.

"Like a line," she said slowly. "Something straight in the middle of everything that curves and twists. A direction that is not just away from danger, but toward something."

He was quiet for a moment. "It feels like that for me too."

She opened her eyes and turned her head slightly, catching his profile in the dimness. "Then maybe this is why the bond is calmer. It recognizes the line."

"Let us hope it approves of our route," he said. "I am not eager to find out what displeasure looks like on this scale."

She shivered slightly, then shifted closer without thinking. Their shoulders pressed together more fully. The warmth that passed between them through cloak and shirt and skin was steady and grounding.

His breath hitched, just once. The bond brightened subtly.

She felt it.

He felt that she felt it.

Neither moved away.

* * *

The quiet inside the cave deepened, wrapping around them like another layer of warmth. Mira focused on the small details because the larger ones felt too dangerous. The roughness of the stone at her back. The way her breath came slower now. The faint scent of ash clinging to Kael's cloak, threaded through with something sharper, like metal heated and then cooled.

Every place their bodies touched hummed. Shoulder against shoulder. The side of her thigh against his. Their hands resting close enough that the backs of their fingers brushed when one of them shifted.

The bond soaked in all of it, thrumming steady and low.

"You are calmer," Kael said quietly.

"Are you accusing me of being dramatic before?" she replied, the slightest lift in her voice.

"Never," he said. "Merely observant."

She smiled despite herself. "I was not calm before. Not really. I was holding on to too many jagged things. Exile. Rage. Fear."

"Same," he said. "Except my jagged things were in Ashrow colors."

She turned her head to look at him. "And now?"

He thought for a moment, gaze distant. "Now the edges are still there, but they feel less like they are cutting me from the inside. You being here makes them… less sharp."

Her chest tightened. "You are not supposed to say things like that in a cave where I cannot walk away."

"You can walk away," he said softly. "The bond will scream, but you can."

She dropped her gaze to their hands. "I am not sure I want to."

The admission hung between them, fragile and true.

The bond brightened.

"Do you remember," he said, "what Ovrin said about emotional alignment?"

Mira nodded. "That the bond cannot tolerate lies between us."

"Then if it is going to tear us apart," he said, "it will be over something real."

Her throat felt tight. "We are already in too deep for it not to be real."

He turned fully to face her. Their knees brushed. She could not avoid his eyes now, not in this close space, not with the bond as awake as it was. They were dark in the low light, but the warmth in them was unmistakable.

"Mira," he said quietly. "For the sake of the bond, and the Ember and the world and whatever else is waiting beyond the Sanctuary, I am going to say this once, simply."

She swallowed. "I am listening."

"I want you," he said.

Heat flooded her face. The bond surged with startled intensity, then settled into a slow, deep thrum.

He did not look away. "Not as a tool. Not as an anchor. Not because the Ember shoved us together. I want you because you are clever and infuriating and stubborn and brave. Because you make impossible choices and still look me in the eye when they hurt. Because you keep choosing to stay even when every part of your past tells you to run."

Her pulse pounded in her ears.

He went on, voice roughened. "The bond may amplify it, but this exists without it too. I can feel the difference. The bond pulls. I choose."

Mira's lungs felt too small. "Kael…"

"I am not asking you for anything," he said. "I know what danger we walk in. I know a single uncontrolled moment could start a cascade we are not ready to stop. I am not asking you to answer or to promise or to change anything. I am just refusing to pretend the feeling is not there."

A shaky laugh escaped her. "You call this helping us control the bond?"

"Yes," he said. "Because the more we hide, the more it strains. Secrets corrode it. So this is me throwing truth onto the table and seeing if it cracks or steadies."

She stared at him, breathing hard. The bond pulsed again, not with pain this time, but with a sensation she could only describe as relief.

"I am going to say something," she whispered. "And I need you not to use it against me later."

There was a faint curve at the corner of his mouth. "I will try."

She drew a breath. "I want you too."

The words left her feeling oddly weightless. The bond reacted at once, flaring with a warm, luminous heat that rushed through her veins and echoed back from his. Her frost and his fire rose in tandem, not in conflict, but in response to a shared truth finally spoken aloud.

She pressed on before the bond could overwhelm her. "I want you in ways that have nothing to do with survival or shared purpose or the Ember. I want you when you argue with me and when you defend me. When you look at me like I am more than the worst thing that has happened to my house. When you carry your guilt and still choose to stand strange and stubborn at my side."

Her voice shook, but she did not look away.

"I do not know how much is the bond and how much is mine," she said. "But I know it did not start at the lake. It started the moment you refused to let them take me after the Rite. The moment you chose my life over your safety."

Kael's expression changed, something raw and bright breaking through. The bond responded in kind, a wave of emotion that made her eyes sting.

They sat there, truths laid bare between them, the cave quiet except for the wind outside and the racing of their hearts.

Then the magic began to climb.

It crept up slowly at first, a faint tingling in her fingertips, a soft flush of heat under his skin. The bond, fed with honesty, turned greedy. Frost curled around the edges of her vision. Flames whispered along his arms. The air shifted, becoming thick and charged.

Kael noticed it the same moment she did.

His eyes widened slightly. "The bond is reacting."

She nodded, throat tight. "It is feeding."

He swore under his breath. "Of course it is. It thinks this is alignment. It does not understand that there are limits."

Mira forced herself to pull her magic back from the edges of her skin, fighting the rising frost. The bond resisted, wanting more. Her breath came faster. "We have to stop."

He clenched his jaw. She felt him trying to bank his fire, to channel it inward without smothering it. The effort shook him. "We just agreed not to lie," he said through gritted teeth. "So here is another truth. If I move closer, I will not stop at almost this time."

Her stomach flipped. "If you move closer, I will not want you to."

The bond flared again, sharp enough to make them both gasp.

Mira squeezed her eyes shut. "We cannot."

"No," he said. "We cannot."

Pain and longing tangled so tightly she could not tell them apart. The bond shivered with frustration, unanswered and restless.

She drew in a breath and forced the words out. "If we give ourselves fully to this before the Sanctuary, the bond will deepen. It will root. Every emotional spike will echo through the Ember. We will become a weapon or a weakness before we know how to be anything else."

"And if we wait?" he asked hoarsely.

"Then we walk into the Sanctuary with a chance," she said. "A chance to learn the structure before we let feeling fill every gap."

He laughed once, harsh and soft all at once. "Only you could make waiting sound like a tactical maneuver."

"It is," she said. "For both of us."

He stared at her, every line of him pulled taut.

Then he nodded slowly. "All right."

Her heart stuttered. "All right?"

"We hold the line," he said. "We do not deny what is there. We do not bury it. But we do not give the bond the fuel it wants until we know it will not set the world on fire."

A breath she had not realized she was holding left her lungs in a shaky rush. "Agreed."

"Agreed," he echoed.

They sat in silence again, the charged moment gradually ebbing into something gentler. The bond, though disappointed in its wordless way, seemed to accept the new boundary. The surge retreated. Her frost settled back into place. His fire dimmed to a steady, manageable glow.

After a while, Kael let out a tired sound. "You realize we have just made a pact to make our lives significantly harder."

She let out a quiet, strained laugh. "Our lives were already difficult."

"True," he said. "We are simply adding disciplined restraint to the list."

She bumped his shoulder lightly with her own. "Spoken like a man who enjoys suffering."

"Spoken like a man who has seen what happens when fire goes unchecked," he replied.

Their shoulders stayed pressed together. Their hands remained close, but not touching. They leaned against the same wall, sharing the same breath, the same quiet.

Outside, the storm roared and then softened.

Inside, they rested against invisible limits they had chosen together.

Mira closed her eyes, feeling the bond's pulse slow to something steady and deep. "When this is over," she murmured, "when we have done what we need to do, when the Ember is stable and the Sanctuary no longer trying to judge us…"

"Yes?" he asked, voice a low thread.

"We revisit this," she said. "Without fear. Without the bond dictating terms."

He did not hesitate. "That is a promise."

"Do not swear lightly," she warned.

"I am not," he said. "I am swearing the only way we can now. In front of the bond that will scream if I lie."

The connection between them gave a soft, resonant pulse. Almost approving.

Mira smiled, small and fierce in the darkness. "Then it will remember we chose this as well. Not just what was forced on us."

They stayed like that until sleep crept over them, slow and quiet. No visions rose to claim them, only the warmth of each other's presence and the knowledge that they had walked to the edge of something vast and dangerous, looked down together and chosen, for now, to step back.

Morning would bring more snow, more miles, more risks.

But it would also bring the same line Ovrin had spoken of. Shared purpose. Shared danger. Shared restraint.

And beneath it all, growing like a steady ember waiting for its rightful flame, something that was no longer just survival, no longer just a broken bond.

Something that felt very much like love, held carefully in both hands until the world was ready for it.

Chapter 16

The shrine rose from the snow like the ribcage of some long dead creature, half swallowed by frost and time. Dark stone pillars leaned at uneasy angles, etched with symbols far older than Veris or Ashrow. Mira felt the ley lines converging beneath the ground, their quiet thrum vibrating through her bones.

Kael felt it too. His fire stirred as if answering a summons.

"We should not stay long," Mira whispered. "Old places like this remember everything."

"Then let us hope they remember mercy," Kael replied.

They stepped between the pillars.

The air shifted.

Heat and cold pulled at the edges of their magic with equal force. Mira felt her frost coil upward like a waking serpent. Kael felt his fire rise in a steady burn. The bond tightened, then burst open with a blinding surge.

The world vanished.

They stood in a vast chamber of light. Frost spiraled down from a ceiling made of stars while rivers of molten gold flowed across the floor. Two figures waited in the center, one shaped from fire, one from ice. Their faces were blurred, their forms fluid, but their presence filled the space with impossible weight.

The Ember.

Its voice was not a sound but a resonance that vibrated through the bond until Mira's breath stuttered.

You are the anchors. You are the line. You are the doorway the world has reopened.

Mira gripped Kael's hand without meaning to. He did not pull away.

Images flooded their minds. Thornvale restored. Her family name cleared. A warm hearth, laughter, safety. Arin waking from her burning illness, smiling in the sunlight. Kael's mother embracing them both. Peace. Healing. Futures handed to them like gifts.

Then a final image.

The two of them standing together, bound by a perfected connection, radiating power bright enough to shape the Ember's flow.

The vision faded into a low, thrumming promise.

Serve the Ember. Accept its guidance. Yield your bond to its pattern. I will give you strength, protection and salvation for all those you love.

Kael's breath caught. "It is offering to save Arin."

Mira felt the sharp ache of longing. "It is offering to restore Thornvale."

The light pulsed once more, warm and cold at once.

Choose. Give yourselves fully, and the path will open. Resist, and the world will choose another way.

The vision snapped.

They staggered back into the physical world, falling to their knees in the snow. The shrine loomed around them, silent and ancient.

Kael pressed a hand to his chest. "It felt real."

Mira swallowed hard. "Too real."

"Arin could live," he whispered.

"My family could stand again," she said softly.

Their eyes met, the bond humming with temptation and fear.

"I want to say yes," Mira breathed.

"So do I," Kael answered.

The bond shivered, waiting for their decision.

But neither spoke the word.

They stayed kneeling in the snow, shaken and silent, knowing the Ember had offered them everything they wanted.

And knowing that accepting it might cost them more than either dared imagine.

Chapter 17

The snow around the shrine had fallen still, as if the world itself awaited their answer. Mira felt the cold pushing into her palms where she knelt, but it barely reached her. The warmth of the Ember's vision still lingered inside her chest, glowing with dangerous promise.

Thornvale restored. Her father's name cleared. A life rebuilt.

A life returned.

She had dreamed of that since the day soldiers escorted her family into exile.

Beside her, Kael's breath shook with something fierce and fragile. His sister's face lingered behind his eyes, pale and fevered, her small hands gripping his sleeve.

Arin alive. Laughing. Whole.

The Ember had shown him exactly what he wanted most.

Exactly what would break him if he reached for it and lost.

Mira forced herself to stand. Her legs trembled. The bond pulled tight, as if sensing she was about to step off a cliff she could not climb back from.

Kael rose more slowly. Snow clung to his cloak. His fire simmered uneasily under his skin, flickering in ways Mira had never seen, restless and hungry.

They locked eyes.

"Mira," he said quietly, almost pleading. "It can save her."

She swallowed hard. "And it can save my family."

They stared at each other, surrounded by the silent bones of the ancient shrine. The cold wind blew through the stones, stirring frost dust into the air. Overhead, the sky was bruised gray, heavy with unfallen snow.

He stepped closer. The bond brightened as their distance closed. "We could take the offer. Just this once. Let it anchor us the way it wants. Just to heal them. Just to set things right."

Her heart twisted. "And after that? When the Ember decides to use us for something else? When it asks us to carry power we do not understand, or to bow to a pattern we cannot control?"

Kael's jaw tightened. He looked away, as if the mountain ridge in the distance might hold an answer he could not find in her face.

"It showed me Arin running in sunlight," he said. "Not burning. Not trembling. Just alive." His voice cracked. "Do you know the last time I saw her run?"

Mira shook her head.

"She was eight," he whispered. "She tripped in the courtyard. Scraped her knee. She cried more from embarrassment than pain, and I carried her to the healer even though she insisted she was fine." His breath faltered. "That was the last time I carried her without fearing I might drop her."

Mira felt tears sting her eyes. "Kael."

He turned to her with raw grief in his gaze. "I am asking for a moment to imagine a world where she survives without paying a price we cannot afford."

She reached out, hesitating only for a heartbeat before laying her hand over his. The bond surged, bright and warm and heartbreakingly gentle.

"When it offered that vision," she said, "it was not giving us a gift. It was showing us the shape of our weakest point."

His composure wavered.

Mira pressed on. "And when something ancient and powerful knows your weakest point, you do not hand it your entire life. You protect it. You protect yourself."

He closed his eyes.

The shrine groaned around them, a low vibration running through the pillars as the Ember's presence lingered, hungry for their answer.

Kael opened his eyes again. His voice was hoarse. "You are right."

She blinked. "I am?"

He nodded once. "If it had shown me Arin dying, I would have resisted without thought. But it showed hope. A future. That is what terrifies me most."

Her throat tightened. "It terrifies me too."

He took her other hand.

The bond tightened around them like a glowing thread.

"But I will not bargain with something that hides its true cost," he said. "And neither will you."

She exhaled shakily, relief and dread knotting together. "Then we refuse."

They turned toward the shrine.

The runes carved into the ancient stone flickered with dim light, as if expecting their submission. Waiting.

Mira raised her chin. "We will not yield our bond."

Kael's voice joined hers, steady. "We choose our own path."

The shrine answered at once.

Light burst from the cracks in the stone like molten gold forced through a shattered vessel. The ground shook violently, throwing Mira off balance. Kael caught her arm just as the bond twisted with such force it stole the breath from her lungs.

A deep, resonant voice rolled across the valley, not in words but in pure, thunderous rage.

Heat slammed into them. Frost clawed at their skin. The air fractured in a violent ripple as magic surged outward in a wave powerful enough to throw snow from the ground and split open the frozen earth.

"Kael!" Mira shouted as the ground buckled under their feet.

He pulled her close, shielding her with his arms. Fire flared from him instinctively, fighting back the violent cold sweeping across the shrine. Her frost rose in response, trying to stabilize the eruption of heat.

The bond screamed.

A shockwave shot through both of them, as if the Ember itself had reached inside and twisted the connection.

Mira cried out.

Kael staggered.

Slowly, painfully, the blast of magic faded. The trembling ground settled to a dull rumble. Snow whipped through the air in frantic swirls. Heat steamed from cracks in the stone while frost spread across shattered pillars.

When silence finally returned, everything smelled of burned snow and ancient magic.

Kael leaned forward, resting his forehead against Mira's as they caught their breath. "That was its anger."

She swallowed. "It knows we refused."

"It will not forgive that," he said.

She nodded once, throat tight. "But it will not force us."

A brittle laugh escaped him. "No. It acts like a god, but it cannot take our will."

Before she could answer, a pulse of sharp energy shot through the bond.

Mira looked up.

Kael stiffened.

Through the haze of lingering magic, Mira felt it first. A distant flare of frost magic. Too uniform. Too trained. Too many signatures at once.

Her stomach dropped.

"Veris," she whispered.

Kael's expression darkened. "Ashrow too. I feel fire on the wind."

They both turned toward the horizon.

Far off, faint but growing stronger, two separate magical presences moved toward their location. Entire groups. Entire squads. Drawn by the violent surge the Ember had unleashed when they refused.

Kael reached for his weapon. "We need to move. Now."

Mira grabbed her satchel. Her heart hammered against her ribs as the bond pulsed with warning.

The explosion of Ember magic had done more than punish them.

It had revealed exactly where they were.

"We are being hunted by both kingdoms," she said.

Kael took her hand. "Then we stay ahead of them."

Together, they ran from the shrine as the shadows of Veris and Ashrow bore down on the ruined valley.

Their refusal had saved their souls.

It might cost them their lives.

But they ran anyway.

Side by side.

Toward the Sanctuary.

Toward the truth.

Toward the only future they still had left.

Chapter 18

Snow whipped in violent spirals as Mira and Kael raced across the valley floor. Their breath came in sharp bursts, each exhale crystallizing instantly in the freezing air. The echo of the Ember's backlash still rang through their bones, leaving both of them drained and unsteady.

They had no time to recover.

Magic signatures were closing in from opposite directions, two tides of force converging on the same target.

"Mira, to the ridge," Kael shouted, pulling her toward a narrow path of rock. "If we gain height, we can break the line of sight."

But the bond surged a warning before Mira could answer.

She spun just in time to see a group of Veris frost soldiers cresting the rise ahead. Their armor gleamed spectral silver, their cloaks crackling with cold enchantment. At their center was a tall figure carrying a sigil staff, the Veris mark of authority bright against the storm-grey sky.

Kael swore under his breath. "We cannot go through them. We go around."

"Too late," Mira said.

The sigil staff struck the ground.

A frost ring exploded outward with blinding force.

The shockwave hit them first. Mira tried to shield herself, but the cold slammed into her like a wall. She staggered. Kael grabbed her, holding her upright, his fire flaring in a desperate counter.

The frost ring scattered in sparks of white light, but the Veris soldiers were already rushing forward.

"Mira Thornvale," the sigil bearer called. "You are hereby taken into custody by decree of the High Court."

She clenched her teeth. "I am not going with you."

"You have no choice," he said calmly. "No one defies a Rite and walks free."

Kael stepped in front of her. "She is not your prisoner."

The sigil bearer raised his staff, light gathering at the tip. "Then you are a threat."

Kael braced himself for the attack, but Mira saw it before he did. Another group was approaching from behind. She felt them through the bond, fire signatures distinct and fierce.

"Kael," she whispered. "Ashrow."

He turned, just as a second wave of fighters burst from the opposite slope. Ashrow cloaks snapped in the wind, bright with ember embroidery. Their blades glowed faint red as they drew heat upward through their arms.

Two kingdoms. One fleeing pair.

Mira felt the bond twist painfully between them. Fire on one side. Frost on the other. A trap closing from both ends.

Kael grabbed her wrist. "We stay together. No matter what."

The bond pulsed in agreement.

But Veris struck first.

A soldier drove his staff into the snow, sending a spear of ice racing toward Mira's feet. She dodged, frost swirling around her hands as she countered with a shard of her own. It struck the ground in front of the soldier, exploding into a cloud of needle-sharp crystals that forced him to stumble back.

Kael swung his arm in a sweeping arc. Fire surged outward, melting snow and forcing the first line of Ashrow fighters to break formation. Their magic cracked the air with heat.

The valley erupted into chaos.

Mira and Kael fought back to back, but they were outnumbered. Every burst of magic drained the strength the Ember had already stripped from them.

Mira's vision blurred. Kael's fire wavered.

They were running out of time.

A Veris soldier lunged at her with a frost-bound chain. Mira tried to twist away, but the ground slipped beneath her boots. The chain wrapped around her wrist and shoulder, locking tight with enchanted force.

"Mira!" Kael shouted.

She threw a blast of frost that smashed the ground and sent shards flying, but the soldier yanked the chain and dragged her forward. She fell hard, snow exploding around her.

Kael charged toward her, fire burning bright along his arms, ready to cut through anything between them.

But Ashrow struck him the same moment Veris captured her.

A flaming hook of molten metal arced through the air and snapped around Kael's torso. He roared in pain as the magic pulled him off his feet. Two Ashrow loyalists rushed forward, securing the binding with practiced precision.

Mira screamed his name.

Kael clawed at the hook, fire burning furiously, but the enchantment resisted him.

"Mira!" he bellowed, dragging himself across the snow toward her.

She struggled against the frost chain, but the Veris soldier tightened his grip and slammed another binding around her legs. "Do not resist. The Court will decide your fate."

Kael surged forward, dragging the Ashrow fighters with him, fire blazing uncontrolled. The hook flared white with heat, and his captors shouted warnings.

The bond hit its breaking point.

Pain tore through Mira's chest. Her magic spasmed, frost racing uncontrollably across her skin. Kael gasped as fire erupted from him in a chaotic burst.

Both forces collided violently inside the bond.

Mira's scream ripped through her throat. Kael echoed it. The pain was not merely physical. It was a wrenching inside their cores, a tearing at the threads binding them.

"Mira, do not let go," Kael choked, fighting the magic that dragged him backward.

"I am trying," she gasped. "Kael, stay with me."

But the armies pulled in opposite directions.

Veris soldiers dragged Mira toward the north.

Ashrow fighters hauled Kael toward the south.

Snow churned beneath their feet as they clawed for each other, fingers reaching, magic surging wildly, the bond shredding with every heartbeat.

Their hands almost touched.

Almost.

Then the armies wrenched them apart.

The bond twisted, snapping tight like a rope pulled across a blade.

Mira felt her vision go white with agony.

Kael shouted her name with a sound that shook her bones.

Light burst between them. The bond screamed in pain.

Then everything went dark.

Chapter 19

Pain lingered long after consciousness returned to Mira.

She opened her eyes slowly. The world resolved into soft frost light, pale walls, and the familiar cold of Veris marble. She lay on a narrow cot, wrists ringed with light-binding cuffs that dampened her magic. The distinct hum of controlled frost currents filled the room. She knew the sound well.

A Veris holding chamber.

Her stomach knotted.

The bond pulsed faintly, as if calling from a great distance. Weak. Strained. Too far.

Kael was alive. That was all she could tell.

But he was not with her.

The moment she tried to sit up, the door slid open and a woman entered. Dark hair braided into a perfect crown, robes immaculate, expression unreadable. High Magister Solenne

Veris. Mira had seen her at court years ago, during her parents' final winter in the capital.

Solenne closed the door with quiet precision. "Mira Thornvale."

Her voice was smooth as polished ice.

Mira forced herself upright. "Where is Kael?"

The Magister smiled the way one smiles at a child who has missed an obvious lesson. "Alive. For now. His kingdom has taken him. You need not concern yourself with Ashrow matters."

Mira pulled against the cuffs. "If you hurt him, you risk destabilizing the bond. You know this."

"Which is precisely why I am here," Solenne said. "To offer you a solution."

Her breath caught. "What kind of solution?"

"One that allows you to walk free." Solenne folded her hands in front of her, posture elegant. "One that allows your family to be restored. Your exile lifted. Thornvale returned to its rightful status."

The words struck Mira like a physical blow.

Solenne stepped closer. "You did not choose this bond. The Ember forced it upon you. We have studied such connection patterns for generations. And we know how to purify them."

"Purify," Mira repeated slowly. "What does that mean?"

"It means removing the unwanted half," Solenne said.

Mira's pulse spiked with horror. "No."

"Hear me out," Solenne said calmly. "You are the frost vessel. Your magic is structured. Stable. His is not. If we channel the Ember's power along the frost line only, the bond will collapse on his side and consolidate on yours."

Mira shook her head. "You are describing his death."

"His dissolution," Solenne corrected. "Painful, yes. But he will not suffer long. The Ember will reclaim what it put into him. You will be whole again."

Mira's throat closed. "And if I refuse?"

Solenne tilted her head. "Your family remains disgraced. You remain in custody. And the unstable bond continues to threaten our kingdom. The Court will not tolerate that. The choice is yours."

Mira's hands trembled.

"Take this offer," Solenne said gently, "and Veris will welcome you home. You will step into your mother's legacy. The kingdom will see you as a savior. Not a danger."

Mira's breath came shallow.

Kael dying meant Arin would die too. He had told her every detail of the curse eating through his sister. The Ember sustained her life only through Kael's magic.

If Kael died, Arin's flame would go out within days.

Solenne studied her face. "Think carefully. For your family. For your kingdom."

Mira closed her eyes as the Magister left the room, her footsteps echoing down the corridor like the ticking of an hourglass spilling sand.

She pressed her forehead into her hands.

She had dreamed of restoring Thornvale for years. Her parents' shame. Her own guilt. Every wound Veris had carved into their lives.

And now she could have everything back. Everything she had lost.

If she let Kael die.

If she killed him.

She felt the bond flutter weakly. A faint spark of warmth. Fading.

She collapsed back onto the cot, shaking.

"I cannot," she whispered. "I cannot choose that."

But she knew Veris would not wait long for her answer.

Kael awoke to darkness, rough stone, and the smell of scorched iron.

Ashrow.

His wrists were chained with binding cuffs that burned cold at the touch, engineered specifically to suppress fire magic. His limbs felt heavy, drained from the bond tearing under forced separation.

The door scraped open.

A tall man entered wearing ceremonial armor trimmed with ember threads. His expression was stern but familiar in a way that made Kael's breath catch.

Commander Rhyken. His father's right hand.

"Kael Ashrow," Rhyken said. "You have caused trouble."

Kael forced himself upright, though pain stabbed through his ribs. "Where is Mira?"

Rhyken snorted. "Worry about yourself first."

"Where is she?" Kael growled.

"Alive," Rhyken said with a shrug. "For now."

Kael yanked against the cuffs, fire flaring despite the suppression. "If Veris harms her, the bond will destabilize. You know this."

Rhyken gave him a cold smile. "Good. Let it destabilize on her side."

Kael froze. "What are you saying?"

"I am offering you a choice," the commander said. "One that benefits Ashrow. One that benefits your family. One that saves your sister."

Kael's heart hammered. "Explain."

"The ritual you began at the lake did more than awaken an unstable bond," Rhyken said. "It also opened the Ember's pathways. With the right pattern, we can channel the Ember's power entirely into a single fire vessel."

Kael felt sick. "Into me."

"Correct," Rhyken said. "If the Ember's energy is claimed fully by your flame, the frost half of the bond will collapse. Mira Thornvale will be consumed. The bond will end. And Ashrow will gain a living conduit of elemental power."

Kael's stomach twisted violently.

"If you refuse," Rhyken said, "Mira remains alive, but your bond will continue to spiral. Arin will die. Your mother will bury her child. And Ashrow will call you a traitor for abandoning your duty."

Kael's breath caught sharply. "Do not talk about my family as leverage."

"They are leverage," Rhyken said. "As is the girl. You know this."

Kael shook his head. "You are asking me to kill her."

"I am asking you to save your sister," Rhyken corrected. "And your kingdom."

Kael's jaw clenched.

He remembered Mira's voice in the snow cave. Her hands in his. Her honesty. Her fear. Her warmth pressed against his shoulder as the storm howled outside.

He remembered how the bond pulsed when she spoke her truth.

And he remembered Arin's smile when she was still healthy. Her laugh. Her tiny hands gripping his as she begged him to tell her one more story before bed.

He closed his eyes in agony.

Commander Rhyken stepped forward. "Choose the ritual. Choose your sister's life. Choose Ashrow."

Kael felt something inside him fracture.

Rhyken turned to leave. "We will expect your answer by nightfall."

The door slammed shut.

Kael stared at the floor, chains digging into his wrists, breath shaking with grief and fury.

Two futures stretched before him.

One where Mira lived.

One where Arin lived.

The bond flickered again, faint as a dying ember.

"Mira," he whispered, voice breaking.

And across the mountains, Mira whispered his name too.

Both trembling.

Both hurting.

Both standing at the edge of the same impossible choice.

Love of family.

Love of each other.

And a bond that would not survive the wrong decision.

Their time was running out.

Chapter 20

Night pressed heavily over Veris and Ashrow territory, yet neither kingdom slept. Both had captured half of a living bond they barely understood, and both feared what would happen if they failed to control it. Soldiers patrolled the halls. Wards tightened. Magic hummed through the walls like a restless storm seeking resolution.

Mira stood in her cell with her palms against the cold marble, heart trembling inside her ribs. The light-binding cuffs kept her frost power numb, as if wrapped in wool. Her thoughts spun, a storm of fear, guilt, longing and terrible clarity.

Veris had offered her salvation. Her family. Her name restored. A future she had begged the stars for during every lonely winter since exile. All she had ever wanted stood in front of her like a door cracked open.

But the door demanded Kael's death.

Her stomach twisted.

Across the mountains, she felt the faintest tug of the bond. Weak. Flickering. But alive. Always alive. That thread had become the one constant in a world that kept shifting beneath her feet.

She pressed her forehead against the cold stone. "I choose you," she whispered. "Even if it destroys everything else."

The bond quivered at her words. Not strong enough for understanding. But it felt her resolve, and it glowed faintly in response.

She lifted her head.

She would not give Veris her silence. She would not let them shape her destiny. She would not sacrifice Kael, not even for her parents' redemption.

Her loyalty was her final truth.

Kael's cell in the Ashrow fortress was carved from volcanic stone that thrummed softly with living heat. The walls glowed faintly with ember enchantments designed to weaken frost or force obedience from reluctant fire wielders. But the suppression cuffs around his wrists bit like ice, numbing the very thing that made him who he was.

He sat on the floor, back against the wall, breathing through the pain pulsing in the bond.

He had thought choices were simple in childhood. Protect your people. Guard your family. Serve your kingdom. But adulthood had given him a price he never expected.

Kill Mira to save Arin.

Submit to a ritual that would make him a conduit of power, a weapon shaped by the Ember and controlled by Ashrow.

The girl who had told him her truths in the quiet of a storm.

The girl who had reached for him when the world's weight had crushed them both.

The girl the bond itself leaned toward as if she were the missing half of something ancient.

He could not kill her.

He would not.

His voice was barely audible when he whispered, "I choose you, Mira. Always."

The bond shuddered. Then something changed.

A spark.

A flicker of light.

A thin, trembling line of connection that pulsed in his chest as if someone far away had tugged the thread with desperate hope.

Kael's eyes snapped open.

"Mira?" he breathed.

A faint answering warmth brushed across his thoughts.

She had chosen too.

The bond surged, heat and frost twisting together like joined heartbeats.

And with that surge came something else.

Connection.

A sudden flash of Mira's cell.

A sigil etched into Veris stone.

A guard walking past her door.

The pressure of the cuffs on her wrists.

The way she braced herself against a rising wave of fear she refused to let show.

She was searching for him.

He reached back as far as the bond allowed.

Show me where you are.

The magic between them flickered. Then Mira's thoughts pushed back, shaky but strong enough to form a clear picture.

Her cell.

The corridor outside.

The placement of the guards.

The weakening of the frost wards near the ceiling.

The exact moment the binding cuffs loosened during each cycle of the suppressive spells.

Kael felt her instruction like a whisper.

Break your cuffs when the next pulse falls.

He inhaled sharply. "Mira. That will burn me."

Her answer trembled in his skull.

It will hurt. But it will work.

He closed his eyes, centering his breath. He waited for the familiar pressure. The suppressive magic pulsed like a heartbeat, rising and falling in steady rhythm.

And then, as Mira had said, there was a moment.

A breath between pulses.

A small gap in the air.

A crack.

Kael seized it.

He pushed fire into his hands with all the strength he had left. The cuffs flared bright white, molten heat battling suppression. Bolts of pain tore through his arms, up his spine, into his teeth.

He screamed.

The cuffs shattered.

Fire burst through the air, ripping across the walls like a living creature finally released from a cage.

Kael collapsed to one knee, panting, vision swimming. The heat had burned him, blistered the skin of his wrists, but he was free.

The bond sang.

Mira felt it. She gasped as the surge answered her own attempt.

She had been waiting, breath held, praying the bond would carry her warning correctly. When she felt him break his restraints, she forced herself upright and pulled frost into her blood with violent force.

Solenne's voice echoed in her memory.

Purify the bond. Kill the fire.

Mira whispered, "Not today."

She pushed frost up her arms.

The cuffs froze.

She slammed her wrists into the stone wall and shattered them.

Cold cracked up her skin in thin white streaks, but she ignored the pain. She pressed her hand against the frost ward at the top of her cell door. The ward flickered, weakened by the Ember backlash earlier that day.

The bond pulsed, and she felt Kael push fire toward her from afar.

She used that heat to destabilize the ward from the inside.

It burst open.

Her cell door swung outward.

Guards shouted in the corridor.

"Thornvale is loose!"

Mira lifted her hands. Frost spiraled outward, coating the floor in glassy ice. The guards slipped as she dashed past, running through the hall with zero hesitation.

The bond tugged her north.

Kael was moving too.

She felt him pushing through Ashrow corridors. Fire lashed out at enemy blades. Heat melted locks. He moved with the precision of a soldier, guided by the bond's instinctive pull.

Her heart pounded.

Through linked magic they saw flashes of each other's escape.

Kael's fist breaking through a weakened window lattice.

Mira freezing the hinges of a tower door and shattering it with her boot.

Kael using the butt of a smoldering sword to knock out two guards blocking his path.

Mira creating a wall of frost to stall a Veris mage who tried to intercept her.

Linked magic.

Shared instinct.

Perfect coordination.

When they reached the open world, both were breathless, shaking, half burned or half frozen.

Snow fell lightly from a moonless sky.

They ran.

Across ridges, down ravines, through forests stripped to skeletal branches. Their magic left trails of frost and steam, impossible to hide but impossible to stop.

And all the while, the bond grew stronger.

The distance between them shrank.

Every breath pulled them closer.

Every pulse of magic drew them nearer.

Finally, at the edge of a frozen lake, Mira saw a figure in the distance sprinting toward her.

Kael.

He saw her at the same moment.

He stumbled to a halt, chest rising and falling like he had been running for his life. When she reached him, she threw herself into his arms before she could think.

He caught her.

His arms wrapped around her, holding tight, holding desperate, holding as if he expected her to vanish.

The bond flared in a burst of warmth and cold so bright she felt tears sting her eyes.

"Are you hurt?" he whispered into her hair.

"Not enough to matter," she said. "You?"

"No," he said. "Not anymore."

She leaned back enough to cup his face. "They wanted me to kill you."

His jaw clenched. "They wanted me to kill you."

She nodded. "Then we both chose right."

He pressed his forehead to hers. "I will not let them touch you again."

"I will not let them take you," she answered.

The bond responded like a heartbeat.

A bright, new pulse of energy rose between them. The kind that had not existed before. Not the chaotic surge from the Rite. Not the painful tearing from separation. Something new. Something steady.

A promise forming in magic.

"I know what we have to do," Mira whispered.

Kael nodded. He felt it too. "The Ember will not stop until it has control of us. Until it has a vessel."

"So we face it," she said, voice grounding in quiet resolve. "At the original binding site. The one Ovrin told us about."

"The sanctuary of embers," he said. "The birthplace of the first bond."

"Where all of this started," she agreed.

"And where we end it," he finished.

Together.

The wind howled over the frozen lake. The stars blinked through thin cloud cover. Somewhere behind them, Veris and Ashrow soldiers scoured the land, searching for them.

But none of it mattered.

The only thing that mattered was the choice they made and the road ahead.

Kael took her hand.

Mira squeezed back.

They turned north. Toward the ruins of the old world. Toward the place the Ember first gave power to a bonded pair. Toward an answer that might save them.

Or kill them.

They did not flinch.

Act II ended under the frozen sky.

Hand in hand.

Two hearts.

One bond.

And a decision that would shape every world the Ember touched.

Part 3

Confrontation and Reshaped Destiny

Chapter 21

The northern horizon stretched in a cold, pale sweep, a world carved from ice and shadow. Mira and Kael walked side by side through the deepening frost, their boots crunching over crusted snow, their breath forming thin clouds that vanished instantly in the bitter air. The wind rose in slow, hollow waves, carrying the strange metallic scent that had marked their path ever since they fled imprisonment. It was the scent of the Ember stirring far below the earth, restless and waking.

The bond pulsed between them in unsteady rhythms, sometimes warm, sometimes sharp as a blade dragged along glass. Mira felt each shift like a change in her own heartbeat, a reminder of how close the world had come to breaking them apart. She stole a glance at Kael as they climbed a ridge of black stone streaked with frost. His jaw was tight, but his eyes scanned the land with unwavering focus.

He felt it too.

The air was not still. The world was not quiet. Something beneath the frozen crust trembled in long, slow waves. The closer they walked to the Ember Mouth, the more each tremor pressed against their ribs like an unspoken threat.

Mira pulled her cloak tighter. "It feels stronger today."

Kael nodded, his gaze fixed on the distant valley ahead. "It knows where we are going."

"Because we refused it," she said.

"Because we broke its script," he corrected. "The Ember spent centuries choosing vessels and shaping them. We changed the pattern."

Mira felt her frost magic flicker along her fingertips. The cold no longer obeyed her as it once had. Some days it surged, desperate to shape the air. Other days it dulled, as if sensing the Ember's presence beneath the earth and hesitating to approach too quickly.

"You think it fears us," she murmured.

Kael stepped over a jagged crack in the ground. "I think it does not understand us. That may be worse."

The bond gave a sharp pulse. Mira winced.

Kael immediately slowed. "Did that hurt?"

"No," she said, though her breath hitched. "Not exactly. It feels like pressure. As if it is pushing against the inside of my chest."

He reached out, brushing his fingers lightly along the back of her hand. The bond steadied at once, the pressure easing into a faint, pulsing thrum.

"Better?" he asked.

She nodded. "Always."

His touch lingered only a moment. Then he released her, but the warmth of his fingers stayed long after the contact broke.

They descended into a shallow ravine where the snow deepened to their calves. Frost clung to the edges of Mira's cloak. Kael's fire rose subtly in response to the cold, but even that heat felt warped. It pulsed in irregular bursts, reacting to forces neither of them could see.

The wind thickened. Snow spiraled upward in unnatural columns.

Mira frowned. "The storms are following us."

"They are not storms," Kael said. "They are symptoms."

"Of what?"

"Of the Ember losing patience."

Mira's heart tightened. She remembered the vision of the first bond, how the ancient pair had been swallowed by their connection, how their individuality dissolved until nothing remained of who they had been.

She glanced at Kael again.

He met her gaze without hesitation. "We will not let that happen," he said softly.

The bond warmed, a gentle pulse that settled deep in her chest.

They continued across the ravine. Their shadows stretched long beneath the gray sky. The land around them shifted from snow to black stone, from black stone back to snow. Strange fissures cut the landscape like veins of forgotten fire.

Kael crouched at one of them, touching the warm edge with careful fingers. "This should not be active," he murmured.

"Do you think the Ember is forcing heat upward?" Mira asked.

He nodded grimly. "It is trying to pull us in. To push us off balance. The fissures, the storms, the tremors. These are not accidents."

Mira knelt beside him. The stone pulsed faintly under her palm. Frost reacted instinctively, curling in a soft spiral before dissipating in a shimmer.

She swallowed. "It is calling us."

"Calling," Kael said, "or warning."

They stood and continued north.

Hours passed in tense, cold silence. They crossed plateaus where the wind carved ridges into the snow like frozen waves. They climbed slopes of obsidian that cracked underfoot with brittle sound. Twice they had to stop and brace themselves as tremors shook the land, causing plumes of steam to rise from small vents in the earth.

The sky darkened early, though no storm clouds formed. The sun was simply swallowed by the strange haze that hovered above the distant horizon. The light grew diffused, heavy, tinted with faint red and silver.

Kael paused, lifting his face to the wind. "Do you feel that?"

Mira did.

The bond flared with sudden, intense heat, followed by a spine chilling cold. Her breath caught as the contradictory sensations raced through her chest.

"It is close," she whispered.

Kael took her hand, steadying her through the spike. "Not much farther now."

She tried to smile, but her heart was pounding too fast. "Kael… if it grows worse…"

"It will," he said quietly. "But we go anyway."

She nodded and squeezed his hand.

They moved again.

Dusk crept across the land, turning frost into shards of pink and blue crystal. At last they reached a ridge overlooking a vast plain of obsidian rock. The air rippled with heat, rising in soft waves that distorted the world. Snow melted the instant it touched the stone.

In the center of the plain, a long scar split the ground.

The Ember Mouth.

Even from the ridge they could feel its pull, like a low hum vibrating along their skin. Heat and cold churned out of the fissure. Streams of glowing light pulsed beneath the surface like veins of molten gold and blue ice intertwined.

Mira stared, her breath stolen by the sight.

"This is where the first bond was forged," she whispered.

Kael's voice was low. "This is where the first pair died."

Mira felt the bond pulse, almost painfully. It recognized the place. It leaned toward it, as if it carried memories in its magic that belonged not to them but to the ancient world.

Kael placed a steadying hand on her back.

Mira closed her eyes.

The world shivered.

The fissure glowed brighter.

The bond tightened, a desperate pull, as if urging them to step forward, to surrender, to complete the legacy the Ember believed they owed.

Kael's hand tightened on her shoulder. "Mira. Look at me."

She forced her eyes open.

He stood close, his breath warming the cold air between them. "We are here on our terms," he said. "Not its."

Her chest loosened. "Our terms."

He nodded. "Always."

The wind surged around them, carrying erratic pulses of heat and cold. Storms began to form in the distance, rotating around the Ember Mouth like hungry shadows. The earth trembled, long, slow quakes spreading through the ridge.

Mira braced herself.

Kael did too.

Then, in the silence between tremors, the bond surged again. Hard. Sharper than before. Mira gasped, stumbling forward. Kael caught her before she could fall.

"Mira," he breathed. "It is pulling."

She gripped his tunic. "I know."

The Ember Mouth flared with sudden light.

A vision slammed into them before they could prepare.

Not a memory, but a warning.

Not a warning, but a summons.

For a moment they saw flashes of an ancient world. Fire erupting from mountains. Frost storms ripping across valleys. A figure stepping into the fissure. Another reaching down from the ridge. Their bond, the original bond, blazing with white fire.

Then the vision shattered.

Mira fell to her knees.

Kael dropped beside her, breath ragged.

The sky pulsed in red and silver.

The land trembled again.

The Ember was waiting. Watching. Calling.

And they had reached the threshold where their fate would be decided.

* * *

The ridge trembled beneath their hands, a long, rolling quake that seemed to rise from the spine of the earth. Mira pressed her palm against the black stone to steady herself, but the bond pulsed again, dragging her attention downward toward the glowing fissure.

Kael crouched beside her, gripping her shoulder with one strong, steadying hand. His fire shimmered along his skin, a trembling halo barely contained. She saw how hard he battled against the Ember's pull. His face was tight with strain, jaw clenched as if resisting a force that wanted to reach inside his chest and seize his heart.

Mira whispered, "It wants us."

He nodded, breath ragged. "Yes."

"It wants us to finish what the first pair began."

He swallowed. "And it does not care if we survive."

A gust of wind slammed into them, carrying the scent of scorched earth and ancient ice. Snow spiraled upward instead of falling. Frost patterns cracked across the obsidian ridge in jagged paths. Heat pulsed through the stone in washes of crimson.

Mira steadied herself against Kael. His presence kept her grounded, his warmth an anchor. The bond calmed slightly, though its pull remained fierce, like a rope tugging at the inside of her chest.

"We need to keep moving," he said quietly. "Before the next quake hits."

She nodded and pushed herself upright. Together they followed the ridge toward a lower slope where the descent would be possible. The Ember Mouth stretched beneath them in a dark, uneven gash in the land. Ribbons of molten gold and icy blue glowed faintly from deep within, pulsing in uneven rhythms like a heartbeat out of sync.

The wind carried the sound of distant cracking stone.

Kael slipped slightly on loose gravel. Mira caught his arm. He steadied, eyes flicking to her with a grateful softness he did not voice.

The bond vibrated.

She felt it as a sharp thrum in her throat.

He felt it as a rush of heat up his spine.

Both froze for a moment.

"It is growing stronger," Mira whispered.

Kael's eyes darkened. "It is growing impatient."

The slope opened into a narrow path carved by centuries of storms and shifting earth. They moved cautiously, the ground trembling without warning under each step. At times Mira felt frost gather spontaneously in her palms, curling upward in spirals she had not intentionally shaped. Kael's magic responded in kind, flickering into visible embers along his arms.

They tried to keep space between their powers, but the bond kept pulling them closer.

After several minutes of unstable descent, Mira paused, leaning against a shard of obsidian. Her breath misted in front of her in fast bursts. "Kael. Something feels wrong."

He turned instantly. "Where?"

"In the bond." She pressed her hand to her sternum. "It feels like we are carrying too much. As if the connection is filling more quickly than it can settle."

He frowned. "As if the Ember is pouring something into us?"

"Or dragging something from us," she whispered.

A tremor rippled through the ground again.

The fissure roared.

A burst of hot air surged upward, sweeping across them in a wave. Mira stumbled. Kael caught her with both arms, pulling her close as the heat blasted across the ridge.

For a moment she was pressed to him, her heart pounding against his chest, his breath hot against her hair.

The bond flooded with light.

Mira gasped as the surge rushed through her.

Kael groaned, clutching her tighter.

Their magic flared together. Frost and fire spiraled outward in twin waves that struck the obsidian with a ringing impact.

The ground beneath them cracked in a sharp scatter of chips.

Then the surge passed.

They sagged into each other, panting.

Kael slowly loosened his grip but did not release her entirely. "That was not us," he said.

Mira looked up at him, cheeks flushed. "That was the Ember pushing through the bond."

His gaze flicked to the fissure's distant glow. "It is trying to complete the connection. It thinks we are already stepping into our role."

"We are not," she said, voice trembling. "Not yet."

"No," Kael agreed. "Not like this."

He helped her stand again. They continued down the slope, forced to rely on each other for balance as the earth trembled beneath their feet.

The air grew hotter as they descended, then colder, then hotter again. Mira felt sweat bead at her temples even as frost formed along her hair. Kael wiped his brow with a shaking hand. The shifting temperatures hit him harder, distorting the natural rhythm of his fire.

"Kael," Mira said gently. "You are overheating."

"I know," he muttered through clenched teeth. "I am trying to contain it."

She reached for him, laying her palm against his forearm. Frost flowed from her skin into his, cooling the frantic burn beneath. He exhaled a shaky breath and leaned into her touch.

"Do not let go yet," he whispered.

She kept her hand there until his fire steadied.

They moved again.

Soon the path opened onto a vast plateau of mixed ice and stone, stretching toward the heart of the Ember Mouth. Pillars of frozen steam stood like tall, ghostly statues. Cracks ran through the ground in glowing veins of light. The air shimmered with stray motes of heat and frost colliding at random.

As they crossed the plateau, Mira noticed something else.

The landscape was becoming symmetrical.

Streaks of frost mirrored streaks of heat. Columns of ice stood opposite cracks of fire. Light rippled in spirals that reflected one another.

"It wants balance," she murmured. "This place is shaped by the bond."

Kael stopped beside her and studied the ground. "Or by what our bond is becoming."

She hesitated. "Is that why it is unstable? Because we are not giving it what the Ember expects?"

His expression hardened. "We will never give it that. We saw what happened to the first pair. I will not let us become another echo of them."

Her heart tightened.

She reached for his hand. "We choose our path."

He interlaced their fingers. The bond steadied, warmth flowing through them like a shared breath.

They walked onward across the plateau, guided by the faint hum of the ley lines and the deep, rhythmic throbbing of the Ember below.

Every step brought new signs of disturbance.

A column of frost suddenly shattered beside them.

The sky cracked with light.

The earth split open with a groan.

Storm winds lashed at their cloaks. A swirling vortex formed overhead.

Kael glanced up. "The Ember is losing control."

Mira shook her head. "No. It is trying to make us hurry."

The funnel of wind tore across the plateau, carrying shards of frozen steam. Mira ducked as a sliver cut past her cheek. Kael wrapped an arm around her, shielding her as the wind howled.

Through the chaos, Mira shouted, "It wants us to accept our role now, before we see the truth!"

Kael's voice was rough. "Then we will refuse again."

The wind screamed.

Heat crackled through the fissure.

The bond surged so hard Mira saw white.

Kael cried out as fire erupted along his arms.

The surge nearly drove them to their knees.

Then the storm died abruptly.

Silence fell.

They stood at the last rise before the Ember Mouth.

Kael took Mira's hand again. "Whatever waits down there. Whatever it offers. We decide."

Mira lifted her chin, gaze fixed on the glowing fissure's core. "We decide."

Together they stepped forward, approaching the threshold where the first bonded pair had surrendered their lives to stabilize the world.

The air pulsed around them, thick with ancient memory.

The ground glowed brighter.

The bond throbbed in warning and anticipation.

They had reached the point of no return.

The final ridge curved inward like the lip of a great bowl, enclosing the fissure in a wide circle of obsidian and ice. Mira stepped to the edge, Kael close beside her, and felt heat rising from below in deep, steady waves. A strange hush filled the air, so absolute that every crack of stone beneath their boots echoed like a heartbeat.

The Ember Mouth stretched beneath them in a sweeping valley of blackened rock broken by glowing lines of molten gold and pale blue frost. The fissure itself ran through the center, pulsing with alternating streams of fire and ice. Wisps of hot vapor rose like smoke, curling into the frigid air before vanishing.

Mira felt the pull immediately.

A sharp tug inside her chest.

A flare of pain.

A rush of power.

The bond strained, throbbing as if drawn toward the fissure with magnetic force. She stumbled, her vision blurring for a moment. Kael caught her elbow, steadying her again.

"Mira."

"I felt it," she whispered. "Like something trying to pull me down."

Kael exhaled slowly. "It feels like gravity."

The fissure pulsed in answer. A rush of air swept upward, carrying sparks that shimmered like tiny falling stars. The sound that followed was low, almost musical, like a distant hum resonating through the bones of the earth.

It reverberated in Mira's chest.

Kael's jaw tightened. "That is not the wind. That is the Ember."

Mira swallowed hard. "It is calling."

He stepped closer, close enough for their shoulders to touch. The contact steadied the bond for a moment, though the pull from below still thrummed with quiet insistence.

"Mira," he murmured. "If we approach the core, it will try to take us again. It has already shown us what it wants."

She shivered at the memory of the first bonded pair. "But we know what we have to do. We saw enough to understand what this place is."

"We saw their end," Kael said softly. "We must find a way to end the Ember without becoming another story carved in stone."

She looked at him.

The firelight rising from below cast amber along his cheekbones, making the shadows under his eyes look deeper. His hair was windtossed, frost clinging to the edges of the strands. Despite exhaustion and strain, he stood steady, unyielding, every line of him ready to face whatever waited.

Mira took his hand.

"We do this together."

He squeezed her fingers. "Always."

The ground beneath them trembled, a sudden violent shake that nearly threw them from their feet. Mira cried out as Kael pulled her backward from the edge. A crack tore through the stone at their feet, splitting the ridge in a jagged line. Heat burst upward through the gap, followed by a swirl of frost that froze the rock edges.

Kael tightened his grip on her waist. "It is losing control."

"No," Mira said, voice trembling. "It is testing us."

The quake subsided. A sourceless whisper threaded through the air, brushing the back of Mira's mind with the faint echo of words she could not decipher. The bond reacted violently, aching with pressure.

Kael steadied her. "We should move. The fissure is worse on this ridge."

Together they descended toward a lower bench of stone. The path was narrow and uneven, steep in places where the ground had folded upon itself from centuries of magical strain. The closer they walked, the more intense the bond pressure became.

First it felt like a tug.

Then a pull.

Then a tightening coil around their ribs.

Mira gasped as the force spiked suddenly, forcing her to brace her hands against the stone. Kael reached for her immediately, but the moment he touched her, the bond surged again.

Light burst between them in a quick flash.

Mira's heart hammered.

The bond was changing. Sharpening. Becoming something new.

"What is happening?" she whispered.

Kael bent near her, bracing a hand on the wall beside her. "It is trying to rewrite us. It wants to complete a pattern."

"We are not letting it."

His gaze met hers, fierce and steady. "No. We are not."

They pushed onward.

At the base of the slope, the ground flattened into a rough plateau of mixed frost-cracked stone and heat warped earth. Motes of drifting light floated through the air. The fissure's glow illuminated the entire plain in shifting waves of blue and gold.

The sound of the Ember was louder here. A rhythmic pulse that beat in time with the bond, overwhelming, relentless.

Kael's voice was tight. "Feel that."

Mira nodded, clutching her chest. "It is syncing with us."

"That is not something we should allow."

She agreed, but the bond did not. It thrummed in eager harmony, rising in strength the nearer they walked to the center of the valley.

Mira forced herself to focus. "We need to find the core fissure. Ovrin said it would be the narrowest point, where fire and frost first collided."

Kael scanned the valley. "Look there."

At the far end of the plain, a massive outcrop of black stone jutted from the ground like the spine of a buried beast. Directly beneath it, the fissure narrowed into a sharp slit, pulsing with intense blue and gold light.

Mira's breath hitched. "That is the place."

Kael nodded. "The origin."

A deep tremor rippled through the stone. The fissure flared violently, sending a column of light arching into the sky. Storm clouds spiraled around the flash, forming a vortex above the valley.

Snow began to fall sideways.

Mira shielded her face as the wind ripped at her cloak. Kael stepped in front of her, bracing them both against the sudden gale. The air was thick with magic, every gust filled with sharp particles of frost and heat. Sparks danced across the ground, crackling like embers in a windstorm.

Mira leaned into him for balance. "It is trying to push us away."

"Or pull us in," Kael said.

The bond tightened again. Mira felt panic inch up her throat as heat burned under her ribs. Kael hissed in pain as frost streaked down his forearm, biting into the skin.

"Hold on," he said through clenched teeth. "I have you."

She gripped his tunic. "I am here."

The wind cut across them again, fiercer than before. Snow and embers spiraled together in a white and red blur. The fissure roared, the sound vibrating through the very air.

Mira could not tell where her magic ended and Kael's began. It swirled through the bond in waves, pulsing with frantic urgency.

"We have to move," Kael shouted above the storm. "If we stay here, it will overwhelm us."

Mira nodded, teeth chattering. The storm tore at her braids, ripping strands of hair loose. She pressed herself to Kael's side for stability.

Together, leaning into each other, they pushed forward across the trembling plateau. Their boots slipped on the slick stone. The air stung their skin. Magic flared around them in chaotic bursts.

With every step, the pull grew stronger.

Mira felt as if invisible hands were tugging at her from below. At moments she swore she heard faint whispers curling through her mind. Her vision blurred, shapes shifting in the corner of her eyes.

Kael's breath came harsh. "Do not look into the fissure yet. Focus on the ground. Focus on me."

She nodded and kept her gaze forward, fixing on the sharp line of his jaw, the tension in his neck, the firelight dancing along the edge of his cheek.

The bond steadied.

Not calm.

Not gentle.

But steady.

They reached the last rise before the fissure's core.

The light exploded upward again, brighter than before. Heat and frost clashed in violent spirals. The wind shrieked across the valley.

Mira grabbed Kael's arm. "Kael. It is too strong. We should not be this close yet. It feels like it is trying to strip something out of us."

He tightened his grip on her hand. "Then we hold on until it fails."

She stared up at him, chest tight. "We do not let go."

"Not unless the world falls apart beneath our feet."

"Then not at all."

A final tremor ripped through the land, nearly knocking them off their feet. Kael caught her. She steadied him in return.

Together, shaking, breathless and burning, they reached the rim of the core fissure.

The light rose in a blinding arc.

The bond surged.

And the Ember, ancient and furious and waiting, felt them arrive.

* * *

The glow from the fissure pulsed in violent waves as Mira and Kael stood at its rim. Light spilled upward in long ribbons, bending as if caught in some unseen wind. The colors shifted without pattern. Blue frost. Golden fire. Silver streaks of energy that hummed with strange, old power. The entire valley shivered under the weight of the Ember stirring below.

Mira felt the pull again, but this time it was stronger. Overwhelming. A slow, relentless pressure that pushed and pulled like tides digging into her bones. Her magic rose instinctively, frost curling along her arms in spirals she did not command. Her breath misted in uneven bursts, trembling and sharp.

Kael took a step closer to her, closing the small space between them so their shoulders touched. His fire flared in answer, a thin line of heat along his skin that seeped into her like a warning.

"Mira," he said quietly. "Stay with me."

She nodded, but her eyes were fixed on the glowing maw beneath them. The fissure seemed bottomless, a window into the raw heart of the world. Heat wafted upward in slow waves, tinged with scents of minerals and something older. Cold rose between them in sudden bursts, leaving streaks of frost across her boots.

The Ember was split inside.

Half heat.

Half ice.

Both fighting for dominance.

Kael followed her gaze. "This is where the first pair stood."

Mira's throat tightened. "Where they lost themselves."

He turned to her, his voice steady. "We will not repeat their ending."

Another tremor shook the ground, forcing them to brace themselves. A pillar of frost burst upward from the fissure, shattering into a cloud of sharp fragments. A stream of fire answered, twisting around itself before sinking back into the abyss.

Mira clutched Kael's arm to keep her balance. "The instability is getting worse."

He steadied her. "The closer we come, the more it reacts."

"It is not reacting," she whispered. "It is preparing."

Kael did not contradict her. He simply took her hand again, lacing their fingers together with quiet resolve.

The bond pulsed, a slow wave that rolled through them like the beat of a second heart.

Mira inhaled shakily. "What if it pulls us in?"

"Then we hold to each other."

"What if it tries to strip the bond apart?"

He lifted her hand to his chest, pressing her palm over the rhythm of his heartbeat. "Then it fails."

She closed her eyes for a moment, letting his warmth calm her trembling breath.

The wind rose around them again, spiraling across the plateau. The vortex overhead thickened, pulling storm clouds into a slow rotation. Bolts of white lightning cracked through the sky, illuminating the fissure in flashes of cold brilliance.

Mira reached out with her senses, feeling the ley lines beneath the valley. They vibrated wildly, crossing and uncrossing with chaotic speed. The Ember was pushing power through them in frantic pulses.

Kael felt it too. "It is trying to force us into alignment."

"It thinks we are ready."

"We are not," he said. "Not like this."

Another burst of heat erupted from the fissure. Kael flinched, staggering back. Mira grabbed him, her frost cooling the sudden surge of fire.

"You said earlier that it was pouring something into us," he said, voice strained. "I think you were right. It is trying to load its force into the bond."

Mira's breath hitched. "Why now?"

"Because it believes we are standing where the first pair surrendered."

Mira stared at the fissure. The pull from below tightened again, sharp enough to make her gasp.

She stumbled.

Kael moved instantly, catching her and pulling her against him. His arms circled her waist, his breath warm at her ear.

"Stay here," he murmured. "Stay with me."

She gripped his shoulders. "Kael, it is dragging on me. Harder than before."

"I know."

His hold around her tightened.

The light flared.

The bond surged with such intensity that Mira cried out. Frost burst from her palms in twisting spirals. Kael shouted as fire licked up his arms, burning through his sleeves.

The magic collided between them in an explosion of sparks. Mira felt herself yanked forward. Kael pulled her back with a desperate sound, anchoring her against the pull.

The fissure roared.

A voice rose from below, not in sound but in pressure. Mira felt it press against her thoughts, a cold and hot presence that breathed through her mind.

Kael's voice broke through it, harsh and urgent.

"Mira. Look at me. Now."

She forced her gaze upward.

He took her face between his hands, steadying her trembling jaw. His touch warmed her skin. His eyes burned with fierce determination.

"Do not let it inside your thoughts."

"I am trying," she whispered, shaking.

"Fight it. With me."

Their foreheads touched. The bond steadied, then flared stronger.

Her breath synced with his.

For a moment, everything fell silent.

Then the fissure erupted again.

A column of pure light surged upward, engulfing the ridge in radiance. The wind howled. The valley shook. Frost and fire churned together in a storm of raw magic.

Mira clung to Kael as the force washed over them. Kael braced himself against the stone, refusing to let either of them fall into the fissure's grip.

Light burned across their skin.

Mira felt the bond stretch like a taut thread pulled to breaking.

Kael's voice reached her through the roar. "We hold. Do you understand? We hold."

She nodded, tears streaming down her face. "I will not let go."

The storm raged.

The fissure pulsed.

The ground split beneath their feet, sending shards of obsidian flying outward. Mira and Kael staggered together, digging their boots into the trembling stone.

Magic lashed through the bond, searing and freezing at once. Mira cried out. Kael roared in pain. Their fingers slipped for one agonizing second.

Then Mira lunged forward, grabbing his hand with both of hers.

The bond snapped into alignment for a single heartbeat.

A pulse of white light burst outward.

Silence fell.

Their knees hit the stone at the same moment. They clung to each other, shaking, breath ragged. The fissure dimmed. The vortex overhead eased. The valley settled into a heavy, trembling quiet.

Mira pressed her forehead to Kael's shoulder, trembling uncontrollably. "I thought it was going to take us."

Kael pulled her against him, sliding a hand up her back in slow, steady strokes. "It almost did."

She clung to his tunic. "We are not ready."

"No," he whispered. "But we will be."

The bond throbbed gently now, calmer. Waiting.

Kael lifted his head and looked at the glowing fissure.

"Mira," he said. "The Ember is losing its grip. It is unstable. But it is not finished."

She followed his gaze.

The fissure shimmered with dangerous light, pulsing slowly like a wound that refused to close.

"We have to learn everything about what happened here," she said. "What happened to the first pair. Why it chose them. Why it chose us."

Kael nodded. "And we have to learn fast. Before it tries again."

Mira took a deep, steadying breath. "Then our next step is clear."

His fingers tightened around hers. "We face the Ember. On our terms."

They turned from the fissure, both exhausted but unbroken. The path forward was lit in faint silver glow, the storm clouds slowly drifting apart above them.

Their journey had brought them to the threshold.

The next step would take them into the heart of the truth.

Together they walked away from the fissure's edge, hands clasped, the bond steady for now.

Behind them, the Ember stirred once more.

As if preparing for what came next.

Chapter 22

Night settled over the Ember Mouth in a strange, luminous hush. A cold that was not natural seeped into the air, softened by faint waves of rising heat that pulsed from the ground like a heartbeat. Strange patterns of light drifted over the valley as Mira and Kael made camp against the lee of a black stone pillar. They huddled together for warmth while the wind carried thin streaks of glowing frost.

Neither slept easily. The bond had been strained nearly to breaking during their confrontation at the fissure rim. It still thrummed with uneven pulses, as if the Ember itself pressed against the connection from the other side, waiting for a moment of weakness.

Mira sat with her knees drawn to her chest, wrapped in her cloak. Frost curled and uncurling across her sleeves in restless spirals. She stared at the faint shimmer drifting from the fissure and felt a deep unease coil inside her.

Kael watched the valley too, his eyes reflecting the flickering gold light from below. "It is quieter than before," he said softly.

Mira nodded. "Like it is holding its breath."

His hand brushed hers. The bond steadied for a heartbeat before another tremor rippled through it, making Mira exhale sharply.

Kael shifted closer until their shoulders pressed together. "You feel that too?"

"Yes," she whispered. "It is tightening again. Slowly this time."

"Like it is preparing."

She leaned her head against his shoulder, exhausted. "Kael, what if it is waiting for us to sleep?"

His voice dropped. "Then we do not sleep alone."

She looked up at him. "You think a shared dream will come?"

"I am certain of it."

He was right.

The moment Mira finally surrendered to fatigue, the moment her eyes closed and her breath slowed, the bond tightened around her like the draw of a deep tide. She felt Kael reach for her across the link, his magic brushing her consciousness in a soft, grounding pulse.

Then the world dissolved.

No sound.

No wind.

No cold.

Only darkness.

Then light.

Blinding light.

Blue and gold.

Frost and fire spiraling around her in slow, graceful arcs.

Mira gasped as the vision took shape. She felt herself standing on a plain of polished stone. The sky above was impossibly vast, filled with swirling bands of color that moved like the auroras of northern Veris, only brighter and alive with energy.

Kael appeared beside her, breath catching with the same shock she felt. His hand instinctively found hers, anchoring them both.

The plain stretched out toward a distant horizon where jagged mountains glowed with shifting light. Frost spirals rose from the earth like curling vines. Rivers of molten gold flowed silently between them. Everything felt impossibly ancient, untouched by time.

Mira's voice came out in a whisper. "Kael... this is not the Ember Mouth."

"No," he said. "This is older."

The ground beneath them hummed. Lines of light streaked outward from their feet, traveling across the plain in branching patterns. The sky rippled in answer. Mira felt pressure rise inside her chest, not painful, but insistent.

"It is pulling us," she said, clutching Kael's arm.

Then the vision shifted.

Not slowly.

Not gently.

The world snapped into a new shape.

They stood on a cliff overlooking the very first version of the fissure. It was smaller now, less violent but more alive, glowing with contained power. The land was younger, unscarred by centuries of imbalance. Snow lay in thin sheets across the stone.

Two figures stood at the edge.

Mira froze.

Kael's breath caught.

The first bonded pair.

The man and woman were not quite fully defined, as if the Ember preserved their truth while erasing their names. The woman's cloak was made of woven frost crystals that shimmered softly in the wind. The man's armor glowed faint gold, lines of ember weaving through the metal.

They stood close but not touching, their bodies tense, their faces drawn. A terrible weight pressed against their shoulders, visible even in the dream. Mira felt the echo of their emotions through the bond with brutal clarity.

Fear.

Hope.

Duty.

Love.

But also dread.

The woman spoke first, her voice soft but resonant. "If we do this, we will not return the same."

The man reached toward her but stopped before his fingers touched. "If we do not, the world breaks."

Mira felt her heart twist. The woman's hands trembled as she lifted them, frost swirling around her in delicate patterns. The man's fire flickered along his arms.

Their bond pulsed between them in a glowing thread of white light.

Kael exhaled, voice low. "They were in love."

Mira nodded, throat tight. "And terrified."

The vision shifted again, sweeping them downward into the memory.

They stood at the fissure's core. The woman stepped forward, her eyes bright with tears. "I can feel it calling. It wants us both."

"Yes," the man said, voice breaking. "But it wants to strip us apart to take us."

"Then we refuse," she whispered.

He caught her hand. "We refuse together."

For a moment the bond between them burned fiercely, pulsing with defiant unity. Mira felt the swell of emotion like a pressure wave through her own chest. Kael's hand tightened on hers.

But the Ember did not accept refusal.

The fissure flared, sending a surge of heat and frost outward. The woman screamed as the magic tore through her. The man pulled her into his arms, fighting to hold the connection steady.

Their bond, once pure and bright, twisted desperately, reshaping itself to carry the Ember's burden.

It could not hold.

Their thoughts merged.

Their fears became one.

Their voices blurred into a single scream.

The vision shifted into chaos. The cliff shattered. Frost and fire collided in violent bursts. Mira clutched Kael, gasping as the agony of the bond collapse rippled through both of them.

She saw the woman dissolve into light.

She saw the man crumble into embers.

She saw the bond collapse into pure force.

Then she saw the Ember surge upward, taking the pair's essence into itself.

A cold realization rose inside her.

"They did not survive," Mira whispered, tears streaking down her cheeks.

Kael wrapped an arm around her, breath shaking. "No. They were consumed."

The vision shifted again.

This time the world reformed around a stone chamber lit by dim crystal globes. Ancient Veris priests knelt at the edges of the room, their faces grim. A shimmering figure hovered above the center: the fused echo of the first pair, a being made of fire and frost with no clear shape.

One of the priests bowed. "The Ember is willing to guide us."

Another asked, voice trembling, "At what cost?"

The fused being did not speak. It pulsed once, and the priest nearest to it collapsed in terror.

The oldest priest rose shakily. "We must control it. If we do not, it will destroy us."

The being pulsed again, its light dimming. Its form flickered, shaking violently as if caught in torment.

Mira realized with horror that the fused consciousness was suffering. The first pair had not simply been absorbed. They were trapped inside the Ember.

Forever.

Beside her, Kael whispered, voice raw, "They were used."

The vision blurred. The world disintegrated into swirling light.

And Mira and Kael were thrust back toward the present.

Toward the valley.

Toward the fissure.

Toward the truth they had witnessed.

But the Ember was not done.

As the vision dissolved, a final whisper brushed their minds.

A whisper from the fused consciousness of the first pair.

Do not repeat our fate.

The words echoed long after the light vanished and darkness claimed them again.

Mira woke with a sharp inhale, as if she had been drowning and finally broken the surface. Cold air hit her lungs, thin and biting. She lay on her back against hard stone, eyes staring up at a sky streaked with pale gray. The faint light of dawn brushed the edges of the horizon.

Her heart raced. Frost curled around her fingers, clinging to the ground.

For a moment she could not tell if she was still in the vision or truly awake. The memory of the first pair's suffering still burned behind her eyes. She could feel the echo of their bond, the way it had imploded under the weight of the Ember, twisting into something that had nothing to do with choice or love.

"Mira."

Kael's voice drifted in from her right. She turned her head.

He sat beside her, knees drawn up, forearms resting on them. His face was pale, eyes shadowed, as if he too had not fully left the dream. His gaze was fixed on the distant fissure, but his attention was on her.

"You saw it," he said quietly.

She nodded, throat tight. "All of it."

He rubbed a hand over his face. "The first pair did not join the Ember willingly in the end. They tried to hold themselves apart. It crushed that boundary."

"And fused them," Mira whispered. "Trapped inside it. Forever."

The bond pulsed faintly, as if in sympathy.

Mira pushed herself up slowly, her muscles stiff. The stone was cold beneath her. The valley lay quiet, but the Ember's glow seemed dimmer than she remembered, as though the act of showing them the vision had drawn energy from its core.

She wrapped her arms around herself. "That voice at the end. Did you hear it too?"

Kael nodded. "Do not repeat our fate."

She shivered.

For a few moments they sat in silence, listening to the faint hum beneath the ground. The vision had stripped away illusions she had not realized she still carried. The Ember was not simply a force. It was a prison. A cage built on sacrifice and maintained by lies.

"The Veris priests built their system on that torment," she said, anger warming her voice despite the cold. "They saw what happened to the first pair and decided to use it anyway. To control it. To weaponize it."

Kael's jaw tightened. "Ashrow is guilty too. They took whatever knowledge they could steal about the Ember, then used it to justify rituals and curses. They built an empire on managed fire, without caring what lay at the center."

Mira looked down at her hands. The frost on her skin pulsed with faint light. "We were not just unlucky. We were selected by a pattern that was corrupted on purpose."

"And neither kingdom ever intended to tell us," Kael said.

The bitterness in his voice cut through her.

She looked up. "Kael. If they had their way, they would push us into the fissure and call it salvation."

"I know." He turned toward her fully. "Which is why we cannot let them near this place. Not Veris. Not Ashrow. Not any of them."

Mira thought of Solenne's offer. The so called purification. She thought of Rhyken's promise to Kael. One host. One kingdom blessed. One sacrificed.

All lies.

"Everything they offered was built on what happened to the first pair," she said. "They wanted to turn us into tools that upheld the same broken pact."

"And the Ember," Kael added softly, "wanted to turn us into replacements."

The thought made her stomach twist.

She looked at him intently. "We cannot just end the Ember's central will for our sake alone. We have to end this cycle. No more pairs. No more sacrificial anchors."

His expression softened at the fierce resolve in her eyes. "Then we do what they could not. We break the pact instead of serving it."

A tremor ran through the ground, subtle but noticeable. The fissure pulsed, flickering with a strange, unstable rhythm. The bond twitched in response, but did not surge this time. It felt as if the Ember had heard their intent and did not like it.

Mira tilted her head, listening. "It is weaker."

"Or more fragmented," Kael said. "The vision we saw was not clean. It was broken by pain. The Ember's will is not a single, coherent voice anymore. It felt like fractured echoes."

She thought back to the fused figure in the chamber, flickering in torment. "The first pair has been trapped inside it for centuries. Maybe they have fought it. Maybe that is why the Ember feels unstable."

His gaze sharpened. "You think they have been resisting from within."

"Trying to loosen its grip," Mira said. "Trying to reach whoever comes after. To warn them."

He was quiet for a moment, considering.

Then he nodded. "If that is true, then we are not only ending something monstrous. We are freeing them."

The idea brought a strange, aching relief to her chest. "They deserve that much."

The bond pulsed in quiet agreement.

Kael shifted closer until their knees brushed. "What we saw also answers another question. Why the Ember offered us such perfect visions. Our families restored. The kingdoms kneeling. All of it shaped to our desires."

"Because it learned," Mira said. "From the first pair. It has centuries of practice now. It knows how to tempt instead of simply taking."

He gave a humorless smile. "Progress."

She looked at him sharply. "The visions it used on them were raw. It pressed its will on them. It did not yet know how to promise, only how to consume."

"And now it promises," he said, "because consuming directly cost it something. It burned itself to fuse with them. It does not want to burn like that again."

"So it tries to get us to step willingly into the same role," Mira finished. "To surrender without resistance."

They shared a long look as the weight of that realization settled over them.

Finally Kael spoke again, voice quieter. "What we do next matters."

"I know."

"Not just for us," he said. "For every mage who will ever touch these lines. For Arin. For your family. For everyone who lives under skies shaped by this thing's mood."

Mira's throat tightened. "If we fail..."

He met her gaze steadily. "If we fail, it finds another pair. It tries again. And again. And again. Until someone either surrenders or breaks."

She shut her eyes briefly, feeling the enormity of their path pressing against the back of her mind.

Then she opened them and said, "Then we do not fail."

His lips curved slightly. "You say that as if the world always obeys stubbornness."

"It has not met mine yet," she replied.

He huffed a quiet laugh, the sound soft and real. "Fair point."

The small shard of humor settled something inside her. For a brief moment, the valley did not feel quite so suffocating.

They sat there in silence for a while, shoulders touching, breathing in the cold air. The fissure pulsed faintly in the distance, but it no longer felt like an inevitable grave. It felt like a challenge. A wound that could be healed, even if the healing cost them dearly.

At last Mira spoke again. "We know the truth. We know what they did. We know what the Ember wants."

"And we know what we will not become," Kael said.

She nodded. "Then the last thing we have to decide is how we face it."

His eyes grew distant, thoughtful. "Ovrin said the first pair were meant to stabilize the Ember. To spread its power, not hold all of it. But the pact corrupted that intention. The Ember clung to them. The priests twisted the knowledge. Everything that followed became about control."

"So we undo that," she said. "Not by giving the Ember a new cage, but by breaking the lock."

"Dispersal," he murmured. "Instead of containment."

Mira turned that word over in her mind. Dispersal. A release rather than another prison. "If we are connected enough to handle its core, then we are connected enough to send it outward."

He looked at her, respect deepening in his gaze. "Using the bond as a channel instead of a vessel."

"Yes," she said. "Not to keep the Ember for ourselves, but to force it to spread through the ley lines, too thin to gather into one hungry will again."

The idea scared her. It would require them to stand in the path of the greatest force the world had ever known. To let it flow through them, tempered by frost and fire working in harmony.

Kael frowned slightly. "It will try to cling to one of us. It may choose a side."

"Then one of us steps closer," she said softly. "And the other pulls back, but not away. Anchored. Holding the bond steady so the other is not swallowed whole."

He studied her. "You have already decided who will step into the fissure."

Mira dropped her gaze. "I know my frost. It holds. It contains.

It binds. If it tries to choose me, I can slow it long enough to push it outward."

He shook his head. "And I know my fire. It moves. It carries. It travels along lines faster than your frost can. If the goal is dispersal, I am the conduit."

She looked up sharply. "Kael, no."

"We knew there would be a risk," he said. "We knew one of us might have to stand in the center of this storm. I am better suited to that role."

"And you think I am suited to watching from above while you burn?" she asked, voice breaking.

He flinched at the pain in her words but did not look away. "I think you are strong enough to hold the bond so I do not fall."

Silence settled between them. Heavy. Full.

The fissure trembled faintly, as if reacting to their debate.

Mira clenched her fists around the fabric of her cloak. "We are not sacrificing you."

"We are not sacrificing either of us," he said firmly. "We are creating a plan. One that gives both of us a chance to survive."

Her eyes stung. "You cannot promise that."

"No," he said softly. "But I can promise that if one of us walks into that fissure alone, the other follows."

She stared at him.

Then she nodded slowly.

"Together," she said.

"Even if it kills us," he replied.

The bond pulsed.

It felt like an oath.

They sat like that, bound by shared purpose and a truth larger than any individual desire. The vision of the first pair still hovered behind their thoughts, a warning lit in fire and frost.

They would not repeat that fate.

They would face the Ember on their own terms.

And when the time came, they would risk everything not for power, not for crowns, but for an end to the cycle that had destroyed so many lives.

Mira leaned her head against Kael's shoulder once more, feeling the steady rise and fall of his breathing. The bond hummed quietly between them, fragile and fierce and wholly theirs.

"We will free them," she whispered. "The first pair. Ourselves. Everyone chained to this."

Kael's voice was a low promise. "Yes. We will."

The fissure glowed in the distance, a wound in the world waiting for its reckoning.

They would go to it.

Soon.

Together.

Chapter 23

Sleep came slowly that night, uneasy and brittle. Mira lay curled against Kael beneath the lean shadow of the obsidian pillar, her head tucked beneath his chin, their legs tangled for warmth as cold winds rattled across the plain. His arms wrapped around her, not just for warmth but for stability, the bond humming faintly between them like a fragile thread trying to mend after being stretched too far.

Neither spoke. There was nothing left to say until morning. They had seen the truth of the first pair. They had rejected every false salvation either kingdom had offered. The only path left was the one no sane mage would choose.

Break the Ember. Free the trapped echoes. Change the world.

Mira closed her eyes, listening to Kael's heartbeat under her cheek. It steadied her, grounding her in the moment rather than the enormity of what awaited them. She drifted slowly toward sleep, comforted by the warmth of his chest and the quiet strength of his presence.

Kael tightened his hold slightly. "I am here," he murmured.

She whispered back, "I know."

Sleep reached for her.

Darkness folded around them both.

Then the world changed.

She opened her eyes not to the cold plateau, but to a soft, golden glow that filtered through tall windows draped with velvet curtains. Warmth brushed her cheeks. The scent of fresh bread curled through the air. The sound of laughter drifted in from a distant hallway.

Mira sat upright in a bed she had not seen in years.

A familiar bed.

A bed from Thornvale Manor.

Her throat tightened. She pressed a trembling hand to the quilt, running her fingers along the embroidery.

Her mother's embroidery.

Footsteps approached. The door swung open.

"Mira," her mother said, smiling with soft affection. "You slept late. Breakfast is ready."

Her father appeared behind her mother, dignified, unburdened, clothed in full Thornvale colors that he had not worn since before their disgrace. His shoulders were straight. His face was relieved.

Whole.

Mira's heart lurched. "This is not real," she whispered, voice cracking.

Her mother stepped forward and cupped Mira's face in her hands, warm and gentle. "Of course it is real, darling. Everything is as it should be."

The bond pulsed faintly in Mira's chest, confused. Foggy.

Her father smiled, placing a hand on her shoulder. "You have been under so much strain. Rest. You are home."

Mira's breath came in sharp, uneven bursts. This was everything she had dreamed. Her parents restored. Her name cleared. Her home returned. Thornvale, warm and safe and whole.

The temptation stabbed deep.

She swallowed hard. "Where is Kael?"

Her parents exchanged a puzzled look.

"Kael?" her mother echoed. "Sweetheart, the Ashrow boy? Why would he be here?"

Her father's brow furrowed. "He is far away, I imagine. Wherever Ashrow sends its soldiers."

Mira stood quickly, moving back from them. "No. That is wrong. He should be here."

Her mother's expression softened. "You are still tired. You do not need him. You do not owe him anything."

The walls brightened. Warmth pressed in. Everything smelled like home.

Everything felt like surrender.

No, she thought. This is the Ember.

Her pulse raced. She backed toward the door.

"Where is Kael?" she repeated.

The manor trembled.

The lights flickered.

Her parents' faces shifted slightly, their eyes dimming into something smooth and hollow, their smiles slipping around the edges like masks that did not quite fit.

Mira felt a breath of cold crawl along her spine.

"False," she whispered. "This is false."

Her mother's mouth curved into a placid smile. "Stay with us, Mira. There is no need to struggle. No need to fear. You are safe here."

Mira felt frost curling around her fingertips.

She did not remember summoning it.

The air dimmed.

And then the room went silent.

Kael blinked against a gentle light as he sat up. He was in a courtyard garden filled with blooming ashflowers. Sunlight spilled over stone walkways. The fountain burbled quietly with warm water. The air was fragrant, peaceful.

Arin stood a few steps away, wearing a loose dress and laughing as she chased a bright orange bird that flitted between the branches of an apple tree.

Kael's breath caught. She looked healthy. Strong. Alive.

"Arin," he whispered.

She turned toward him with a bright smile and ran to him, throwing her arms around his waist. "Kael. You overslept."

He closed his eyes, burying his face in her hair. He felt the warmth of her. The solidity. Her pulse. All the things he feared he would lose.

"You are well," he breathed. "You are alive."

She pulled back and grinned. "Of course I am. You saved me."

The words cut him deeply.

And yet they healed something inside him too.

He brushed a hand along her cheek. "Arin… little ember… this cannot be right."

She giggled and tugged at his sleeve. "Come. Mother is waiting for us by the fire. She made your favorite tea."

Kael froze.

The courtyard shimmered slightly at the edges.

Arin tugged harder, laughing again. "Stop worrying. Everything is perfect now."

The bond inside his chest flickered, thin and muffled. Mira felt distant, as if wrapped in fog.

Kept away.

"Arin," he whispered. "Where is Mira?"

His sister's smile dimmed. "Why do you keep asking about her? She is not here, Kael. She is not part of our life now."

His stomach twisted.

Arin's voice shifted in tone. Softer. Persuasive. Too smooth. "You do not need her anymore. You do not need anyone. You have everything you have ever wanted."

Kael stepped back. "That is not true."

Arin reached for his hand. "Stay. Be happy."

He felt heat in the air. Pressing. Shaping.

"Arin," he whispered, voice breaking, "this is not real."

The courtyard flickered again. The trees wavered. The ground blurred.

He clutched his chest as the bond pulsed sharply, like a distant cry.

"Mira," he breathed. "Where are you?"

The illusion trembled.

And the Ember's pressure thickened like smoke.

Mira staggered backward as the Thornvale manor dissolved into drifting motes of light. Her parents' faces twisted, crumbling into glittering dust. The walls cracked open like thin ice.

Beneath it, darkness coalesced. Light swirled in spirals of blue and gold.

A voice filled the air.

Not spoken.

Not human.

A chorus of whispers layered over a single rising note.

Accept peace. Accept inheritance. Accept the future shaped for you.

Mira trembled. "I will not."

You want this life. You have always wanted it.

"I want my family safe," she said fiercely. "But not if the cost is my will."

The light brightened.

Then accept the bond fully and walk into the fissure. I will shape the world around you. You will want for nothing.

She felt a cold pressure against her thoughts. A warm promise. An impossible dream.

She pushed back with all her strength.

"No," she whispered. "Real peace is not given. It is chosen."

The Ember went silent.

The pressure shifted.

A new image appeared.

Kael.

On his knees.

Surrounded by fire.

Reaching for someone not there.

Her breath caught. "Kael."

The vision flickered out before she could reach him.

Mira's frost pulsed violently through her body, fighting the Ember's hold.

But she felt one thing clearly.

Kael was resisting too.

And the Ember would not let either of them go easily.

* * *

The world around Kael flickered again. The courtyard dimmed, its colors draining into mist. Arin stood before him, but her smile faltered, her outline shimmering as though she were made from thin threads pulled too tight.

Kael backed away. "You are not my sister."

Arin tilted her head. "Do you not want me?"

The question twisted through him like a blade. He shut his eyes, overwhelmed by the ache of longing. Arin whole. His mother alive. His father at peace. A warm home without fear or fire that turned inward and burned.

He forced his breath steady.

"I want you alive," he said softly. "I want my family safe. But not at the cost of my mind. And not by surrendering Mira."

Arin's expression shifted. Her eyes darkened, losing their reflection of sunlight. "You choose her?"

Kael's throat tightened. "I choose myself. And Mira. And the truth."

The illusion wavered violently.

Heat surged upward like a furnace door thrown open. Fire flared around the false Arin, twisting her features into a smooth, unreadable mask. Her voice changed, deepening into something layered and hollow.

You deny what you want most.

Kael stood his ground. "I deny a lie."

You could have a world where she laughs again. A world where your mother lives. A kingdom that kneels to your bond.

He shook his head. "Not like this."

The air trembled.

The Ember pressed again, harder. Images flooded around him. Mira kneeling at the fissure's edge. Thornvale restored. Arin smiling. Kael crowned in firelight. Mira crowned beside him. Peace shaped like a perfect dream.

All false.

All tempting.

All poison.

The bond pulsed, faint but steady.

Kael clutched his chest. "Mira," he whispered.

Her voice flickered in the link, tangled in fear and stubborn clarity.

Kael. Do not believe what it shows you. It is shaping illusions.

He steadied, grounding himself in her presence. "I will not bend."

The Ember's illusion shattered.

The courtyard dissolved into darkness. Arin's form crumbled into embers. The warm air vanished, replaced by frigid cold.

Kael exhaled shakily. "Mira. I am coming."

The bond pulled at him again. He followed.

Mira ran through dissolving hallways, walls fading into vapor as the Thornvale manor collapsed behind her. The Ember had shaped everything with surgical precision, stitching her deepest desires into rooms she had dreamed of since childhood. But now the illusion was falling apart. Light bled through the cracks. Frost formed on polished floors. Heat rose in sudden bursts.

She pushed forward until she stumbled into an endless expanse of mist.

No walls.

No sky.

No ground.

Only a ghostly horizon of swirling blue and gold light.

Her breath sounded too loud. The cold cut into her lungs.

"Mira."

The voice came not from the Ember, but through the bond.

She spun around.

And there he was.

Kael emerged from the fog, stepping toward her with firelight flickering along his skin. His face carried exhaustion and fierce resolve. His expression was raw with relief when he saw her.

Mira's knees almost buckled.

She ran to him.

He caught her in his arms, holding her tightly against him, breath shaking hard against her hair. She clung to him with everything she had.

"You are real," she whispered.

"You too," he said, voice thick.

The bond flared between them in a rush of heat and frost, pushing back the fog. The Ember recoiled. Pressure rippled across the illusion.

Kael pulled back enough to cup her face in his hands. "Did it show you your family?"

She nodded. "Yes. Whole. Safe. Alive."

"And you know it was not real."

"Yes."

He swallowed. "Did it hurt?"

Her voice cracked. "More than anything."

He rested his forehead against hers. "It showed me Arin. Running. Laughing."

Mira pressed her eyes shut. "I am sorry."

"I almost believed it," he whispered. "For a moment I wanted to stay."

Mira touched his cheek. "I almost did too."

He grabbed her wrist gently. "But we did not."

"No," she said. "We chose each other."

The illusion trembled around them. The mist thickened, folding inward like breathing lungs. Light pulsed violently. A low, resonant hum filled the air, rising in pitch.

The Ember was angry.

Mira felt it push against her thoughts again, harder, stronger, trying to wedge itself inside. Kael's grip tightened on her hand. Fire and frost rose around them, clashing and merging into a barrier that pressed back.

A voice echoed through the mist.

You reject harmony. You reject salvation. You reject the world shaped for you.

Mira lifted her chin. "We reject a cage."

Kael's voice sharpened. "We reject control."

The fog swirled around them, forming tendrils of blue and gold that twisted like serpents. The light pressed closer, wrapping around their ankles, climbing their legs, threatening to pull them apart again.

Mira gasped. "It is trying to separate us."

Kael yanked her closer. "Then we stay together."

He pulled her into a tight embrace, arms locked around her waist. She clung to him, pressing her face to his shoulder, their bodies merging into one point of resistance.

The bond erupted with light.

A wave of heat burst outward from Kael.

A ring of frost exploded from Mira.

The forces collided, weaving into a spiral that expanded across the dreamscape. The fog recoiled as if struck. The Ember's presence flickered, its pressure wavering.

Mira felt strength rush through her, fueled by their unity.

She lifted her voice.

"We choose our path. We choose each other. We choose freedom."

Kael added his own voice, steady and unbreakable. "You cannot shape us. You cannot own us."

The vision cracked down the middle.

Light seeped through the fracture.

The Ember voice trembled.

Then you choose destruction.

Mira's hand tightened on Kael's. "No. We choose truth."

A roar filled the mist. The vision shuddered.

And then, in a blinding flash, everything collapsed inward.

A rush of freezing air hit her. Heat followed. She tumbled backward, falling through light and shadow, through crackling frost and burning embers.

She landed hard on cold stone.

Kael landed beside her with a groan.

They were back in the real valley. The fissure glowed fiercely beneath them. The wind howled overhead. The sky swirled with storm clouds.

Kael rolled onto his side, panting. "We broke its hold."

Mira pushed herself up, shaking violently. "It will not try that way again."

He reached for her hand. "Mira. We resisted the perfect dream."

She looked at him, breath trembling. "We did."

He gripped her hand more firmly.

"And now we do the impossible."

She nodded. "We break the Ember."

Their eyes met.

The bond pulsed with quiet certainty.

Tomorrow, everything would change.

And they would face that change together.

Chapter 24

The valley trembled before dawn, long before the first pale light touched the frozen ridges. Mira and Kael stood at the rim of the Ember Mouth once more, facing the fissure that pulsed with unbearable force. The air vibrated with power, a constant low hum that settled in their bones. Heat and frost surged upward in spiraling waves, clashing in bursts that sent shards of steam and ice scattering across the plateau.

Mira's heart thundered against her ribs as she gazed into the churning light below. The fissure no longer glowed in gentle rhythm. It blazed. It demanded. It raged.

Kael stepped closer behind her, his presence solid and grounding. "This is it," he said softly.

She nodded, unable to find her voice for a moment. The wind whipped her hair across her face, carrying the scent of scorched stone and sharp winter.

He touched her shoulder gently. "Your plan can work."

"It is our plan," she said, eyes fixed on the fissure. "And it is the only one we have left."

Below them, the Ember throbbed with fierce intensity, as if sensing their intent. Light cracked across the valley in jagged lines. Frost exploded upward. Fire curled along the ridges. The very land seemed to writhe under the strain of what lay beneath.

Mira's breath shook. "Once it begins, there is no stopping. No going back."

Kael's hand found hers, warm and steady. "Then we start together."

She turned to face him fully. His eyes were fierce, determined, and soft in the edges where fear and love lived side by side. She cupped his cheek, tracing the warm line of his jaw with her fingers.

"If it chooses me," she whispered, "do not follow into the core."

His hand rose to cover hers. "You know I will."

"If you step too close you might be pulled in too," she said, voice cracking. "Kael, I cannot lose you."

"You will not," he said firmly. "Because we will not let the Ember decide who burns and who does not."

He held her gaze. Unshaken. Unwavering.

She realized that whatever happened, he would not walk away from her. Not now. Not ever.

Mira inhaled sharply and turned toward the fissure. "Then we do this."

They approached slowly, boots crunching across fractured stone. Tremors rippled beneath their feet, shaking the ground in short bursts. The fissure widened with each quake, glowing brighter and brighter until Mira's vision blurred from the intensity.

By the time they reached the narrow stone ledge that overlooked the core, the heat was sweltering. Frost formed on Mira's skin and evaporated instantly. Kael's fire flickered wildly, reacting to the unstable energy.

Mira lifted her chin, eyes narrowed against the glare. "This is where the first pair fell."

"We do not fall," Kael said. "We stand."

Together they stepped onto the final platform.

Magic roared upward in a violent surge. Mira staggered. Kael grabbed her arm but did not pull her back. Their feet remained planted. Their expressions remained fierce.

The Ember rose.

It did not reveal a face or a form. It appeared as a spiraling column of frost and flame, twisting like a living storm. Light pulsed through it in waves that burned the air and froze it in the same breath.

A voice followed, rippling through their minds.

You refuse the vision. You refuse the path. You refuse harmony.

Mira shouted over the roar. "We refuse surrender."

Kael stood tall beside her. "We refuse to feed your cage."

The spiraling core flared violently, its light almost blinding.

You choose destruction.

Mira lifted her arms, frost gathering in a swirling arc. "We choose freedom."

Kael answered her with fire erupting along his skin. "For everyone you have taken."

The fissure screamed, a sound like breaking earth and shattering steel. Light burst outward in a torrent. The bond surged so violently that Mira fell to one knee. Kael dropped beside her, gripping her hand.

The Ember struck.

The force slammed into them, a tidal wave of magic that tried to drag them into the core. Mira screamed against the pressure. Kael roared. Their magic flared, resisting with every instinct they had.

Frost spiraled outward from Mira in a wide arc, attempting to contain the surge. Fire erupted from Kael, pushing back with raw momentum.

They held.

But the Ember pushed harder.

The ground cracked beneath them. Heat scorched their skin. Frost numbed their limbs. The bond twisted and shook under the immense strain, flickering between breaking and strengthening with each pulse.

Mira felt the Ember grasp for her essence.

Kael felt it reach for his spirit.

It wanted to claim them both. To bind them as it had bound the first pair. To complete the cycle.

No.

Not this time.

Through the roaring chaos, Mira squeezed Kael's hand with all her strength. "Now," she gasped. "Kael, now. Take it and carry it."

He met her gaze, and in his eyes she saw complete trust.

He stepped toward the core.

The Ember lunged for him instantly, threads of fire and frost whipping out to coil around his arms and chest. He cried out as the force surged into him. Mira grabbed his other hand and anchored herself, frost spiraling outward to steady him.

They became a conduit.

Magic flowed through Kael like a river set ablaze. It burned and twisted and tore at him, but Mira's frost held the edges, directing the flow into the bond.

Together they channeled the Ember upward. Not into a vessel. Not into a prison.

Into the ley lines.

Mira shouted, calling frost from every root of her being. Kael thrust his free hand skyward, fire blazing from his palm.

The bond erupted into brilliant white light, a fusion of fire and frost that tore through the fissure like a spear.

The Ember screamed.

The valley shook violently. Cracks raced across the ridges. Pillars of steam burst upward. The fissure widened.

But the flow changed.

Light poured outward instead of inward. It spread into the land, into the lines beneath the earth, into the sky.

Not contained.

Not controlled.

Free.

Mira felt the Ember's will thrash wildly, trying to cling to them, trying to bind itself to Kael.

She gritted her teeth and pushed harder, frost swirling around her like a storm. "Let go," she shouted. "Let go. You do not own him."

Kael roared as the last of the force surged through him. He staggered. She pulled him back from the collapsing edge, holding him with every ounce of strength she had left.

The light dimmed.

The ground stilled.

The core fell silent.

The Ember broke.

A final pulse rolled through the valley, soft and gentle, like a sigh after centuries of strain. The swirling core dissolved into drifting particles of gold and blue that floated upward into the sky.

Then it was gone.

Mira collapsed to her knees. Kael fell beside her, panting hard, sweat and frost covering his skin. For several long moments they leaned against each other, their bodies trembling with exhaustion.

Mira pressed her face to his shoulder. "You are alive."

Kael let out a ragged breath. "Because you held me."

She held him tighter. The bond was dim, flickering with fatigue, but unbroken.

Above them, the sky cleared into a calm stretch of pale morning.

The Ember's central will was gone.

They had survived.

Together.

Chapter 25

Silence spread slowly across the valley in the wake of the Ember's collapse. Not the tense, vibrating silence of something waiting to strike, but a deep and natural quiet that felt almost wrong after the storm of magic that had torn through the world moments before. Frost drifted in soft spirals where fire had once erupted. Warm air rose in thin ribbons where the ground had frozen solid minutes earlier.

Mira and Kael remained on their knees at the edge of the fissure, their bodies trembling from exhaustion.

Mira's breath came in uneven pulls. Her chest burned from the strain of channeling so much power, and her palms were raw where the frost spiraled uncontrollably. She blinked against the stinging in her eyes and lifted her head, scanning the valley.

The fissure looked different.

Not alive.

Not pulsing.

Not demanding.

It sat quiet, its edges glowing faintly like a wound finally given the chance to heal.

Kael leaned forward, bracing his hands on the stone. He coughed once, breath shaky, then pushed himself upright. Mira immediately reached for him, steadying him by the arm.

"Easy," she whispered.

He gave her a tired, crooked half smile. "I am trying."

The bond flickered between them, weak but steady. It felt stretched thin, but not unstable. If anything, the instability that had plagued it since the rite felt less jagged. Less dangerous.

Kael followed her gaze to the fissure. "It feels different."

Mira nodded. "It is no longer one voice. No longer one will."

He frowned slightly. "What do you hear?"

She closed her eyes briefly, listening to the thrum beneath the stone. "Nothing. For the first time since the Winter Rite. Nothing pressing. Nothing calling."

Kael let out a breath that seemed to release years of tension. "Then we did it."

Mira swallowed. "We broke the pact."

The weight of that truth hit her with unexpected force. Her knees gave slightly, and she sank to sit on the stone. Kael joined her without hesitation.

For a long moment neither said anything. They simply breathed and tried to understand the world as it now was.

Then Mira sensed something else.

A subtle shift beneath the earth. A soft pulse that was not oppressive but natural, spreading calmly through the ley lines.

Kael straightened. "Do you feel that?"

She nodded slowly. "The lines are equalizing. Without a central will dragging them together, the frost and fire streams are dispersing. Becoming what they were before the first pair."

"Separate," Kael murmured. "Balanced. Not forced into a single purpose."

Mira's eyes filled with tears she had not expected. "They are free."

Kael reached over and took her hand, intertwining their fingers. He did not speak, but the bond pulsed with quiet gratitude. Relief. Astonishment.

And then something shifted inside Kael.

He gasped, leaning forward with a hand pressed to his chest. Mira grabbed him instinctively.

"Kael? What is wrong?"

He closed his eyes as a wave of heat rolled through him, then another, but not painful heat. Not destructive. This fire felt calm, humming with a different rhythm.

He looked at her, stunned. "The burn that has been eating at me since the Winter Rite. It is gone."

Mira's breath caught. "Completely?"

He nodded slowly, eyes wide. "Completely."

She released a shaky laugh and cupped his face with trembling hands. He turned into her touch, eyes closing briefly, overwhelmed.

"That is not all," he said quietly.

She lowered her hands. "What else?"

He swallowed hard. "Arin."

Mira froze. "What about her?"

"The curse." He exhaled, trembling. "The sickness in her blood. I cannot explain it, but I can feel it. The fire that had tangled inside her soul. It is loosening."

Mira covered her mouth with both hands. Tears spilled down her cheeks. "Kael. She might survive."

His voice cracked. "She might."

He leaned forward, pressing his forehead to hers. They stayed like that, breathing each other in, letting the enormity settle between them.

Then Mira felt it.

A faint warmth beneath her ribs. Not heat, but something like a soft glow. Her frost responded, curling gently around her wrists in slow spirals.

Kael noticed. "What is that?"

She touched her chest, startled. "I do not know. Something changed in me too."

"Does it hurt?"

"No." She shook her head. "It feels like... potential. Like something settling instead of spiraling out of control."

Kael studied her with concern and awe. "Your magic feels calmer."

"So does yours."

He let out a soft laugh. "Maybe breaking an ancient force recalibrates a person."

She nudged him weakly. "Do not make jokes. I can barely breathe."

He grinned faintly. "If I do not joke I might collapse."

She leaned into him, letting his shoulder support her weight. The exhaustion pressed heavy against her limbs, but it was a peaceful exhaustion.

For the first time in her life, the magic around her felt quiet and natural. Not a weapon. Not a curse. Not a destiny someone else forced upon her.

Kael looked across the valley again. "The kingdoms will feel this."

"All of them," Mira said. "Every mage. Every priest. Everyone tied to the old systems."

He nodded slowly. "The world will not know what happened yet. But they will know that something changed."

"And someone will come looking," she said.

A shadow of concern crossed his face, but he nodded. "Yes. Both kingdoms will send scouts. Investigators. Perhaps entire battalions."

She leaned back to look at him. "Then we should not be here when they arrive."

He hesitated. "We should rest first."

She nodded. "But not too long."

He wrapped an arm around her, pulling her close. The warmth of him melted the lingering cold from her skin.

"We survived," he murmured.

She closed her eyes and rested her head on his shoulder. "Yes. Somehow."

He tightened his hold around her, his voice quiet but steady. "Whatever happens next, we faced the worst. Together."

The bond fluttered gently, no longer strained, no longer chaotic. It felt... quiet. Peaceful. Not controlling them. Simply connecting them.

Mira's voice softened. "Kael, do you think it will stay this way?"

He brushed a thumb along the back of her hand. "I think it has become what it was meant to be."

She exhaled shakily, a weight lifting from her chest.

The valley shifted slightly beneath them as the ley lines continued to settle. The air filled with drifting motes of gold and blue, remnants of the Ember's released essence.

They sat in silence, holding each other, until the sun crested the distant ridge.

The world they knew had changed forever.

And so had they.

* * *

As the sun climbed higher, the valley transformed under its light. What had once been a battlefield of elemental chaos was now a quiet expanse strewn with glittering fragments of blue and gold. The drifting motes settled gently over the stone, melting into the cracks as if being absorbed by the land itself.

Mira stood slowly, legs trembling from exhaustion. Kael rose beside her, steadying her with a hand at her waist until she found her balance. Her cloak was torn along the hem, her gloves frayed, and her hair matted with frost. Kael did not look much better. Ash streaked his jaw and his sleeves were ragged, though the fire that once licked at his skin now lay calm beneath the surface.

They both looked toward the fissure.

What remained of the Ember's core pulsed faintly like the last heartbeat of a dying star. The heat had cooled to a lukewarm glow. Frost curled at the edges without urgency. The opposing forces no longer fought each other.

It looked peaceful.

Mira approached the edge carefully. Kael followed a step behind, watchful. She peered into the depths, expecting to see a lingering trace of the fused consciousness that had haunted it for centuries.

But she saw no suffering.

No echo of trapped souls.

Only light dispersing downward in thin streams.

"They are free," she whispered.

Kael joined her, his expression softening. "The first pair."

She nodded. "I could feel something loosen when the Ember broke. As if a knot untied itself inside the core."

Kael's arm brushed hers. "Then they are finally at rest."

The wind carried the faint scent of snowmelt. Somewhere deep within the valley, a small stream of water flowed where earlier there had been only cracked stone. The world was shifting, adapting to the absence of the force that had shaped it for centuries.

Kael exhaled slowly. "Veris will sense this."

"And so will Ashrow," Mira said. "Any mage attuned to the lines will feel the change."

"They will come wanting answers."

Mira turned to him. "And they will assume we caused everything."

Kael gave a tired laugh. "We did."

"Not everything," she corrected softly. "We just broke the part that should never have existed."

He looked at her then, eyes filled with something tender and fierce. "You saved them. The pair trapped inside. The mages born after. The families who would have suffered next. You freed all of them."

She shook her head. "Not alone."

He reached out and threaded his fingers through hers. "No. Never alone."

The bond pulsed gently, no longer pushing or pulling, no longer burning or freezing. It felt warm and quiet, a steady rhythm that hummed beneath their skin.

Mira touched her chest, startled. "Kael. The bond feels different."

He frowned in concentration. "It does."

"It is quieter," she whispered. "Not demanding. Not trying to fuse us or tear us apart."

Kael closed his eyes briefly. "It feels... honest. It feels like it belongs to us now."

Her heart tightened. "Not the Ember."

"No," he said. "Us."

The relief swept through her so strongly her knees almost buckled again. Kael held her close, wrapping his arms around her. She did not hold back her tears this time. They spilled freely, soaking into the fabric of his cloak. He pressed a kiss to her temple, lingering there.

"We did not lose ourselves," he whispered. "We did not become what it wanted."

She clung to him. "We chose our future. Not its vision."

Their embrace was interrupted by a faint pulse beneath their feet. Not violent. Not painful. A gentle thrum, like the settling of a great beast finally allowed to sleep.

Mira steadied herself and pulled back. "We should leave before scouts arrive."

Kael nodded. "Do you feel strong enough to walk?"

She tested her footing. Her strength had returned partially, though her muscles still felt like water. "Strong enough to stay ahead of a brigade? Absolutely not."

Kael smirked. "Good. Then we take it slowly."

She gave him a flat look. "Slowly means we get caught."

He shrugged. "We broke the Ember. We get to choose how we walk away."

She sighed, though a faint smile tugged at her lips. "I suppose that is fair."

They began moving toward the narrow path that wound along the ridge. The air shifted around them in faint waves of balanced magic, frost and fire blending into something easier, something gentler. The weight that had pressed against both kingdoms for centuries had lifted.

As they climbed, Mira paused to look back one last time.

The Ember Mouth was no longer a threat, no longer a prison, no longer a place of inevitable sacrifice. It was simply a scar in the world, healing at its own pace.

She whispered, "Goodbye."

Kael touched her back lightly. "Come on."

They continued upward. The ridge narrowed, and Mira reached for his hand to steady herself. He laced their fingers together without hesitation. They moved in quiet unity, each supporting the other when needed.

As they reached the final turn in the path, Mira felt something shift in the bond again. A soft, warm flutter.

She stopped.

Kael looked at her with concern. "Mira?"

She touched her chest. "Something is settling."

He stepped closer. "Does it hurt?"

"No," she said softly. "It feels like a choice forming."

Kael held her gaze, a quiet understanding passing between them.

The bond was waking into its new shape.

Not forced.

Not burned into them.

Not demanded.

Claimed.

Mira reached up and brushed Kael's cheek. "Whatever this becomes from here… it is ours."

He covered her hand with his. "Yes."

The wind whispered through the valley. The ley lines pulsed in slow, steady harmony. The world waited for what they would do next.

Kael squeezed her hand gently. "Ready?"

Mira nodded.

Together they stepped over the last rise, leaving the Ember Mouth behind and walking into a future that had never been written for them.

Chapter 26

The journey back to the outer valleys took three days. Snow softened under warm winds that had no business blowing this early in the season. Frost melted along the ridges. Hot spring streams cooled to gentle warmth instead of scalding heat. The land healed itself in quiet rhythms Mira had never felt before.

They were not alone in feeling the change.

By the time they crossed into the lower passes, word had spread. Villagers stepped from doorways with wary eyes, sensing something different in the ley lines. Children pointed to the sky where faint blue and gold trails shimmered like harmless ribbons. Elders muttered prayers of confusion or awe.

No one dared approach Mira and Kael directly, but all watched them pass.

Mira felt the weight of their gazes. "Veris will want answers."

Kael's expression tightened. "Ashrow will demand them."

She nodded. "But neither can shape the truth for long. The magic itself has changed. People will feel it."

"Some will fear it," Kael murmured. "Some will want to claim it."

"And some," Mira said softly, "will want to destroy us for being part of it."

He reached for her hand. "Then we face them together."

They continued walking until the forest thinned and the frozen lake of the Winter Rite came into view. The surface had shifted. Thin cracks shaped like delicate lines of light spread outward from the center, remnants of the bond's earliest flare. But instead of threatening the ice, the cracks glowed faintly, like veins of living crystal.

Mira stepped onto the lake slowly. Kael followed, his boots leaving impressions in the thin frost.

A quiet breath escaped her chest. "This is where it began."

Kael's eyes softened as he looked down at the glowing lines beneath their feet. "And where we decide what comes next."

She turned to him fully, the wind brushing her hair across her cheeks. "The kingdoms will not accept this easily."

"They do not have to accept it," he said. "They only need to understand that the Ember no longer belongs to them."

"And neither do we."

He nodded, voice quiet. "We choose our own path now."

For a long moment they simply stood there, hands clasped, the cold brushing gently around their ankles. The bond hummed with calm certainty, no longer pulling or tearing, simply existing between them with quiet strength.

Mira stepped closer, resting her forehead against his. "Whatever they demand of us. Whatever future rises from this. We stay true to what we fought for."

Kael's breath warmed her lips. "And we stay true to each other."

Their kiss was soft, steady, unhurried. A promise carried in warmth rather than flame. Frost curled around their boots. Light rippled beneath the ice. The world around them shifted in a quiet acknowledgement.

When they parted, Mira looked toward the distant horizon.

"What do we do now?" she asked.

Kael followed her gaze, expression thoughtful. "We watch. We learn. We guide where we can. The kingdoms will change with or without us. But we can help shape what grows from the ashes."

Mira nodded. "And if something rises from the Ember's remnants?"

"Then we face it," Kael said softly. "Together."

The wind carried their breath across the lake. Faint golden sparks drifted on the air, settling onto the ice like small blessings.

Mira squeezed his hand. "Then let this be our beginning."

Kael smiled, the warmth in his eyes brighter than any fire. "It is."

They walked across the lake, side by side, stepping into a world that was already shifting under their feet.

A world waiting to see what they would become.

A world they had remade.

A world still capable of wonder and danger in equal measure.

Behind them the lake glowed softly, the last echo of the Ember's power flickering like a distant heartbeat.

Ahead of them, the path opened wide.